CROSSED HEART

Dick Donaghue

Copyright © 2019 Dick Donaghue

All rights reserved.

ISBN:
ISBN-13: 978-1-0918-6302-6

The rights of Dick Donaghue to be identified as the author of this work
has been asserted in accordance with Section 77, of the Copyright, Designs and Patents Act 1988.

All characters, places, institutions and events are the invention of the author and bear no relationship to
and real person or place

For Marja
***

And Kathleen who encouraged me to start it
and Nuala who encouraged me to finish it.

Dick Donaghue

Acknowledgments
A special thanks to Amy, Billy
and Shirley for their help.

Cover designed by D-Zine
Cover photographs pexels.com

The CROSSED HEART

1

Rosemary woke in a sweat. She had slept fitfully and dreamed erratically, fragments that didn't seem to fit together. The only recollection she could muster was a hazy vision of herself as a young girl which seemed to melt as she tried to focus on it. She shook her head violently on the pillow in the attempt to fling the cloying feeling from her. But the remnants of the hazy images hung in her head. She wished she were still asleep, but without dreams.

Without opening her eyes she sensed that it was already bright. She turned in the large bed and faced the wall, avoiding the urge to face the other way. The clock was on that side. It might read some unearthly hour - like six, and she would have to lie on until a reasonable hour to get up. Or it might read eleven or twelve and she would feel guilty for having overslept. Either way she did not want to know. She wanted to be asleep. But even with her eyes closed she knew it was no use. She was wide awake and in a foul humour.

She turned with a moan and looked at the clock. Almost nine-thirty. Oh well, the alarm was set to go off on a few minutes anyway so she might as well get up now. She threw back the covers roughly and lay until the cold settled on her. Then she sat up on the edge of the bed for a few moments, her hands on her knees, her head hanging and her long black hair dangling like dishevelled curtains on either side of her face. She stood, pulling on her dressing gown, a pale golden coloured Japanese kimono, with a picture of a fiery dragon embroidered in bold colours on the back and pulled aside the orange curtain that separated the kitchen from the small bed-sit.

It wasn't really a kitchen, as in a separate room. It was more an alcove with a large window, which looked out onto a narrow concrete space with a high wall rising to ground level, with a row of black railings on top. The little ceramic sink was built-in under the window and there was a small cooker to one side and a few shelves jammed on the other. It gave only enough room to stand in the center and do the washing or the cooking, and all this in view of the busy street above. Rosemary had hung a lace curtain over the window replacing the nylon one that hung there when she had taken the room. The large orange curtain she normally kept closed.

The buzz of the city filtered down to her.

She took a carton of milk from the mini-fridge which was wedged beneath the sink and poured some into a saucepan. Preoccupied with her thoughts she slammed the saucepan down on the cooker, slopping some of the milk onto the hot-plate.

'Hell..!'

She wiped up the spilt milk and turned on the cooker. While it was heating she sat back on the bed and brushed the knots out of her hair.

When she had finished her breakfast, hardly aware that she had tasted any of it, she heaped the dishes in the sink. She pulled the curtain closed and sat back on the edge of the bed. The light from the window was defused through the curtain giving the room a mellow glow. But it didn't dispel her gloom.

From underneath the bed she pulled a sketch pad and fished in the bed-side locker for a pencil. She was no artist. She was aware of that, but somewhere she had read that drawing was therapeutic and she had bought the pad for days like this. Days when she was on edge.

And she would spend long hours filling in pages with rough, childish scribblings, oblivious to the bustling city outside. Mostly the drawings were meaningless, but on occasions she had been amazed at her meagre attempts. And sometimes she was alarmed at some of the images which had appeared on the page, almost as if they had conjured themselves up from the undertones of her brain with no real consciousness of their origin.

But lately she was beginning to admit to herself that she did know and that she was going to have to face it, if she was to make anything of her life. It had to do with her father, and that dream. It was like some foul thing she had buried at the bottom of the garden many years ago and didn't want to think about but knowing she would have to dig it up at some time.

It was a bad start to her day, but she would not let it get the better of her. She sat back on the edge of the bed and gathered herself. What was it she had planned to do today?

Three things. She fought with herself to think straight. Three things. One. Do some drawing. Well that had taken its own course. Two? Shopping. Yes shopping. You wanted to get something. What? A coffee percolator. Yes. And Three? See Jack. And ask him something special and private. He hasn't called for some time, now. Has he abandoned me, she wondered?

Jack amused her. He could be a bit of a clown at times and although she didn't laugh at him right out, she enjoyed his attempts to try and make her do so. She always put on her serious face for Jack. She didn't know why. She liked him enough and his endeavours to lighten her up did amuse her even if she refused to allow it to show. It was, in a way, Rosemary's way of keeping him a little at arm's length. She wasn't ready to get involved with him more than on a friendship level at the moment. He didn't seem to mind, or if he did, he didn't show it. But today she had a proposition to put to him. A special favour, and if it worked maybe these moods and bad dreams would leave her. There was no-one else she could ask, Jack was a special friend. He would understand and appreciate why she wanted this special favour from him. But she didn't want to think about it right now. It seemed to be related to the dream and she didn't want to be reminded of that now.

***

Jack Weasel had moved flat recently. He had not seen Rosemary for about two weeks, what with the moving and settling in. He was now sharing with Doc, whom he knew for a number of years through soccer. They had met on several occasions through the workers street league, Jack at full-back for *'The Jammy Dodgers'* from the jam factory where he had worked and Doc as striker with *'The Microbe X1'* from the university, where Doc lectured in microbiotics. Jack had marked him on the pitch and the initial rivalry had turned to admiration as they were both fairly good players. They had struck up a friendship which continued off the pitch when the teams would resort to the pub to replenish their energies and replay the match in bawdy good natured argument.

Doc was an early riser, and Jack, who had fallen into the lazy habit of sleeping on in the mornings since losing his job, decided to rise with him as part of his new daily routine. After breakfast he would saunter into town, buy the newspaper and have a coffee. To keep it interesting he decided to have his coffee in a different place each morning. The way things were going, he joked to himself, as far as finding a new job was concerned, he would soon be having his morning coffees in the suburbs.

He was sitting in a pub not far from Rosemary's. It was early and he was the only customer. Jack settled himself at a table away from the bar. The barman eyed him disappointedly as he had been ready for a chat. But Jack ignored him and took the newspaper out of his back pocket and opened it at the Situations Vacant and spread it out on the table. He scanned the columns quickly. Nothing doing again. His kind of genius wasn't being sought after today. 'Aw well. Maybe tomorrow. And then again, if not tomorrow, there was always another tomorrow...!

Jack hadn't worked now for almost nine months. The 'novelty' of having his 'freedom' hadn't quite worn off yet. At twenty seven he had put nine years of labour under his belt. When he thought back on it, it amazed him that he had actually spent nine whole years in the same room in the same building. And it hadn't gotten him very far. Working on the assembly line in the jam factory had come nowhere near achieving his life's ambition. Not that he could pinpoint that ambition. He wasn't even sure if he had an ambition. But he knew it didn't lie in jam making. So, he told himself that a little more 'holidays' at the Nation's expense wouldn't hurt anyone. When he had been laid off at first he had felt some panic, but when the fatal day arrived and he had no more assembly line to attend to, he breathed a sigh of relief. His jam making days were over. They were getting him nowhere anyway. He was sure that the break might turn up something more adventurous, but what that might be he had no idea. But he felt sure that there was more to life - his life anyway - than manning a jam making machine. Looking back on it now, if he had stayed there any longer, he would have ended up like a machine himself.

With his redundancy payment and a small return on a pay-related Insurance policy and his Social Welfare entitlement he had survived. He had only himself to look after. His only real regret was having to sell his second hand car. And now, nine months later his savings were wearing thin and soon he knew he would be totally reliant on what he received from Social Welfare.

Her turned to the front page of the newspaper and scanned the headlines. 'More Summit Talks'. 'Unemployment Figures Still Rising'. 'Milk Levy Tactics'. 'Child Killed By Joy Riders'.

He rolled himself a cigarette and amused himself by re-writing the headlines in his head.

Summit Talks Huge Success.

Unemployment Figures Fall Dramatically.

Milk Prices Stable.

Nobody Killed Today.

Somebody, he thought, should publish a 'Good News' paper!

As he smoked and skimmed over the news items his thoughts turned a corner. In this alleyway of his mind lay the puzzle of his unusual name - *Weasel!*

He had been given the name by his mother. At least he assumed it had come from his mother. He had never met her. When he was found on the steps of the St. Anthony's orphanage a slip of paper had been among his blankets and scribbled on it was the legend - *WEASEL*. Although it was barely legible the nuns were in agreement that that was what it read - *WEASEL*. And as it presented the only clue to his origin they had christened him with it. Whether it was a clue to his ancestry no-one could be certain. But it was, at the time, a brave move on their behalf to christen a child thus.

They were a unique order of nuns. It was also unusual that he had been reared by nuns. It was customary for male foundlings to be reared by the Religious Brothers. But Saint Anthony's *was* different. It was an e*xperimental* orphanage. And at the time a very progressive one at that. St. Anthony's orphanage was set up in 1949 by Sister Imelda O'Riordan, who as a young nun had campaigned for ten years for an orphanage to admit both girls and boys under one roof as they would have been in a proper family. It was not until the passing of the *Republic of Ireland Act* in 1949 that the energetic *Department of Children's Welfare* had given the go-ahead for her dream, but as a closely monitored experimental project. Imelda O'Riordan was then in her thirty ninth year and installed as the youngest Mother Superior in the history of her order. The orphanage of St. Anthony's was not widely known, and had not opened in a blaze of publicity. Sister Imelda, in her wisdom, had made that a proviso, and indeed the Bishop and the government Minister had been very supportive, both for their own reasons, to keep it so.

Would his Mother have known about it, he had often wondered... Had she worked for the Department...? Had she been privy to classified information...? Or was he abandoned at random...? Whether she knew or not, she had obviously been desperate to leave him - *dump him* - like that, twenty seven years ago, back in October of 1956. But no evidence of who she might have been ever came to light.

The nuns gave him John as a first name. But his fellow inmates had quickly changed that to Jack after he had played a *Jack-in-the-Box* in the school play at the age of six. So here he was - Jack Weasel - *Jack-In-The-Box-*

Weasel!

He had known only institutionalized life for so long that he had found it difficult to relate to the outside world for a long time after. He shook the thought out of his head. What the hell! That was his name? What did it matter anyhow? It could be something worse.

He drained his coffee, folded his newspaper and stuffed it in his back pocket and headed for the door. It was drizzling rain outside. Jack zipped up his jacket and buried his hands in the pockets of his jeans. So, he asked himself, looking at the overcast city sky, where to from here? Somewhere out of this drizzle. The Library? Art Gallery? No. He wasn't in the mood for books or pictures. Well? Something to shake the drizzle, unemployment and the feeling of abandonment from his thoughts.

He decided to look around the new shopping centre which had recently opened in a blaze of publicity, claiming to be the biggest shopping centre in the country. Though he had little money to spend Jack liked looking at things, anything really. It was more like dreaming that one day he might just be able to afford some luxuries in his life. He didn't plan to stay unemployed for much longer if he could help it.

As he approached the main mall of the centre and stepped in out of the rain, in the distance he was sure he saw Rosemary hurrying into a large department store. But when he got there and had a quick look around, and not seeing her, he thought he had been mistaken. So he amused himself moochin' about the counters and then headed for the roof-top restaurant.

2

It was twenty minutes to closing time. The pub was crowded. The atmosphere was thick with cigarette smoke and loud animated conversations. The television blinked high up in a corner but nobody was paying any attention to it. Jack and Doc and Jack's former flat-mate Paul, a tall lanky fellow with yellow hair, were jammed on the curve of a corner seat. Doc was flanked on either side by the two lads and his small eyes blinked behind the circles of his little round specs. He was in full flight on one of his theories and had Jack and Paul in fits of laughter at his antics as he stabbed the air with his finger and jumped up and down the more excited he became with his ideas.

'So, OK, man. Look at it like this. Take the barman, there... You go up to the bar... and he says to you... "There's ten pint glasses here behind the counter. Right..? And only one of them is full. Will you bet me the price of a pint you can pick out which one it is? He jabbed his finger in Paul's face. 'Pick a number. One to ten. Go on.' Paul shook his head laughing. 'Doc, you're incorrigible. There's no answer to that.' He buried his face in his pint. Doc turned to Jack.

'Well...? His little eyes were black dots behind his glasses.

'Well, all I can say,' said Jack. 'Is, that if that was the case there'd be very little drinking done here to-night.'

Doc bounced with glee on the seat. 'Yes. Exactly. But we're not talking about drinking, man. We're talking about backing horses. And the pub makes its money from selling full glasses.' He drummed the table with his finger. 'But the bookies, they make their money on the empty glasses, the horses that lose! Our *losers* are their *winners!*

He rocked back and forth in his seat as if he were on a racing horse. '*And the pints are under starter's orders. And they're off. Ten-to-one the half-filled glass. Two-to-one-on the empties. And they're on the counter and they're streaking to the finish and it's Half-Filled by a short head followed by Empty followed by...*'

'Slow down. Doc. You're rocking the table.' Jack laughed and pulled him down on the seat. Doc grabbed his glass and took a long swig. He made a face and looked from Paul to Jack. 'And more horses lose than win..! Didya ever see a *three-horse-race... Huh...?* 'A mug's game. Man, I'm tellin' you. A mug's game.'

Paul put his hand on Doc's shoulder to steady him. 'But it's not as cut and dried as all that. You can study the form with horses. The jockeys. The condition of the track. The weather, eh...' He began counting the arguments on his fingers. Doc rounded on him.

'And who's driving the *effen* Merc's, man? Who? The bookie or the punter? Huh? You can count *them* on your fingers.'

'Well, it's certainly not the punters,' Jack said dryly, taking a sup of his pint. 'I backed a horse once and I'm still on '*Shank's Mare*'.'

'And if you backed a horse one hundred times, man,' Doc jabbed at him. 'You'd probably still be on *effen* Shank's. Given the law of averages?'

Paul and Jack raised their hands in front of them in mock horror. ' Oh. No. Not the *Law-Of-Averages again*!

'You're a gas man, Doc. But spare us the law-of-averages.'

Doc ignored their dramatics. He said flatly. 'If the barman asked you to bet on a glass, you'd tell him to come outside and you'd kick the stuffin' outta him.'

'If you were big enough...'

'Or sober enough...'

They laughed.

'Fair play to you Doc.' Paul drained his pint. 'Did you hear the one about the 'heavy' who came into the pub and says to the barman, "D'ya wanna know how to sell more beer?" "How?," asks the barman. The 'heavy' grabs him across the counter by the shirt. He says. "Fill the freakin' glasses." '

'Tell us a new one.' They jeered at Paul. 'Look,' Doc said, raising his empty glass. 'Talking about more beer. Who's round is it anyway? It's almost closin''.

'Can I talk to you for a minute.' The soft low voice close to Jack's ear took him by surprise. He hadn't noticed Rosemary slipping in beside him on the edge of the seat.

'Jesus! Rosemary!'

'Can I, Jack. Just for a minute?' Her pale blue eyes fixed on his.

Jack recovered from his surprise. 'How are you? I haven't seen you for ages. I think I saw you in town this morning... but that's another story.' He indicated his friends. 'Do you know the lads. Doc and Paul. This is Rosemary.'

Doc and Paul said 'Hi'. Rosemary flicked her eyes in their direction for an instant and them back to Jack.

'Jack...?' She hemmed him in with her look. Doc and Paul were staring at her in bewilderment. They knew was taken out of the fun of it for him, and anyway he could see Rosemary wasn't in the least interested. Put Paul insisted. His initial reaction to Rosemary's dramatic entrance had been off-putting but he was prepared to at least try and involve her in the banter. After all, she was a friend of Jack's. He began to explain again. Doc stared at the ceiling, exasperated. Rosemary had all but spoilt his night. She sat so remote amid the pandemonium of last orders at a few minutes to closing time looking like a zombie in a graveyard, with her pale face, black hair and long black coat.

But Rosemary wasn't listening to Paul. Her eyes darted around at the other drinkers. She had no interest in horse racing, or theories about it. It was only 'pub' talk. Wasted breath. It was of no consequence to her. There were other things, important things, on her mind. She was all keyed up. She knew the lads night out was upset now, but she had been looking for Jack and needed to talk to him while she still had the courage to explain to him. She realized Jack's drinking buddies were bored with her, but he should have let one of them go to the bar for the drinks instead. She looked for Jack at the bar, wishing he would come back so that they could get out of here.

Finally Jack came back and warily placed the drinks on the table. 'Thanks for the help. It was like battling my way up the Amazon.'

His friends raised their glasses solemnly. 'To the Amazon.'

Rosemary didn't join in the toast. She said to Jack, 'Will we be going soon...?

'We?'

'I want to talk to you, Jack.' Her tone was edgy. 'I need

to…'

'Well, here I am. Talk.'

'Jack. Not here.' She gave him a stern look. 'Anyway you're drunk.'

'Me?'

'Yes.'

'Well...maybe I am. A bit.' He gave her a big grin and made to put his arm around her shoulders. She shrugged him off. 'Jack...!'

He changed tack. 'So. Have you been around the pubs looking for me?' He was a bit drunk, all right. He knew he shouldn't have asked Rosemary that question. He was right. She shook her shoulders in agitation. 'Don't be stupid. I knew where to find you.'

Jack raised an eyebrow at her. 'Are you psychic or something?'

'Maybe.' Rosemary let it pass. 'What time is it? Are we going soon?'

'I just got a pint in. Drink your orange. Relax.'

But Rosemary couldn't relax. Jack drew a breath. Rosemary was beginning to get on his nerves. He put down his pint and turned to her. 'Rosemary,' He said pointedly in a hushed voice so that Doc and Paul wouldn't hear. 'Take it easy. I'll be going when I finish this pint. OK.' He pointed to her drink. 'You haven't touched your orange.'

'I didn't really want it.'

'OK. But if you're not in any great hurry I'll just finish mine. I don't want to rush it.'

Rosemary picked up her glass and took a quick

Then, almost inaudibly she said. 'Jack? Who's the girl in your flat?'

'Girl? What girl?'

'The blond girl?'

Jack stared at her, puzzled. What was she talking about? He screwed up his face. He had no idea what she was playing at. Rosemary continued to look at the floor.

'Well,' he began, tentatively, his brain still a little fuzzy. 'Eh... If there is a woman in my flat... eh...' Then it began to dawn on him. He gave a little laugh. 'Rose, my love.'

Her head shot up. She glared at him sharply. 'Don't call me that!'

Jack raised his hands in mock defence. 'OK. OK. But, when were you ever in my flat?

When she didn't answer he continued. 'You don't even know where I live.'

'I do.'

'No you don't. You've never been there. Though you *have* been invited. So...'

'But I know.'

He grinned. 'The old psychic trick again? How do you do it?' But he was thinking. This is ridiculous. I know and she knows she has never been to my place. So, what is she on about? He eyed her. 'When did you call?'

'Today.'

'Today? And was I there?' He shook his head at her. 'No I wasn't. Why? Because I moved two weeks ago. So.'

Rosemary tossed her head in annoyance and snorted. The towel came undone. She wrapped it up again.

'So, the girl in my flat...my old flat...that is...is the new tenant. And, if you went to the right place, and as you've never been there before, as far as I recollect, you may not have. Anyway, the girl you're so worried about is Aisling. Paul's girlfriend. Satisfied?

The towel came undone again and Rosemary pulled it off her head and threw it in a corner.

'You could have told me.' She shook out her hair. 'So where did you move to?'

'Doc's. The guy in the pub with the glasses. The other guy was Paul.'

'Well, you could have let me know you were moving.'

'Rose, love...'

'Jack. Don't call me that!'

'All right. All right.' He sat up. 'If I thought you'd call up and see me sometime I probably would have. But you never...'

'Well, you could have dropped in a note or something. *I* haven't moved.' She glared at him. This conversation was getting her nowhere. It was turning into a pointless argument. But now she was getting annoyed with herself. She wasn't sure now, *how* Jack felt. The fact that he hadn't bothered to let her know he had moved and the scene in the pub..! What had seemed to her a simple idea earlier, to invite him round and talk to him, confide in him, had now changed in the light of what had happened. Perhaps she had expected too much of him? Had she assumed too much of his friendship? She would have to backwater a while...

Then she remembered the percolator.

She hopped off the bed. 'Would you like a coffee? I have the real stuff. I got it today.' She indicated the new percolator, pulling back the orange curtain with a flourish. 'What d'you think?

Jack nodded. 'Looks good. But where did you get that kind of money?'

'Oh ho! That would be telling!' Her voice dropped to a conspiratorial whisper. 'Actually, I stole it.'

She giggled.

Jack shook his head slowly from side to side. The recollection that he had thought he saw her in the department store flashed through his mind. 'Oh, no, you didn't...'

She threw her head back and cocked her hand on her hip like a 'B' movie queen. 'You don't believe me?

'Nope,' he drawled back like a 'B' movie cowboy.

'And where d'you think I'd get that kind of money?

'Howda hell would Ah know. Robbed a bank! Got a present from someone? Ah dunno?'

'A present. From who?'

Jack shrugged. 'Ah dunno.'

'He'd want to be some friend.'

'I never said 'he'.' Jack wagged his finger at her. 'You said 'he'.'

'Well. What if I did? A girl can have friends?' She wiggled her hips coquettishly at him.

'Who then?'

Rosemary burst into a fit of giggling. 'Oh. Never you mind. Never you mind.' And she turned and disappeared behind the orange curtain.

Jack sat back in his chair and closed his eyes. Well, at

least Rosemary's mood had changed for the better.

As he waited for the coffee his thoughts drifted back to the first time he had met her about seven months ago. She had been in front of him in the queue at the Social Welfare office. Jack had only been on the dole for a short time and was applying for a rent allowance. He sat nervously waiting his turn. Most of the others were sitting quietly, smoking or simply staring into space. Even the children with their mothers were somewhat subdued, as if they too felt the ominous atmosphere. The room was dull and sparsely furnished with tubular steel chairs. Posters from the Department of Social Welfare adorned the walls, mostly warning applicants against giving *False Information*, and a *No Smoking* sign, which was being blatantly ignored. The girl in front of him was getting more and more fidgety as she got closer to the door marked Social Welfare Officer. Her eyes flicked around the room, at the posters, and the other people waiting. She caught Jack's eye. He said 'Hi'. She asked him if he had been here before. He said, No it's a first. She was very attractive but her clothes were drab. She told him later that she always dressed down when she came for her visits. 'No point in giving them anything to think about.' She had advised him not to volunteer any information. 'They'll get you on it again.' She sounded like a veteran to Jack. 'Don't act too bright.' And then it was her turn. She wasn't in for too long and as she was passing him on her way out she gave him an encouraging smile. Jack's interview didn't last long. He just filled in the form and didn't volunteer any unnecessary information. He was told to expect a visit at his flat during the following week.

Out on the street he found Rosemary waiting. She inquired how he had done. OK, he shrugged, and after a pause asked her if she'd like to go for a coffee, to pay her back for all her good advice. She declined at first and then agreed. They went up town and had their coffee in a classy little cafe. Over the next hour he told her his story. Rosemary listened attentively. It was only later he realised that she had told him almost nothing about herself. Rosemary seemed to have the knack of changing the subject if he questioned her about her own upbringing. Or she would ignore the question altogether. As he got to know her better, he realised she could be annoyingly moody and tantalisingly vague at times. But she seemed to like him a lot - and moody or not, he found her very attractive. But for some reason she never visited *his* flat. After one or two initial queries as to why, and getting an evasive answer he gave up trying to find out. They made no commitments to each other. Though he found her very appealing and would have loved to take their relationship one step further, she gave him no encouragement in that area. He began to look on her as a sister he never had. Rosemary seemed happy with that arrangement. But secretly Jack hoped that she would change.

He came out of his reverie as Rosemary passed a mug of delicious smelling dark coffee under his nose. He took a sip. 'Wonderful.' He held up his mug in salute. 'Compliments to the chef.' Rosemary sat on the edge of the bed and took a sip of hers then placed the mug on the floor at her feet. She reached under the bed and took out her sketch pad.

'I didn't know you were an artist, too. When did you take that up?' Rosemary didn't answer. 'What are you drawing? Not me I hope?

'Stay quiet.'

Jack closed his eyes.

'Open your eyes.' Jack opened his eyes.

'No. Not like that. Half open. Like you were.' She sniffed the air and jumped up. 'I left the cooker on... Damn.' She threw the sketch pad on the bed and went to turn off the cooker. Jack lazily reached over and lifted the sketch pad off the bed to have a look. 'Hmmm, not ba...' Like a flash Rosemary turned and snatched it from him.

'Don't touch it.' She shrieked.

'I was only...' Jack began, but Rosemary ripped the page out and screwed it into a ball and flung it across the room.

Her eyes blazed. 'An artist's work is *private!* Until they decide to show it!

'Jesus, Rosie, I was only looking.'

She flung the pad under the bed.

Jack tried to make light of her sudden outburst. 'And, anyway, you were drawing me without my permission.'

'An artist doesn't *need* permission.' She picked up her coffee. 'Drink your coffee.' She ordered. Jack picked up his mug with an exaggerated finesse and made a face. 'Yes ma'am.'

They were both quiet for a while. Jack was too tired to be bothered arguing. He had had a pint too many and needed to go home to bed. And eying Rosemary over the top of his mug, looking so enticing, he wished it was *that* bed. Rosemary finished her coffee and placed the empty mug on the floor again.

'So why did you move?' she asked, her tone placid again

Jack didn't answer for a moment. 'I thought you would have guessed.'

He rubbed his face. It hurt, but so did being called a bastard. 'There was no need for...'

'Get out.'

'Rose?'

She sprang off the bed and screamed in his face.

'GET OUT.'

Jack took a step back. 'Rose. What's all this about. C'mon?'

He didn't get to finish. He jumped back as he felt the wind of Rosemary's fist swing past his face. The back of his knees hit the chair and he stumbled back into it. Before he could recover Rosemary was on top of him knocking him and the armchair over. Her fists were raining blows on his back as he fell. He hit the floor and twisted to face her, bringing his arms up to shield his face.

'For Chris'sake, Rose. Lay off. What the hell...!'

But she still came at him, her fists flailing blows on his forearms. In her fury she fell on top of him, winding him. They rolled over, getting jammed against the wall. Jack was incredulous, thinking, *Never pick a fight in a bed-sit. Nowhere to run!* But Rosemary seemed to be very serious. What the hell had brought this on?

With great effort he managed to push her off and struggle to his feet. But she recoiled and came at him with her nails, groping for his face. He backed off, just keeping out of reach. The back of his knees came in contact with the edge of the bed. He put his hand back to steady himself and at that instant Rosemary lunged at him knocking them both onto the bed. He caught her arms and using his legs for leverage succeeded in twisting his body until she was pinned beneath him. She stopped struggling and lay under him, her head turned away. They were both breathing heavily.

Jack let her arms free and pushed back from her. Her kimono had come undone and the sweat was trickling down her naked body. She made no move to cover herself. The aroma of sweat and perfume mingled in Jack's nostrils. He became excited by her heat and her smell and her nakedness. His passion began to rise.

He mumbled softly. 'Rosemary...' A touch of huskiness tinged his voice. He could feel the heat of her body down the whole length of his own through his clothes. 'Rose...' His voice now an urgent whisper.

She turned to face him. Her eyes were wild. She swallowed a few times and he thought she was going to spit at him. Then, with one swift motion that took him by surprise she drew up her legs and, twisting them around pushed at his chest, at the same time heaving and rolling him onto the floor. She sprang to her feet and stood over him, her shoulders hunched and her fists tightly clenched like a street fighter. Where the hell had she learned those tricks, he wondered.

'Don't you ever try that again.' She spat, her voice seeming to come from the pit of her stomach. Her eyes were wild.

Jack edged back from beneath her. He was really getting scared now. He backed up to the wall and leaned against it. He was amazed by her strength. She was only up to his shoulder, and slim, but the fury of her attack had given her the strength of a tiger. He stood, gaping at her. He didn't know what to think or say. He was aware of Rosemary's temper, but this violent outburst was beyond his understanding. Rosemary stood rigid, her breath heaving, watching him like a wild cat.

Jack took a step towards the door.

'Jack.' Her voice was small. 'Jack. I'm sorry.' Her body seemed to deflate and her hands dropped to her sides. Like a lost child. All the fury of the previous few minutes had vaporised.

Jack sucked in a breath and expelled it slowly. He made a gesture of helplessness. He reached out and touched her lightly on the shoulder. She didn't move or brush it away. He shook his head gently and taking a step closer put his arms around her. She didn't resist. She was so warm; so soft. God! This is what he had wanted all along. He pulled her gently towards him and hugged her closer. But she was like a statue; her body unyielding. He didn't want to let her go and gradually he could feel her rigidness subside, the heat of their bodies blending together.

They stood like this for a time; Jack hugging her close; she leaning against him. Jack was excited, more excited than he had thought he would be. He breathed in the fragrance of Rosemary's sweet, sweet body. He wanted her there and then. He wanted to pick her up and lay her gently on the bed and explore every inch of her, slowly, carefully, lovingly. But Rosemary just stood there limply in his embrace. She didn't try to push him away, nor did she raise her arms to return his embrace. She did nothing. But the fact that she was still there, enfolded in his arms gave him hope and courage. He hugged her tighter, loving the feel of her. He lowered his head and kissed her neck. The taste was warm and salty with the vaguest hint of lavender from her shower. It reminded him of how long it had been since he tasted the warm, moist, tang of a woman's skin. He kissed her again, this time letting his tongue roll across her shoulder.

She stirred. 'Jack...'

'Yeah...' His voice deep in his throat.

'Jack. I think you'd better go.'

He hugged her tighter, not wanting to hear the words. Not wanting to let go. Needing her...

'Jack.' She raised her arms and pushed him gently away. He held on to her, fighting for time.

'Jack. Please?' She looked away, unwilling to meet his eyes. The anger gone.

'Rose, love...'

'No, Jack. It's no good.'

Reluctantly he let his hands fall to his side. Rosemary took a step back. Jack was in turmoil. He wanted to grab her and kiss her passionately. He wanted to feel the heat of her passion kissing him in return. He wanted to tear his clothes off and feel her hot skin on his. But she was lifeless. She gave him no sign. No help. No encouragement... He reached out and touched her cheek. Could she not see the need in him? She raised her hand and brushed his fingers aside.

'I'll see you tomorrow...' Her eyes were focused somewhere between his feet.

One last try. Love, desire, pleading, all mixed up in his voice. 'Rosemary?'

But she seemed already far away.

Jack was bewildered. He was stranded. Lost. And finally, dismissed. Christ! What had he done wrong? He didn't want to leave like this. He wanted... Oh, he knew what he wanted, but how to get it? How to retrace his steps. How to unravel this tangled mess and get back to a mutual starting point where they could start again on equal terms? But Rosemary had cut off. Shut down.

Rosemary was confused too. Her plan had backfired. She couldn't fathom exactly at what moment it had gone wrong. But it looked as if it had started to go wrong as soon as Jack had appeared on her doorstep. It seemed, now, as if it had all been a great big mistake. How could she have thought...? She brushed the thought aside. All she wanted now, was to be on her own. She wanted Jack gone. God! She had enjoyed his closeness. She had wanted to respond. She had wanted him then. But she couldn't - wouldn't - bring herself to respond to him. Why...? Wasn't that the exact reason she had invited him in the first place...? Wasn't that her plan...? But not like that! Not like that... So why..? Why..? Why could she not...? Did it have to be on her terms...? Or what..? Or *what*? Why did she have to attack him? What demon had taken hold of her? But she knew. She *did* know. She felt as if she were splitting in two. Oh God! Just leave. Leave me. But another voice inside her was screaming... *Help me...! Don't leave me...!*

But all she could say was. 'I'll see you tomorrow.'

Tomorrow? She didn't want to know 'tomorrow'.

Jack was standing awkwardly with his back against the door, his eyes on the floor. He sighed and shrugged. There was nothing left to do but leave.

'Well... I'll see you, then.' He opened the door and slowly backed out. 'Next time you want a boxing match...' He forced a grin. '...Give me a bit of notice. I'm out of shape.' It was the best he could do under the circumstances.

Rosemary just nodded. 'OK.' But inwardly, don't leave, please don't leave. *Oh, God, don't go...*

Jack hesitated. Poor Rosemary! Standing there. If he could only read her thoughts. 'Will you be all right?

'Yes. I'll be all right.' Why couldn't she say what she really wanted to say? But no. She wouldn't back down now. Better that Jack leave. She needed time to think; space to breath...

'Right. OK. I'll see you tomorrow.' He pulled the door slowly closed behind him. He didn't go up the stairs right away. He stood with his cheek pressed against the door, his fingers still on the handle, hoping Rosemary would fling open the door and fall into his arms. But there was no sound from within.

Not a movement.

He went up the stairs and out into the night.

4

He'd blown it.

Out on the street Jack rolled a cigarette. His fingers fumbled with the paper and tobacco. He was still shaking from the tussle with Rosemary. His hands were unsteady as he lit it and turned down the empty street. He was in no mood to go home so he headed into town. He sucked on the cigarette, the hot smoke rasping in his throat. He threw it away in disgust. It wasn't a cigarette he wanted. The perfume of Rosemary's sweating body still clung in his nostrils. He kicked himself mentally for being such a fool; not reading the signs...! Damn, she had told him to go home and like a lamb he had obeyed.

What did she really want? He didn't know. She seemed so mixed up that her way of giving him the come-on got twisted so that she kicked and scratched instead of luring him on. Or was she afraid of getting involved and her defences became an attack? But, dammit, it had been her idea... Perhaps he should go back and... Perhaps she needed gentle persuasion... Perhaps..! But he was hurt and he couldn't go back and face her. She threw you out, Jack! It was too late now... A snide little play took to the stage in his head...

'Jesus, Jack, you were slow off the mark.' Wink!

'I wasn't trying to get off my mark.'

'You'll never get it that way, old son.' Guffaw!

'Look, I wasn't trying to get anything I was only talking, OK.'

'It's not talking they're after.' Nudge!

'Do you ever think of anything else...?'

'Sometimes. But not often.' Roars of laughter!

'Lay off, will you, there's more to it than *that*.'

'Oh, really. Like what, old son? Y'know, Jack, you're one blind twit. She was asking for it. Asking for it. And you stood there discussing the weather or something...'

'I wasn't discussing the weather. As a matter of fact we were talking about... Oh forget it...'

'That's my problem, old son. I can't forget it. I find it hard sometimes. Know what I mean?' Choking on his pint at his own cleverness. 'Get it Jack?' Digging him in the ribs. 'But of course you didn't get it? '*HAWHAWHAW*. 'You think that thing dangling between your legs is for stirring your porridge!'

Exit.

The bustle and brightness of the night city broke in on the shadows of Jack's thoughts. Buses. Taxis. Couples. Music. Lights. Rushing. Strolling. Laughing. Jostling. Singing. It was all around him. The movement surged over him. Beckoning. Discos. Burger Joints. Cafes. Cinemas. Come on, boy. Relax. Shake out of it. Give us a smile. Have a laugh. Forget your worries. It roared in his face. It tugged at his elbow. It offered relief.

Jack battened down the hatches against its sucking tide, burying his hands deep in his pockets and pushed against the flow. Suddenly he felt hungry. The door-way of a Burger Joint was sucking people in and spewing them out again with burger-filled wrappers crammed in their hot faces. He allowed himself to be sucked in. The loud pounding beat of the music, the glaring lights and the plastic decor assaulted his sensibility. Young girls in striped waistcoats and paper hats pretended to be actresses in TV commercials as they served the burger-hungry queues that snaked towards them. Jack joined the tail of one of the snake. Have-a-nice-day. Have-a-nice-day. *Ice*-day, more likely...

Back on the street he plunged through the jostling crowds, with their shiny laughing faces and their carefree smiles. He swallowed his burger in a few bites. Fast food Indeed! He walked on, and it seemed to him that everyone was going the other way. His thoughts came back to Rosemary. Yes, he should have stood his ground. He should not have given up so easily. He should have pushed his luck... But what did he really know about her? Practically nothing. Where she came from. She had never told him. What she did for a living, outside of the dole. He didn't know. And there was that thing with the percolator...? Must have cost about fifty pounds! Or...? But there she was. The woman with no past, as far as he was concerned. And the woman with no future...? That was how he saw her. *Jesus!* What if she did something crazy...? Like slit her wrists or take an overdose in frustration...? But you don't do those things with frustration...? You lash out...! Don't you...? And she had certainly lashed out at him. But... Damn! She could be lying on the floor this minute dripping blood all over the carpet. *For fuck sake, Jack, come off it! Rosemary's not like that. She just had a bad day...She's gone to bed and it'll be OK in the morning...*

I'll go back. I mean. What was the reason for her eruption in the first place? Was it his refusal to take her up on her offer...? God! She had taken him by surprise, or, was it something else...? I mean. A beautiful girl comes into the pub. Asks you to call and see her. Asks you to stay with her. Then attacks you. Then asks you... NO, orders you...throws you out! *What do you make of that Jack, m'lad?*

I'll go back. Maybe she's just all screwed up and needs

some help. To talk it out. Or maybe she *is* on the floor. What if she had simply gone to bed to sleep it off? A right fool you'd look!

"Oh, Rosemary. I thought you were slashing your wrists.

Oh, Jack. I didn't think you cared.

But, Rosemary, I...

Piss off.

But Rose...

Shag off. OK.

But..."

SLAM.

Here he was acting it all out, much to the amusement of a few drunks on the bridge. He hurried on.

Whatever it is that guides people's feet when they are walking and deep in thought, not paying any attention to the scenes around them, brought Jack along old familiar streets and before he knew it he was standing at the front door to his old flat. So familiar were the surroundings to him that it took a full minute to realise he didn't live here anymore. He put his keys back in his pocket and turned to go. As he did his gaze rested on the old church across the street. His little old church, as he used to call it, with the narrow vaulted windows and the long thin spire reaching up between the three storied tenements crammed on either side. It was closed. Always had been when he lived here. And the soaring spire seemed to be reaching to the sky in a cry for help. How often had he sat in his third floor window and gazed at this little old orphaned church. It was a bit like himself. Out of place. Lost in the progress of bricks and mortar and time.

As he was about to leave he looked up at his old window. The light was on. Paul was probably home. Reading late. Paul would sit up half the night sometimes, reading. And a few times Jack had found him asleep in the morning with a book on his lap. Jack would waken him and Paul never seemed to be surprised. It was as natural for him to waken with a book clutched in his hand as it was for other people to wake up in bed. He had been doing it all his life.

This had been one of the reasons for the bad feelings between Jack and Paul's girlfriend when she moved in. Not that Jack had any argument with Aisling living there. The flat was big enough. If Paul wanted her there that was all right with him. If Paul wanted to read all night that was all right with him too. But it wasn't all right with Aisling. When she had gone on and on about it Jack had come to Paul's defence. Aisling had turned on him.

'It's none of your *goddamn* business. Just keep out of it,' she roared. When she was riled she would roar. She was an actress and she could certainly use her voice. When she had only been a visitor to the flat it hadn't been so bad but now that she was entrenched it was hard to take.

'But I live here too,' argued Jack. 'And it doesn't bother me. You go on too much about it. He's been doing that all his life...'

'It's got nothing to *do* with you. This is our affair and I'd thank you to keep your *goddamn* nose out of it.'

'But I don't see why you have to go on at him about it. That's all I'm saying.'

'If Paul and I are to *live* together, we have to try and under*stand* each other. We have to *com*promise. If I do something to upset him, I'll try to change to make life more bearable for him. And furthermore, it's *bad* for him. It's bad for his health and it's bad for his posture, slumped in a chair all night like that. We didn't buy that expensive new bed for *nothing*.'

'But you said you both had to try and understand each other. Surely you have to understand that if Paul wants to read and sleep in a chair that's his business. It doesn't seem to have done him much harm so far.'

'It's not *now* it will do him the harm. It's later. Dammit. I've *studied* these things. I *know* what I'm talking about.'

'I'm sure you're right. But Paul is not a child and as far as I'm concerned he can do as he pleases.'

Of course, during all this Paul said nothing. It wasn't that he was afraid or anything. He just couldn't be bothered arguing. Aisling's outbursts seemed to have no effect on him. Jack wasn't the type to pick an argument, normally, but something in Aisling made him retaliate. He didn't know what it was. He just didn't like her. After she moved in Jack had tolerated her for Paul's sake. He and Paul were old friends; almost like brothers. But when she began to include Jack in her criticisms and point out *his* bad habits, it became too much for him. So when Doc casually mentioned in the pub one night that he had a spare room in his flat, Jack had a quiet word with Paul and moved. There was no animosity between them. Paul understood. When Aisling heard about it she took it personally as a rebuke on herself, and Paul had to take the brunt of her outburst. Secretly, she was delighted. Jack hadn't seen her since. He had settled happily at Doc's.

And now, two weeks later, he was standing at his old doorstep at half past one in the morning. He rang the bell. What the hell, he'd have a talk with Paul. Get it of his chest. He imagined Paul, his nose stuck in a book, slumped in a chair, slowly unfurl himself and come to the window to look down and see who was ringing at this hour. He craned his neck as he heard the window open. But instead of Paul's face it was Aisling's.

Damn!

'Yes,' Her voice floated down in the stillness. 'Who is it...?'

'Hi. It's me, Jack.'

'Oh it's *you*.' She didn't sound too pleased. 'Paul's not in. I thought he was with you?'

'He's not there? Yeah. I saw him earlier. I thought he had gone...' He assumed Paul had come home. He must have gone to Doc's. 'He's probably at Doc's. Sorry for disturbing you. I was just passing.'

'Passing.?' The disdain in her voice bounced of the buildings opposite. 'Well he's not here. I'll tell him you called. Any message?

'No I'll see him again.' He turned to go and heard the window closing. Then 'Hey, any letters,' he called. But she probably hadn't heard. Just as well, he wasn't expecting any. He didn't know why he said it. But the window opened again. She must have super hearing. Her voice ricocheted in the quiet street.

'What.? Letters?'

'It doesn't matter. It's OK. You can give them to Paul for me.'

'I'll come down and have a look.' She seemed determined to play this out. Why, Jack could not imagine. Perhaps to complain to Paul later about him calling at this ungodly hour in the morning looking for letters...

'Don't bother,' he called, but she was already on her way. The light went on the top landing, then the middle, then the fanlight over the door. The door opened a few inches, the chain lock in place. Did she expect him to jump in on top of her? Her round moon-like face appeared in the gap.

'Sorry.' He could see she was enjoying this for some reason. 'Nothing for you.'

Jack decided not to respond to the jibe in her voice.

'Thanks anyway' He said as courteously as he could and made to go.

'By the way. Someone called for you earlier.'

He stopped. 'For me...?'

'Some *girl*.' There was a hint of a smirk on Aisling's face. 'She said she was your *cousin* or something. She was in an awful hurry. Said she'd probably bump into you later.'

'My *cousin*?' What was all this about? His *cousin*? But he didn't have a cousin. Or any relation that he knew of. But, maybe...*Christ!*

'Are you serious. She said she was my cousin?'

Aisling shrugged. 'That's what she told *me*.'

'Did she give a name.?' Maybe it *was* true. For a moment he hoped it might be possible.

'No. No name.'

'What did she look like.?'

Aisling made a face. 'Ordinary looking. Black hair... longish. She was very nervous about something.'

'*Rosemary*!' He thought. Of course. So she *had* called.

'What?'

'Nothing. It's OK. I know who it was.' He turned away quickly, not wanting Aisling to see his annoyance and the vague possibility dashed. But he knew it had to be Rosemary. Hadn't she told him she had called to see him to-night. But he hadn't really believed her. He heard the door bang shut.

Rosemary! What business had she in saying she was my cousin? She had no right to say that. The first time she calls up to see me and I'm not there and she pretends to be my cousin. He snorted. *Damn!* She had no right to do that! If this was her idea of a joke, well it was a sad joke indeed.

He buried his fists in his pockets and headed home.

5

A party was in full swing by the time Jack arrived back at Doc's. He could hear the stereo as he mounted the stairs. He was cold and tired and miserable and the drizzle had soaked through his light denim jacket. He thought seriously for the thousandth time about buying a proper overcoat but he hated to be encased in too many layers of clothes. But this was the second time today he had gotten wet. Doc would probably give him a lecture about it like the last time. *About the effect of damp clothes affecting human tissue and muscles and the resulting inflammation and his lungs changing from the air filled sacks that they were to a solid consistency and...etc...etc...* But Jack didn't mind Doc's haranguing. Unlike Aisling, there was no malice in Doc, he was a natural clown and his *'motherly lectures'*, as Jack thought of them, were highly entertaining. Doc didn't expect anyone to *take* his advice, he was more interested in them enjoying his performance in *giving* it.

The last time, Doc had jokingly suggested, that as Jack had no mother to keep him on the straight-and-narrow, that he, Doc, would act as surrogate mother, *and* father, if the need arose. The lecturing had been delivered in the form of a pantomime Dame and Jack, instead of taking exception, had been highly amused. He had laughingly suggested that Doc could give Aisling acting lessons. He wasn't annoyed by Doc referring to his lack of parents, either. Doc had a way about him. It was just unselfconscious good fun coming from him. On the few occasions that Aisling had been in Doc's company, although she couldn't help herself laughing at Doc's anomalous behaviour, later she would criticize him as immature and frivolous. Jack thought she was simply jealous of Doc's natural mimicry and acting ability. He trudged up the stairs wondering why the neighbours weren't queuing at Doc's door to strangle him, with all the noise he was creating. But it seemed, Doc could get away with murder.

Jack's feet were killing him. He had done a lot of walking today and it had taken its toll. Since losing his job and his old car he had landed on his feet, as he jokingly told himself. He didn't like buses and he couldn't afford taxis. He didn't like wearing those 'runners' that so many people seemed to find fashionable. Doc had dubbed them the *Casual Athletes*. And most of them, he said were as out-of-shape as he was. Jack liked well made leather brogues and he had been tempted to have a pair hand made at one time when he had some money. But at over a hundred pounds a pair he had kept putting it off. He was sorry now. They would 'stand' to him now. He smiled at his little pun as he approached his door and the noise.

As he pushed open the door he could hear Doc's voice above the music. Doc was standing in the center of the room with his back to the door, a huge cigar in one hand and a glass in the other. In front of him sitting on the sofa, and taking up most of it, was a huge man. He was sprawled, spread-eagled, a glass on one hand and a huge cigar stuck in his mouth. There was a half-filled bottle of brandy on the floor between his feet. He made the sofa look like dolls' furniture he was so large. On first glance he reminded Jack of pictures he had seen of Oscar Wilde, only this man, sprawled as he was, lacked the finesse. He was grinning through his cigar with his tombstone-like teeth at Doc's antics, expounding a new theory on something or other...

'...and *that* guy, man, who discovered that the *majority*

of investors only needed to utilize about *ten* per cent. *Ten Per-bleedin' Cent, man,* at any one time, of their millions... *He* was one smart fucker indeed, he...'

In front of the stereo, a slim, willowy, but somehow shapely woman with masses of untidy orange hair was gyrating spasmodically to the blaring music. She seemed to have her own ideas about the rhythm as she was totally out of sync with what was coming out of the speakers. But that was the way with some of Doc's Jazz-Rock records. Jack was hard pushed sometimes to make out the rhythms himself. He wasn't as 'up' on these things as Doc of course who had given him another lecture on the Pygmy rhythms of Australia, where at times, Doc informed him, you could have up to thirteen different rhythms playing at the same time... *'In the same fucking tune, man...'* But this woman moved as though she might understand it! She also looked as if she was trying to bore through the floor to the flat below.

None of them noticed Jack standing in the doorway, wide eyed and with the steam now rising off him. Then, as he tried to readjust his brain to the scene before him, two more girls appeared from the kitchen carrying plates of sandwiches. They were both tall, beautiful, and dressed like models out of a magazine. Twin-like. They noticed Jack, standing there, steaming. The one in front ignored him and went and seated herself daintily on the last six inches of the sofa beside 'Oscar Wilde', the second stopped in front of Jack, and flashing him a brilliant smile said, Hi, and offered him a sandwich. Jack thought, *Doc was right. I've got Pneumonia. I'm sick in bed. I'm delirious. And I'm hallucinating... Holy Shit!*

Just then, Doc, gesticulating wildly, turned and spotted him.

'Hey! Man! Jack. Old buddy', He roared over the

volume of the Jazz-Rock. 'Hey, the very man. Come in and join the party...' He was pretty drunk. He swung his arm in a wide ark indicating the others in the room. 'This is Jack. My flat-mate. And this is is the professor, man. Newly arrived in the rat-skinner's department at work. Matthew Rolestom. The Prof. And his wife...' He pointed to the spiralling willow. 'Ma...Ma...Marjory, man. And the girls...eh...well...'

Matthew Roleston heaved himself off the sofa, placing the brandy glass on the floor beside the bottle, and lurched at Jack, engulfing his hand in his immense damp paw.

All his ss's ran together in zz's. 'Pleazzed to meet you. Indeed pleazzed.' He hissed through his tombstone teeth and almost crushed Jack's hand as he over-greeted him like a long lost relative. He released Jack's hand an instant before Jack screamed for mercy, and flinging his arms wide, almost engulfing the whole room, introduced the '*girls*'.

'Thizz delightful creature...' He executed a heavy, slow, wink. '...zztanding too close for comfort bezzide you izz Mary. And...thizz..' He waved in the direction of the girl on the sofa munching on her plate of sandwiches. '...izz Rozze. He swayed dangerously, almost knocking Jack and Mary and Doc to the floor. '...Two *won*derful girlzz of our aquaintanzze. Mary and Rozze. The inzzeperable zzizzterzz...! 'He kissed his fingers. Smack. 'Hmmm *Très bien...*'

Jack thought. *Not only am I hallucinating. I'm bloodywell delirious as well...!*

Belying his huge bulk, Roleston retrieved his glass and the bottle and settled himself once more on the sofa executing a neat pirouette in the process, and not disturbing Rose and her sandwiches in the least.

Mary flashed a broad wicked smile and offered Jack the plate. 'You look starved,' she said sweetly. 'Have a sandwich.' And then she noticed the steam rising out of Jack's jacket. She turned to the others. 'Look. Look. Jack's on fire!.' And she laughed a loud warbling laugh.

Doc turned, letting out a roar and screwing up his face shook his cigar in Jack's face. 'How many times, man? How many times..? Have I warned you...?' But he was too drunk to continue and he roared with laughter. He slopped his drink down his shirt-front. Roleston was on his feet in a flash and replenished the drink, letting out a thundering guffaw that almost drowned out the music.

Jack took a sandwich. Mary smiled at him like he was *a-nice-little-boy* and had *done-the-right-thing*. The smile was like a pat on the head. Jack noticed that Mary's brilliant smile was on a level with his eyes. Now he *was* hallucinating. He had shrunk and she had grown! As he chewed hungrily on his sandwich he casually glanced at her feet. She must be wearing six-inch heels, he thought. She noticed his look. To cover himself he said quickly. 'Good sandwich. What's in it?'

She pouted her scarlet lips. 'Ommm. Smoked Salmon and... um, Tomato and Iceberg Lettuce...Things like that. Good...?'

'Yeah. Very good.' He nodded, wolfing it down.

'Courtesy of the host.' She smiled, indicating Matthew Roleston.

'Fair play to him,' Jack said, taking another.

Mary pointed to it with a well manicured nail. 'Baked ham and Pineapple...and Ommm ...'

'Brilliant,' Jack remarked, beginning to get high on the sweet aroma of Mary's scarlet lipstick. She was standing quite close to him. He could almost feel the heat of her body. If he *was* delirious and dying from Pneumonia he hoped that he wouldn't die just yet. This was too much! He was getting aroused by her closeness and her attention and her striking beauty. *God!* She was beautiful...

He came to his senses.

'I haven't eaten for ages...' he said. He wanted to test out his voice to see if all this was real.

You poor thing, she mimed through her smile and then handed him the plate. 'Why not have the lot.' and 'What would you like to drink...?'

'Beer. Please. If you have any.'

'Sor-ry. No beer,' she sing-songed and shook her head in slow motion. 'Only nasty spirits.'

Jack shrugged. 'Fine. I'll have some nasty spirits, then...' Might as well live it up while the dream lasts, he thought.

'Nasty brandy or nasty rum,' she asked sweetly.

'Rum.'

'And...?'

'And.....?'

'Just Rum?' She gave him an appraising look.

'No... and Coke... Thanks...'

She flashed him another one of those wicked smiles and headed for the kitchen, calling over her shoulder, 'Oh, don't thank me. All thanks to the host...' She flapped long manicured scarlet nails in Roleston's direction.

Meanwhile the host was being highly entertained by Doc and the Willow was still drilling, oblivious to everyone and everything. Rose sat wedged on the sofa skillfully balancing her plate of sandwiches on her shapely knees and Doc was in his element with his audience of one. From where Jack was standing it looked not so much a party as a one-man show with guests and pounding music on the side.

Tired though he was, Jack was enjoying himself. The sandwiches were reviving him and the floor-show was highly entertaining. The company was good and he was getting lots of attention... and from a beautiful young woman... After what he had been through already tonight it was bizarre and unreal! And very welcome. The smoke from the cigars added a filmy haze to the scene giving it the appearance of some surreal stage setting.

Mary sailed back from the kitchen. She handed the drink to Jack. 'I've made it a double...' She winked a slow wink at him. 'Save you a trip.' She gave him one of her dazzling smiles. 'And, help you catch up on the others...' *God,* Thought Jack. *This woman is unreal. This isn't happening...*

He asked. 'You not having one..?

'Emmm. Nooo. Not at the moment...' She turned away towards where the Willow was still gyrating and danced around her, coming back to Jack with a joint. She took a long whiff and exhaled slowly. She raised her eyebrows at Jack and held out the joint to him. 'Sor-ry,' She giggled seeing Jack had both his hands full. 'You have no hands.' She held the joint for him to inhale. He took a blast. Then she took his hand and raised it with the glass to her lips. '...And I'll have a little sip...' She sipped. '...of yours...' leaving a little smudge of lipstick on her side of the glass.

Jack's head swam. What with the tiredness and the rum

and the joint and this *apparition, his brain was beginning to slip*. This whole scenario was beginning to be too much for him. He wanted desperately to go to his bed and lie down. But Mary was giving him so much pleasure. And he was loving it.

Mary was passing the joint between them and making small talk. She took the plate off Jack so that he had a hand free to finish his sandwich. Jack wasn't even trying to make sense of what she was saying. He was getting nicely drunk and stoned and Mary's words seemed to leave her mouth one by one and float around the room and land in his ear. He watched the syllables hover in the air in fascination. He took a bite of his sandwich and a swallow of his drink.

Too Fast! It took his breath. He struggled to swallow the remains of the sandwich, but the rum was taking a wrong turning in his throat. He began to splutter and choke. He could feel the blood rushing to his face. He couldn't breathe. He coughed and spluttered, spewing Mary with half chewed bread and a spray of rum. She jumped back with a yelp. In a flash Roleston was on his feet. His huge hand began pounding on Jack's back.

'Atta boy Jack, old zzon. Cough it up. It'zz only a brick...' He roared, '*En Passant, Oui!*' laughing in Jack's ear. Jack felt as though he was going to have a heart attack. The stereo blared in the background. Mary screeching about her ruined dress and Rolestone attempting to smash his spine with those huge fists of his. *God*! He wanted to throw up but he could hardly breathe. Doc was pulling on his other arm and yelling advice. Now Roleston was grabbing him by the shoulders and shaking him like a rag doll.

'Can't have the patient dying on uzz. What zzay you , Doctor...? *Qui Vive! Oui!* And he continued to rattle every bone in Jack's body.

Jack's windpipe finally cleared and he took a few gulps of breath. Doc went over and turned off the stereo.

'OK now, man?' He came back to Jack.

'Yeah. Shit! I think so. Sorry.' A bunch of tissues were pressed into his hand. He blew his nose and wiped his streaming eyes.

'Thanks. Sorry. *Jesus!*'

Roleston was HAWHAWING and whistling through his teeth. 'HAWHAW...OK now, Jack lad? zzz. Live to fight another day! ZZZ HAWHAW...' He lifted Jack off his feet and deposited him on the sofa beside Rose. It rattled the breath out of him as he landed with a jolt, almost knocking against her as she held onto her plate for dear life. Roleston sat on the arm of the sofa. He gave Jack a friendly thump on the shoulder.

'HAWHAW...Wouldn't want to rizzk another zzandwich. What?? HAWHAW.'

Jack wished someone would take Roleston and...

'WHAT HAPPENED THE SOUNDS...?? Marjory began to wail. 'THE SOUNDS...??

'It's OK,' Doc shouted. 'I just turned it off for a minute. Jack had an accident...'

The sofa lurched as Roleston jumped to his feet and went to console her. 'It'zz all right, dear. HAWHAW. Nothing to worry about. Jack'zz had a little aczzident... Drink went down the wrong way. HAWHAW... Carry on...' And he shook his huge frame at her in imitation of her dancing.

Doc turned the stereo back on, but low. Roleston patted Marjory on the back. 'Carry on, dear. Carry on...'

But Marjory stood stock still. Her face screwed up as if she were going to scream again. Doc tried to put a drink in her hand but she brushed it aside. Suddenly she lurched forward and grabbed the knob of the stereo, yanking the volume up as far as it would go.

Doc screamed. *'HOLY FREAKIN' JAYSUS, MAN. ME SPEAKERS!!'* And he jumped to the player to turn it off. But he couldn't locate the knob. Marjory had pulled it off. Roleston grabbed his wife who had begun frantically gyrating to the deafening beat. Doc collided with them and fell sideways. Roleston pulled at Marjory with one hand and pounded the top of the stereo with the other.

'Marjory! Dearest! For Godsake!' He roared. All his SS's back under control. The needle screeched crazily across the record as the top caved in on top of it.

'JESUS H. CHRIST.' Doc roared as he made a lunge to save it. But the damage was done! The arm was in bits and the record was ruined. *'AHHH. SHIT. MAN!'* In a rage he lifted the player and hurled it to the floor.

Everything came to a dead stop. Everyone stared at Doc in a heap on the floor with the smashed stereo.

'AH HOLY SHIT, MAN. THAT STYLUS COST OVER TWENTY QUID..!'

Roleston got to his feet and fished out his wallet. 'Sorry Old Man. Here...' He pushed some notes at Doc. Doc pushed them away. He was shaking his head slowly from side to side and repeating over and over. 'Ho-ly Shit. Ho-ly Shit.'

Roleston tried to push the money into his hand again. 'Here, Old Man... Please... Accidents will happen. HAWHAW...' But Doc didn't find it funny.

'Accidents! BALLS...!

'Please, Old Boy...I'm terribly sorry...'

Doc lifted the pieces of the stereo back onto the table. Roleston shoved the money in Doc's shirt pocket. Doc pulled it out again and threw it on the floor.

'It's not the *MONEY*, man. It's not the *MONEY*...!'

Roleston stood for a few seconds at a loss. 'Well. Hm. HAWHAW. I think we'd better call it a night. HAWHAW...Yes!'

He grabbed Marjory by the arm and gestured to Rose and Mary and headed quickly for the door, not forgetting to scoop up the remainder of the bottle of brandy as he passed. In seconds they were all gone, closing the door quietly behind them.

Doc was on the floor beside the stereo. He had his specs off and was rubbing them vigorously with a tissue. Jack sat on the sofa watching him. His throat was stinging and his head was light.

They heard the street door bang closed and then the sound of car doors slamming and the engine echoing in the empty street below.

Doc put his specs back on and without a word got to his feet and stomped into his bedroom, slamming the door behind him. Jack's ears were ringing with the sudden silence. After a few minutes when his head stopped spinning, he followed suit and went to his own bed.

The mess could wait until morning…

6

Jack.

I want to apologise for what I did tonight. I know I made you mad and I'm sorry. It's hard for me to explain. I felt awful when you left and I wanted you to come back but after the way I treated you I didn't think you would. If you never come back I wouldn't be surprised. You may not believe this but you're the only real friend I ever had. It's not easy for me to say this. It's like you were a brother to me. And I know that is not the way you think about me but I thought it was until tonight. I realise you wanted more of me than I was able to give. I know I invited you and asked you to stay but I wanted to explain something to you first. I'm sorry it turned out so crazy in the end. I didn't want to fight with you but I don't know why I did. But I was afraid. I knew you wanted to make love to me and I wanted to as well but it all went wrong for me. I know this is confusing. You probably think bad of me for leading you on and then asking you to leave.

I have thought about this for a long time, Jack, and want to explain. It's not going to be easy. Most of the time I don't want to be alive. When I think of how my life is I just want to be dead. I know this might shock you but it's true. I have never told anyone how I really feel.

Jack, you have never really asked me questions about myself. You have never put pressure on me to tell you about my past although you have told me about yours. You have accepted me as I am. I know I have asked you a lot of questions and I know more about you than you know about me. This is one of the things I like most about you. You don't pry into other peoples affairs. I always felt safe with you. Although I have acted strange at times and I will try to explain. If it sounds confused it's because I have never tried to explain it before.

You don't know this but I am an orphan too. This is why I said I thought of you like a brother. But the difference is that I knew both my parents. I hope you are not upset by my saying this. I don't mean any harm by it. But you seem to have accepted the fact that you never knew anything about yours. You remember you even joked about it saying that they probably passed you on the street and didn't know it. But my parents are only dead a short time.

I was an only child. My mother died when I was sixteen. She was a lovely woman and I loved her. When she died it nearly killed me. It was the most horrible thing that ever happened to me. Even though she was sick for years before she died we never expected her to go and when she did it was a terrible shock. I still think about her a lot and I miss her. She never complained. She was a wonderful person. She did everything for me and my father until in the end she was confined to bed. She wouldn't go to the hospital. She wanted to be with us at home. And even then she still wanted to cook and clean but she wasn't able. My father was a good man too. He did all he could for us. You might think from this that as an only child I was spoilt and was lazy. My parents didn't spoil me. In fact they were very strict. More strict than most of my friends parents. They were very religious. I have thought about this and I think it was because I was their only child and a girl and they wanted to protect me or something. I don't really know. I think if they had more children they would have not been so strict. They wouldn't have had so much time for me. But don't think I wasn't happy. We were a happy family. My father and mother never fought. I don't remember one argument they ever had. They never fought with me. They were both quiet people. My father was even quieter than my mother. It was as if he was thinking all the time. But he could be great fun too. He would take me for walks around the city showing me things. Especially the Botanic Gardens. He loved flowers. Especially roses. I thing that's why he called me Rosemary. My Mother's name was Mary. But this is not what I want to explain to you. But it's important that you know a little about them because when I tell you what happened after my mother died I don't want you to think bad about my father.

When my mother died both my father and I were heart broken. My father took it so bad he almost lost his job. There were days when he would wake up feeling so badly he couldn't go to work. He would just sit and stare. And sometimes he got so bad he would thump the table with his fists. He stopped going to Mass as well. Some days he couldn't eat. But he would make sure I would get ready for school. I would be almost crying but he would control himself while I was getting ready but I knew when I left the house he would just sit there thinking about my mother. It wasn't easy for me either. Sometimes I would cry all the way to school. After he had been warned a few times at work about being late and some days not going in at all he got frightened about losing his job and got himself together. But I could see he was not happy. It was as if he had lost the will to live any more.

I stopped going to school and stayed at home to help my father. I did all the shopping and housework just like my mother used to do.

My father settled down too. We couldn't forget my mother but I think we began to accept her death. We would talk about her a lot. My father told me all about how they had met and getting married and me coming along and it was just wonderful to see the look on his face to recall all the happiness he and my mother had. But sometimes he would suddenly go silent and stare at the floor and it was as if he was remembering something dreadful that had happened. What it was he never told me. It puzzled me. It was as if he had a dark secret. I'm not really sure but I had a feeling about it. A bad feeling. I can't explain it.

Jack, I'm sorry for burdening you with all this but I have to tell someone. It's killing me.

Sometimes I would wake up in the middle of the night and I would hear my father walking about in the next room. After it happened a few times I got very upset and I got up and went and stood outside his door and just stood there listening wishing I could do something for him. One night he caught me listening at his door and her shouted at me to get back to bed.

Then one night I woke up and my father was standing inside my door. He was fully dressed as if he hadn't yet gone to bed. I was only half awake and wasn't sure if it was a dream or not. Then I don't remember what happened after that. I suppose I went back to sleep. I never mentioned it to him and he never mentioned it either. Perhaps it was a dream. A while later the same thing happened. He stood there for a long time and then came over and sat on the edge of my bed. He reached under the covers and held my hand. I was falling back to sleep and I heard him saying that I looked just like her. That she must have looked like this when she was my age. You see they got married when they were nearly thirty. Then he bent down and kissed me on the cheek. That was not unusual. Even though he was strict in some ways he was not shy about showing affection either to my mother when she was alive or to me. Then he kissed me lightly on the mouth. At this stage I wasn't sure if it was a dream or not. I must have fallen asleep because the next thing I remember was that he was lying beside me in the bed. And then he was kissing me all over my face. I realized then that it was not dreaming. I tried to make him stop and push him away but I was very mixed up. I loved him and didn't want to hurt him. I knew what he was doing was not right. I was very confused. I didn't know what to do. He kept kissing me and he was too strong for me and the next thing I knew was that he was trying to make love to me. It was horrible and I tried again to push him off. But he was too strong. And then he got angry and kept pushing into me. I was frightened. I didn't know how to make him stop. I was crying and then he began to say nice things to me. But I couldn't stop crying. Suddenly he got off me and went back to his own room. I was sore and hurt and confused. I cried all night.

This went on for a few months on and off. I hated him. And sometimes I was so confused because I really loved him. He was my father. And I thought he must be in pain too. We never talked any more. I just wanted him to be like he used to be. If he would only come in the door like the old days. But I dreaded him coming home. And I dreaded going to bed at night not knowing what would happen. I wanted to run away but I didn't know where to go. But then the nights he would come into my room I wanted to kill him.

We never talked about it. We couldn't. Sometimes looking back on it I can't believe it ever happened. But it did. My father wasn't my father any more. He was a monster. A few months later he died of a heart attack. But I was never able to let a man touch me like that again. And that is why I attacked you I think. I'm sorry Jack. I wanted to explain all this to you tonight but it went wrong on me. And now I don't know what to do.

I don't want you to hate my father. I can't hate him now. He's dead and that's the end of it. Even though he did this to me I knew we could have worked it out in time if he hadn't passed away. I know it was wrong. But I don't think he meant to hurt me. It was wrong but it wasn't bad. Can you understand the difference. Even though he done bad in the eyes of the law he wasn't really a bad man.

But I'm so mixed up about it all that I don't want to live with it any more.

Since my parent's deaths and what happened I don't want to be with people. I thought you were different Jack. But I don't know what to do about it now. After what happened between us this life seems so frivolous and unfair and I don't want any more of it. I don't think I can face you again.

Don't think bad of me.

Rosemary.

. . .

Rosemary folded the letter quickly and stuffed it in an envelope and sealed it. She was afraid if she didn't do it quickly she would lose her nerve. She wrote Jack's name on it in big letters and placed it on the bedside locker where it would be found. She sat for a while on the edge of the bed going over in her head what she had written. She hoped he would understand her torment and what she was trying to say. Then she took a bottle of wine from the fridge. This was to have been for their celebration too. Well, she would celebrate by herself. What did it matter. Everything had been said. There was no more.

She took the bread-knife and sat on the bed again, placing the knife on the covers beside her. She opened the wine, OK, here goes, and took a long gulp. The wine was cold and sweet. She drank some more, forcing it down as she wasn't used to it. After a few minutes she could feel her head growing lighter. She took another mouthful, drinking straight from the bottle. No point in standing on ceremony now. She took another swig. Her eyes started to lose their focus. She felt sleepy. She could feel her muscles softening to jelly. The room was beginning to rise and fall with her breath. The white of the walls shimmered and receded. She reached for the knife. It seemed to be a hundred miles away on the bed covers. She took another swig from the bottle. Her head swam. Her tongue felt thick. Her eyelids were like lumps of lead on her eyes. She held up the bottle and tried to focus on it. Half full. Or half empty. Hah! Just like her life. She took another mouthful. God! Her stomach was churning. It felt as if it would explode. She thought she should go to the bathroom and throw up. But she would have to climb the stairs and she didn't think she could manage that, now. She made an effort to stand. No use. Her legs were like... she couldn't think of the word... Ice Cream...and...! Jelly...! She began to giggle at the idea and fell back on the bed, the bottle falling to the floor. She struggled into a sitting position and watched the remains of the wine glug-glugging out onto the rug. She didn't attempt to pick up the bottle. She knew she would topple over if she did, so she fell back instead.

The bread-knife fell in the grove of the bedclothes beside her hand. She grasped for it and brought it up to her face and studied it for a long time, watching the reflection of light catching in the steel and then the reflection of her eyes, unfocused, staring blankly back at her. She turned the blade to and fro. Now you see me.

Now you don't. Now you see me...

With a lunge she slashed the serrated edge across her wrist. She was surprised to feel no pain. Then it struck. *OH SWEET JESUS..! OH SWEET JESUS..!* Was that *her*? Was *she* feeling this? Was *this* really happening..? She slashed again and again, trying to be sure it was *she* who was feeling this; that it was really *she* who was experiencing this...! Then the other wrist. She saw this girl slashing and slashing and her mouth opened to scream but out came a vile mixture of vomit and wine. She watched as the red liquid came in little short spurts from the girl's wrists. Somebody should get help! Somebody should call..! She screamed and screamed. *C o u l d   a n y o n e   h e a r   h e r . . . ? OH...SWEET...DEVINE...JESUS...*

COULD...ANYBODY...HEAR...HER...............

7

His first awareness of her is the warmth of her body as he settles close beside her in the warm bed. Her softness moulded its glow of feminine sensuality around him. He is not in control of his mind any more. It drifts with the voluptuous movements of her body; his arms reaching around her and his hands caressing the silk of her skin. Roooss - a voice deep down in him moans - Maarree - Roooss... SShhhh - The soothing honey of her voice mingles with his.

Half asleep half-awake dreamlike fantasy passion rising with her moving in waves the sweet ripples of her merging with his own heat blending together until no definition of their extremities exists.

The hotness of her tongue caressing the sensitivity of his neck and under his ear throwing back his head in abandonment and her lips following his movement her lissom body sliding over him he hears himself moan from far away and deep deep hungrily sucking at ears and neck and mouth. Ecstatic shivers running through the length of his body and her heat burning...burning...losing control losing his senses losing sense of time and space...of his brain tumbling down a long dark cavern...

His limbs evaporate until he can no longer fathom depth or width or height...his eyes sightless...no light no dark. A sense of space then no sense no space. Then. Sucking at him. Drowning him. His lungs mucus solid thick slimy the torrent of glutinous fluidity.

His body pulsating as she pushes with strong supple muscularity her strength taking him by surprise. Fighting back with all his strength but she is too strong too strong... His hands groping for a hold something to hold but she is on him now he is inside her inside her moving, moving. Down she pushes overpowering with her strength. Panic. Panic. He can't hold on. Too strong. Too strong. Again frantically fighting to hold on hold on but he is coming coming, coming...

A scream. Hers. A scream. His. Outside him..? Inside him...? He can't be sure. Then again. She bears down. His mind returns he tries to hold back. No strength. No strength. He is coming... Too soon. Too soon. Much too soon... His head! Pulling his head! Hands on his head! Hands everywhere! Cold! Cold! The rush of sounds. Voices. He falls! He rises! Is separated!

His Mother? Where is his Mother?

WHERE IS MY MOTHER. WHERE... MOTHER...? MOOOTHERRRRRRRRRRRRRRR..................

Dark. Where is the light?

Light?

Sweat.

The bedclothes soaked in sweat. His heart pounding. His hands shaking. He labours for air. He gropes for the bedside lamp.

The light floods the pillow. It hurts his eyes.

He is awake. The dream fades.

The terror melts. The room is empty.

All is still.

8

Later Jack awoke to the sound of Doc kicking the broken stereo player around the living room. At first the sounds were mixed up with the faded memory of his nightmare, but the roars of Doc soon convinced him that he was awake. Doc was clattering dishes on the table and playing football with the pieces of the broken stereo at the same time.

Jack rolled out of bed. His head felt a bit awry as he pulled on his old dressing gown and went into the sitting room. The room was a mess and reeked of cigar smoke. Bits of the stereo littered the floor. Doc now sat at the table with his breakfast. A *Do Not Disturb!* scowl hung on his face. He looked pretty hung over from the night before. Unusual for Doc. Probably more to do with the wrecked record player than the drink, Jack thought.

Doc didn't look up. He sat there gloomily munching cornflakes. Jack didn't feel so good either. He said 'Hi'. Doc mumbled without looking up. Jack went through to the bathroom.

He ran the cold tap until it was very cold and splashed the water on his face. That double brandy had had its effect. He wasn't used to doubles. He wasn't used to brandy! And the joint! Achh! He should have known better...!

He reached for the towel. The remnants of the dream clung to the corners of his brain. *Rose. Mary. Sex. Birth. Mother.* The images all rolled into one. He shuddered. A shiver ran down his spine. He gripped the sides of the washbasin to steady himself. Achh! He was still drunk. He studied his puffed eyes in the mirror. Too many pints. The battle with Rosemary. The brandy. The joint. Then the nightmare. His head felt like a junk-yard. His face peered back at him. Who *was* the woman in the dream? Rose..? Mary..? His mother..? What did she look like? Like him? He tried to visualise his face as a woman's. He placed the towel over his head like a scarf. Is this what she looked like? Or his father? He must have had a father. Did his father look like this? He was gripped by a sudden sadness. He shook the towel from his head and flung it away from him. He felt really alone. Everybody seemed to have someone. A brother. A sister. Aunts. Uncles. Cousins... Even most of the other kids in St. Anthony's had someone. And the ones that had got away. To new families...

True, the 'Tony Nuns, as they were affectionately called, had been both father and mother to him, and all the kids. Hadn't the other kids been brother and sister to him? Wasn't that what St. Anthony's had been all about..? But it wasn't the same. It couldn't be the same. When he had lived with Paul's family for a time after leaving the orphanage he could see the difference. For all its Love and Attention and Efficiency there was a clinical-ness to it that didn't exist in real families. It would always be the smell of cabbage mixed with floor polish for him. And didn't he still search for his mother in every woman's face?

He splashed his face again and dried it, then flung the towel into a corner, as if it could take with it all his feelings of loneliness and abandonment and the empty feeling that always lay in the pit of his stomach.

When he came back to the sitting room, Doc was still sitting, eating and scowling. They didn't speak. Jack went into his room and dressed. He came out and sat opposite Doc.

'Good morning,' he said as jovially as he could. But he

didn't mean it. Doc just ate and scowled. Jack poured himself a bowl of cereal.

'So...?' He tried again. But Doc could not be moved. He just shrugged. Jack tried again. He had never seen Doc in such foul humour. 'Is the tea hot?' He asked, feeling the teapot. It was lukewarm. 'Will I make a fresh pot?' Doc shrugged again. He munched. Then. 'If you want to.' He waved offhandedly. 'I've had enough...' He was so mad he could hardly mouth the words. Jack went to the kitchen and made a fresh pot. He had only shared the flat with Doc for two weeks and didn't know all his moods yet. Obviously the wreck of the stereo had bitten him deeply.

When he came back he poured himself a cup of tea and caught Doc's eye. He held up the teapot. Doc held out his cup. 'Yeah. OK...'

They drank in silence for a few minutes. Doc put his cup down with a bang. He snorted. 'That bloody clumsy dope-head...' He picked up his cup again and suddenly flung it with full force at the wall behind Jack's head. Jack ducked automatically as the cup whizzed past his ear, but he knew it wasn't meant for him. It smashed, dousing the wall with tea. He glanced over his shoulder at the tea running down the wallpaper and then back at Doc. He burst out laughing. He couldn't help himself at the expression on Doc's face. It was a mixture of anger and annoyance and bewilderment at his own action. It seemed as if the whole of his face was converging in the center of his eyebrows and would disappear under the bridge of his glasses. Jack tried to stop laughing. But it was no use. The tea dribbling down the wall, Doc's scrunched up face, the debris of broken stereo, he couldn't contain himself. He clapped his hands over his mouth for Doc's sake to stifle the laughter. Then Doc burst out laughing too. He picked up his plate and saucer and they followed the cup... Smash... Crash. He jumped up from the table. 'What the hell...! What the hell...! It's only a record player, man. It was a heap of crap anyway!

He threw on his coat and headed for the door. 'Gotta go. I'm late, man. See you later...' He was gone. Jack stopped laughing. He shouted after Doc. 'Oh, it's OK, *man*. I'll clean it up. After all what else have I got to do..?

He finished his breakfast. Doc was back to his old self again. Fine. He cleared the dishes into the kitchen. Then wiped the wall with a dishcloth. It left a brown stain on the wallpaper. There would always be that shadow to remind them of Roleston and his party. Anyway, Doc had had a good laugh at his own misfortune and he would milk mileage out of the story in the retelling.

Jack cleared the pieces of broken crockery into the bin. He gathered together the bits of the stereo. Whatever damage Roleston and his wife had done to it might have been mended, but Doc, in his rage, had kicked any fixing out of it. He built them into a pile in the middle of the room, thinking that Doc could get a final 'kick' out of it when he got home later. He didn't think Doc would sulk for long over it. He would probably replace it with a more up-to-date model and that would be an end to it.

All the commotion had made Jack almost forget what day it was. Wednesday. Dole Day. He checked his watch. Nine twenty. He signed on at half past eleven. Loads of time. He went back to the kitchen and washed up the remaining dishes and the glasses and plates from the party. He'd call on Rosemary, pass an hour, have a coffee and try to sort out the disastrous misunderstanding from last night.

God! Last night seemed like years ago. And it was

only a few hours! He was still annoyed at Rosemary for telling Aisling she was his cousin. And the row? *God!* Was *that* something! He didn't know how he felt about her now. Last night he had loved her and then hated her. But they had been – no, still were - friends. That, he had decided long ago, no matter what, he would be her friend, regardless. So he would go over this morning and sort this thing out. For all her peculiarities; for all their misunderstandings; for all his uncertainties, he was fond, very fond, of Rosemary.

9

The orange curtain was still closed over the basement window when Jack rang Rosemary's bell. He rang again. He wasn't in the habit of calling on her so early like this but he wanted to clear the air as soon as possible. Perhaps when they had this misunderstanding sorted out they could spend the day together. There was still no movement from below. At least she could shake the curtain and let him know she was getting up. If she was trying to avoid him he wasn't going to go away. He was here now and he was going to get it over with.

He gave it another minute and pressed the bell. A long ring. Still no movement. He looked around for a stone to throw against the window but he couldn't find one. Just then the door opened. It wasn't Rosemary. It was a middle aged man from one of the other flats. Before he shut the door Jack bid him a 'good morning' and slipped in. The man paid him no heed.

The door down to Rosemary's bed-sit was ajar. Jack knocked. No reply. Perhaps she had gone out for milk. He knocked again and called down. No answer. He didn't want to go down and wait. He didn't know if Rosemary would like that and he didn't know what kind of humour she was in this morning. He rolled himself a cigarette. Still, it was odd, her leaving the door open like that.

A woman came down the stairs carrying a shopping basket. Jack nodded to her. The woman nodded back and walked on down the hall. As she was about to open the hall door she stopped and looked back at Jack, scrutinising him for a moment.

'Are you looking for someone,' she asked suspiciously,

looked him up and down.

'Yeah. The girl from the bottom flat. She must have gone to the shop.'

The woman sniffed and scrutinised him a while longer. She seemed uneasy with him standing there loitering in the hallway. The ash from his cigarette fell on the polished floor. The woman's eyes followed it and then back to his face.

She asked sharply. 'Are you a relative...?'

There we are again! Jack thought. This *relative* thing.

'No. Just a friend.'

The woman cleared her throat and then pressed her lips together into a thin line. She said. 'Hmmm.' She seemed to be appraising him. Then she lowered her voice and said in a conspiratorial whisper. 'I'm not sure if I should tell you this...' She glanced up at the stairs behind Jack to make sure all was clear. '...But seeing as you're a friend...' She paused. 'The girl in the basement was taken in an ambulance.'

'An ambulance!'

'Yes. In the middle of the night. There was awful screaming...and thumping. Anyway.'

'*Jesus!* What happened?'

The woman features tightened in annoyance. 'There's no need to take the '*Holy Name*' in vain.' She admonished him. 'Anyway that's all I know.' She turned and opened the door.

Jack shouted. 'What happened..?' But she stepped out and pulled the door closed behind her.

Jack ran to the door and flung it open. She was hurrying down the street. He called after her. '...Which hospital...?' But she simply waved her hand dismissively over her shoulder and scurried on.

Jack froze in the doorway. His mind was a blur. *Jesus!* If only he had returned last night! If he hadn't let his passions run away with him! If he'd only trusted his instincts...! If. If. If... He banged the door shut in frustration and ran down the back stairs. He stopped in his tracks. The bed-sit was a mess. The bed covers were crumpled on the floor. The little table was on its side and there were dishes and ornaments smashed around it. The stale smell of spilled wine and vomit assailed his nostrils. He took a step into the room. The only thing in place was the orange curtain covering the kitchen.

There were dark red smears on the wall opposite the bed as if someone had squashed flies in temper. They seemed to jump out at him from the white walls. He recalled Rosemary saying once how white walls showed up to advantage everything in the room. He hadn't thought much about it at the time, but it struck him with force now. But this was blood. From a human being. From Rosemary!

The room looked like the scene of a violent struggle. They had fought, yes, but he couldn't remember having caused this mush damage! Or, had she been attacked *after* he left? *My God!* This was going on while he was roaming the streets! He was almost afraid to take another step into the room.

Rosemary...Rosemary...! *Good God Rosemary*. What happened...! And to think I could have prevented all this! Why didn't you say...! He bent down and touched the bed covers on the floor. There were stains of dried blood already encrusted on them. *God!* It didn't take long for life to stiffen! Only a short time ago this had been warm blood flowing through Rosemary's veins. He had felt it pulsating through her only a few hours ago when he held her.

Only a few hours ago.

When he had laughed at her.

When he hadn't listened to her.

When he had fought with her.

When he had held her.

And now...?

Now...? Now he had to find which hospital she was lying in.

Which hospital? He thought of the encounter with the woman upstairs. Oh yes, you stupid bitch! You knew *what* happened. The screaming. The banging. The ambulance. *That's* something to whisper and gossip about. But which hospital? *That* vital piece of information was of no interest to *you*.

His raving took its course. It had nothing to do with the woman in the hall. He had no right to harangue her. She had only been an innocent bystander. He blamed himself. *He* could have prevented this. But *she* didn't have to be so smug.

He caught a glint of something underneath the bed, and crouched down to look closer. It was Rosemary's black handled bread knife. He stepped carefully over the debris on the floor and reached under the bed and drew it out. There were traces of blood on the handle and along the serrated edge. His nerves jarred. He could sense the rasp of its jagged edge along his own wrist. He shuddered, staring at it for a long time. He couldn't think. He didn't know what to think any more.

Finally he came back to his senses. He pulled the

sketch pad out from under the bed. He leafed through it. Page after page of weird drawings! He tore a few empty pages out of it and wrapped the bread knife carefully - almost reverently - in it. He had the sensation of partaking in some strange ritual. He tucked it inside his jacket and left the room. There was a pay-phone in the hall. He fished in his pocket for change. He picked up the receiver and then noticed there was no phone book. Typical! He banged the receiver back in place. *Damn!* He stood for a moment glaring at it. He felt like smashing it against the wall.

He raced out onto the street.

The nearest phone box was occupied. He shifted from foot to foot in agitation hoping the woman in the box would notice his urgency. *Come on. Come on.* But she ignored him. He wanted to pull the door open and drag her off the phone. Then he noticed that the phone was one of the old black models. She could be on that for ages. He swore and took off down into the next street. No phone box in sight. He went on, half walking, half running. He saw one. Unoccupied. It was probably free because it was out of order.

It worked. He leafed through the book. Hospitals. He hadn't realized there were so many. He counted his change. He only had enough to ring a few.

On the third attempt he was lucky. Yes Rosemary Carr had been admitted. Yes she was comfortable. Was he a relation? No? A close friend. Hmm... He could visit her. But only for a few minutes. Which bus. Right. He raced to the bus-stop.

St. Chives Infirmary was lost among warehouses in the old commercial end of the city. Jack wasn't familiar with this part of town. The hospital, which predated the surrounding buildings by at least a hundred years, stood out from the turn-of-the-century warehouses and it's once sparkling granite facade was dulled by decades of grime. But it was still like an oasis tucked away between these dilapidated streets. It's high windows and spear topped railings gave it a stately air among the bustle and whine of trucks and fork-lifts. Two hundred years ago it had stood proud, among lush gardens on the fringe of this old merchant city. But now it crouched like a flower choked among weeds.

The receptionist was helpful. Even though it wasn't an official visiting time Jack had no trouble getting to see Rosemary. On the way over in the bus he had made up a story about being an only distant relative, just in case. It struck him, as he went up in the lift, that the hospital was happy to see him - or anyone - so soon after what had happened. He could see Rosemary right away. But only for a few minutes. When he found her, she was propped up on pillows in an old iron bed in the middle of what looked like a disused ward. It was more like a large store-room. There were other beds, unoccupied, pushed up against the walls. And hospital lockers were stacked in one corner. But there was a cleanliness and order to it that could only be found in a hospital. Either the hospital was filled to overflowing or they were keeping her isolated. Jack didn't know which. He had no experience of hospitals.

Rosemary seemed to be sleeping. She was very still. Her eyes were closed but there was a slight grimace of pain sketched across her pale face. Jack stood motionless gazing down at her. She looked unreal. Shrunken. Paler. Jack had never seen her so still before. Rosemary rarely had the same expression on her face for two minutes in a row. She swung from one mood to another, so that her face seemed to be continually in motion. But now, seeing her just lying there, so still, it was like he was seeing her for the first time. The upward slant of her eyes seemed more acute than usual, and that, with her drained, alabaster-like complexion, gave her the appearance of a geisha. The picture of her standing at her door last night, in her kimona, flashed into his head; her standing there with her hair piled up in a towel and him miming and calling her Lotus Blossom and she hadn't been amused. Seeing her now, like this, he wondered, that if he had been asked to identify her he would have had to think twice. He shook the morbid thought out of his head.

Rosemary seemed to sense his presence. 'Jack...' Her voice was drowsy. Her eyes slowly focused on him. 'Jack...'

For a minute he could find no words. She sounded so lost and isolated. He watched as the heaviness lifted from her eyes like a shadow. She forced a smile, a pale smile with painful memories tagged onto the end of it.

He sat carefully on the edge of the bed and touched her hand lightly. He noticed that both her wrists were bandaged and a tube extended from one arm to a plastic container attached to a stand at the head of the bed.

'Hello Rose. How are you?' He said softly, a lump forming in his throat.

She expelled a long breath. '...Poor Jack...' She sighed, her voice low and raw. She swallowed a few times. It was difficult for her and she screwed up her face with the effort. She closed her eyes again as if to keep them open was too much for her. Jack held her hand gently, not wanting to disturb it as she lay there, wan and deathlike. He watched as her eyes opened again and the cloudiness passed in slow motion. Her lips parted slowly, forming the words.

'...How are you, Jack..?'

It was unreal. She was asking him how *he* was. She was the one in pain and she was asking *him*. He gripped her hand tighter. Suddenly he realized how much he loved her. He didn't want to see her in so much pain. He didn't want her to die. He forced himself to smile and she shifted her body slightly, but with great effort closer to him.

'I'm fine, Rose. How are you doing...?' He wanted to bend down and kiss her pale mouth. He wanted to scoop her up in his arms and take her away from here.

Her words were slow and laboured. '...I'm OK... Thanks for coming...' She drew a long breath. '...Is the flat a mess..?'

Jack squeezed her hand. 'Don't worry about the flat. I'll fix it up.'

'...I'm sorry, Jack... I...' She seemed to be talking through a haze, her voice coming from far away. Jack was thinking. When all this is over we'll sort something out. He renewed his resolution to himself that no matter what, he'd never abandon this poor troubled...

'Jack.' She tried to sit up. Panic in her voice suddenly making it strong. 'Jack? Did you find the letter...?' She fell back.

'Letter? What letter?' He didn't remember any letter. Did he miss it in the hall when he left Doc's this morning? He would have noticed it, surely? No. He had seen no letter. He tried to remember. 'Did you post it.' He was puzzled.

'...On the locker...' She said. '...In the flat...' She tried to sit up once more, alarm in her eyes.

'No. I didn't see any letter... For me…?' He visualised the mess in her flat. He didn't remember any letter. All he had seen was the upheaval and the splatters of blood. He hadn't noticed the locker at all. Why hadn't he noticed the locker? And the knife.

The knife! It was still wrapped under his jacket.

The knife. He took it out and unwrapped it.

'Rosemary...' As he held it up for her to see he realized what a fool he was! Why was he doing this? *For Chris'sakes why was he showing her the bread knife!* He wished it would vanish. He tried to stuff it and the wrapping back under his jacket. But Rosemary had pushed herself up and she had seen it.

'What, Jack?'

He zipped up the jacket. 'It's nothing.'

She fell back. She made a weird sound in her throat. Her lips crinkled in a grimace. Jack thought the sound she made was crying. But it wasn't. She was laughing.

'Jack? What are you doing with the bread knife?' The grimace became a pained smile.

Jack felt ridiculous now. What the hell had he been trying to prove? Had he been trying to tell her something? Make her feel something? What? But whatever it was she had shattered it with her question. What *was* he doing with the blasted bread knife, which he had carefully wrapped and carried around town? But he felt compelled to continue. He stammered. 'It's the knife you...cut...yourself with...' Not - *tried to kill yourself with*, or - *slashed yourself with* - But *cut* yourself with. He heard himself saying it and he was disgusted by his pathetic attempt to *make her feel something*.... What, for Chris'sake...!

Hadn't she suffered enough? He felt cheap.

Well. He had done it. She had seen it.

She had asked him what he was doing with it.

And he had no answer.

He stood up. He felt like a fool. He had to get out. 'I'll clean up the flat.'

'Jack? Are you going...?' She tried to raise herself. 'Don't worry about the flat.'

'No. I'll fix it up.' He dug his hands deep in his pockets. He needed to go now and do something to make recompense. 'I'll fix it up. I'll come back tomorrow.'

Rosemary managed a smile and sunk back into the pillow. 'Thanks Jack. Thanks for coming...' Her eyes seemed to take on an extra light. That was what she wanted to hear him say. That was all she wanted. That he would come back tomorrow. Was it really so simple?

Out on the street he found the nearest litter bin and buried the knife and it's wrapping deep in the garbage. He never wanted to see it again. Never wanted to touch it again. It was *unclean*. A reminder of Rosemary's pain and his own foolishness. He couldn't imagine her wanting to use it again to cut bread and he couldn't carry it to the dole office.

Damn! The dole! He checked his watch. Just eleven thirty. He should be there now. He had a half an hour before they closed. If he didn't get there between now and twelve he would have a lot of explaining to do. He could lose a day's money. And they'd want to know why. They were sticklers for time keeping lately. They closed on the dot of twelve. He'd have to take a bus. Two, maybe. But which bus? He didn't know this part of town. He could be waiting ages. He checked the name of the street. If he cut left and went along by the river and ran all the way...

He reached the dole office with just five minutes to spare. The caretaker was standing inside the door. He checked his watch as Jack hurried past him and took his place at the end of the queue. There were only five in front of him. He had never been this late before. Usually there were about twenty ahead of him with twenty more behind. He looked back at the caretaker and saw him with his hand on the door waiting for the clock to move on. *Rotten bastard!* He'd close the door on the button if it was the last thing he did. Jack was catching his breath. The sweat was pouring off him. He was definitely out of shape. He hadn't played football for months. The queue shuffled forward. It was hard to stand there in line when he was hot and sweaty.

He reached the hatch. Last in the queue. The girl gave him a *Made-it-by-the-skin-of-you-teeth* look. She knew he was late. Out of the hundreds that queued at hatch 22 she knew all their times by rote. Dole queuers were as regular as clockwork in their places in the line. A smart remark crossed his mind, '*hatch 22 - catch 22*', just to let her know he didn't care what she thought. But he let it pass and held up his signing card to the grill. He hated saying his name. She handed him the signing slip and looked at her watch. Was she giving him a hint or just checking how long it was til lunch? He scribbled his name and went to the pay hatch. He said, Thanks. The girl just nodded and closed the hatch. Yes. Same time next week unless the Economy suddenly takes a sharp rise, he mumbled, as he headed for the door. The caretaker opened it just enough to let him slip through. It closed on his heels.

Well, he thought, It's not a Five Star Hotel. He doesn't expect a tip.

10

After a fast-food lunch and coffee, Jack went back to Rosemary's flat. He'd forgotten to ask her for a key to the front door. He had been in too much of a hurry to get out of the hospital and reckoned he'd have to take a chance on someone opening it for him. He assumed her flat door would still be ajar.

He waited outside for a while, but nobody came out or went in. He decided to chance ringing some of the other bells. A window on the second floor opened. A woman's voice floated down.

'Yes...?'

He craned his neck but he could only see the top of her head over the sill. 'Oh. Hello. I've come to collect some things for the girl in the bottom flat. She's in the hospital...' He called up, hoping that the woman would respond to the urgency in his voice. From what he could see of her it looked like a young woman, and not the one with the shopping basket he had met earlier.

She called down. 'Have you no key?'

Jack was agitated. He hated having to conduct a conversation like this, shouting in the street. But the woman in the window gave him no choice. 'She had an accident... I need to get some things.' He tried not to show his annoyance. 'She...I forgot to ask her. I'm her brother. Jack...Carr.' He lied.

The woman thought for a moment. She turned back into the room then back to Jack. 'What girl did you say?'

'Rosemary. Rosemary Carr. In the basement.'

He waited, wondering if the woman knew Rosemary, and that she didn't have a brother. He kicked himself for forgetting about the keys. This was a nuisance.

The woman called down again. 'Right. Wait.' The window closed. Jack breathed a sigh of relief. It took her some time to come down. When she opened the door she was holding a young child in her arms.

'Sorry for dragging you down.' Jack said and rushed past. He didn't want to get entangled in small talk. He disappeared down the back stairs without looking back at the woman's raised eyebrows. He heard the street door bang.

The disarray in the bed-sit didn't have the same effect on him as it had earlier, knowing now that Rosemary was safe. The upheaval lost most of its significance for him. Earlier, he had been acutely aware of the lingering charge of violence which hung in the room like a dark veil, but now it simply looked like a cold mess. Although the blood streaks on the wall still made him wince, somehow they didn't seem as large as he had remembered.

The letter...

It wasn't on the locker. Rosemary must have made a mistake. He lifted the small table and threw it on the bed. The letter was not on the floor. He moved some of the broken crockery with his foot, then he went on his hands and knees and looked under the bed. There it was, far in, near the back wall. Rosemary must have flung it under together with the knife.

His name was scrawled in large letters on the front and there was a tiny red smudge on one corner. He replaced the table on the floor and sat on the bed. The envelope was very thick. He turned it over in his hand. Did he really want to know what Rosemary had written..? Written when she had obviously not been in her right...

mind. No! That was unfair. He shouldn't be thinking like this. She had been upset. Very upset. That's all.! He was undecided as to what to do. When she had mentioned the letter in the hospital maybe she had wanted him to find it and destroy it. She hadn't said. He decided not to open it until he saw her again.

He folded it and put it in his pocket. If Rosemary wanted him to read it then, he would.

He started into the cleaning.

It didn't take long to put the room in order. First he tackled the sink where Rosemary had been sick. Most of it flushed away by running the tap, but the rest had to be fished out with old newspapers. It was a disgusting job and he had to tie a small hand towel around his mouth and nose as he did so. The soiled bed covers he stuffed in a black refuse bag and left in a corner. He tidied up the bits of broken crockery and ornaments on the floor and heaped them on the table. He didn't want to dump them. Rosemary might want to mend some of them? He shrugged. He'd ask her later.

The stains on the wall didn't scrub off so easily, he'd need to get some paint later and paint them over. He might as well paint the whole wall while he was at it. That would be better.

By the time he was finished he was hungry. He found some pasta and a jar of sauce in the fridge and it cooked quickly. After eating he cleared the dishes and took a last look around. It was tidy enough except for the stains on the wall and the wine on the rug. He opened the window, with some difficulty, to let in some fresh air.

Rosemary was normally a tidy person. Although, he thought, she could be all-over-the-place in her head, in her room she had a place for everything; her ornaments, her clothes, her few books and all her bits and pieces. He found it hard to visualise her throwing things about and smashing them. But she had! The evidence was all around him.

He pulled the door closed at the top of the stairs as he left. He would make sure to have keys the next time.

Later, climbing the stairs to his own flat Jack felt weary. The events of the past twenty four hours weighed on him. He was drained and wanted to do nothing except sprawl on the sofa and relax. He heard music coming from the top of the house. Doc! He sighed and went on up. As soon as he put his key in the door the music stopped.

'Here, man...' Doc pulled him in and propelled him to the sofa. '...Watch... Listen...!' Doc pointed across the room. The music sprang out of a shiny new racked stereo system, stacked about three foot high, with huge speaker cabinets on either side.

Doc waved his hand in the air. 'Reeemote Contrrrol, man...' He roared above the blare of the music. 'Fucking ACE, man. Latest technology...!' He zapped the system off. 'Whaddya think? Huh..?' Jack was silent. Doc jumped to his feet. 'Well...? Whaddya think, man...? Old Roleston, man, he has contacts everywhere. He's not called The Professor for nothing. Look. Tracks at five grams up-side-down. *Up-Side-Freak-Ing-Down*...!' He punctuated each syllable by jabbing the air with the remote control in his hand. 'Quadraphonic adaptability. Fifty watts per channel. Separate bass booster. Equalization. The only thing it doesn't do, man...' He gave a wry grin. 'is turn the record over...!'

Jack wasn't listening. Doc saw the detached look on his face and stopped. 'Sorry, man, just got carried away.'

Jack winced. 'It's OK. I just had a weird day, that's all.'

'Dole boys get you. Huh?' Doc wagged his head impishly. 'It's a bad scene, man, you need to get into something.' He laughed. 'Even a job, man!' He hopped over to the stereo and turned the record.

Jack sighed. 'I just came from the hospital...'

Doc turned and scrutinized him. 'Hospital?'

'Oh. It's not me. Rosemary. The girl in the pub. Last night...'

'Yeah. I remember. A bit of a looper...'

'Well. She tried to... She slashed her wrists last night.'

'Serious...?'

'Well. she'll be OK.'

'Where you there?'

'No. It was after. I only found out this morning.'

Doc began fiddling with some wires at the back of the new system. He fiddled for a minute and then stopped and looked at Jack through his little round glasses. 'A weird lady, Jack. None of my business, man. But a weird lady all the same.' He re-assembled the wires in silence for some minutes. Jack was too tired to bother saying anything more. Doc stopped what he was doing and put the stereo back against the wall. He took off his glasses and gave them a rub. He put them back on and raised his eyebrows at Jack.

'You and her...?'

Jack ignored the inference. He took out his tobacco and rolled a cigarette. 'Well the main thing is,' he began slowly. 'Is that she's going to be all right. I suppose.'

'Yeah, man. Right.'

'We're just friends. Really. I met her just after I lost the job - I mentioned it - At the Social Welfare office. Got talking.' He lit the cigarette. 'We got on Ok together... yeah, I know, sometimes it's... Ah, what the hell!' He took a long drag of his cigarette. Doc didn't say anything for a minute waiting to see if Jack wanted to say more. He could see Jack was upset. He didn't want to put any pressure on him to talk if he didn't want to.

Jack took a breath. 'It's...well. I don't have any...y'know...people, and hers are dead.' He paused. 'We're kinda like brother and sister. Or something. I dunno. We're not lovers or anything. Though...' He stopped. Doc waited. Jack went on. 'I like her. She's strange... *Different*... Well I suppose I'm different too. But we get on great together. If I'd stayed. Last night. But I didn't. And then she...' He gave a short moan.

Doc said. 'It's OK, man. You don't have to explain. That's your own business.' He closed the top of the stereo.

'I wish I could explain. I don't understand why she... took it so bad. She asked me to... do something for her and I thought it was a joke. At the time. Then it all went wrong. Oh. I dunno.' He thumped the arm of the sofa.

Doc waited for him to continue, but Jack just sat staring at the far wall. Doc shifted uneasily and asked. 'You want to eat? I got a couple of T-bones.' He made a face. 'Kind of celebration. For the new system.' He nodded towards the new stereo.

'No. I'm not hungry. I had something already. I might go out later. Pictures or something.' Doc shrugged. 'Sure, man. Whatever you think.' He disappeared into the kitchen. Jack stretched out on the sofa. He could hear Doc slamming things about in the kitchen. He turned his head and searched the floor, but there was nothing left of the old record player. Not a scrap. He stared at the ceiling and closed his eyes.

11

'Did you find the letter?' Rosemary was sitting up in a bed in the public ward. She had been moved later the previous night. She was looking remarkably brighter and wearing a light blue dressing gown over a white hospital shift. Jack was surprised to see her looking so perky. He pulled up a chair.

'I did.'

Rosemary dropped her head and looked at him under her eyelids. A little girl's face, coy but anxious.

'And?'

Jack took the envelope out of his pocket. 'I didn't open it.' He said. There was a touch of resigned gallantry in his voice. Rosemary noticed it and dropped her coyness. She asked haughtily. 'Why?' And fixed him with her eyes. Jack was taken aback.

'Why...?'

'Yes. Why? Jack.'

He placed the thick envelope on the bed and squared it off along the lines of the candlewick counterpane. 'I wasn't sure...' He was thinking, if she *hadn't* pulled through, it would have been different, of course I would have read it, to find out. But as she *had* pulled through. But he couldn't very well tell her that. He tried to make light of the situation. 'You asked me if I had *found* it. You said nothing about *reading* it.'

She gave him a haughty look. 'And you weren't curious?'

'Of course I was curious.' She had got his back up now. 'But I didn't come here to fight about it. If you

87

want me to read it I will.'

Rosemary's eyes dropped to the letter on the bed. She reached out and touched it, flicking at the corner with her slim fingers. Then she said softly. 'Thanks Jack.' She touched the corner with the little red smudge. Their eyes met. She said. 'Mine I suppose.' Jack nodded gravely. Rosemary flicked the letter over on its back. She shrugged. 'Well it's nothing for me to see my own blood. I see it all the time.'

Jack was taken aback by the hauteur of her remark but tried not to show it. She saw that he was a bit shocked by it and said accusingly. 'You men wouldn't be aware of that.'

Jack ignored her tone. He could play at this game too. He flicked the letter back. 'I reckoned that if you wanted me to know what was in it you'd tell me yourself.' He looked at her challengingly. 'So tell me...?'

She met his look and smiled. She touched his hand. She said. 'Jack...?'

'What?'

'You're sweet.'

He couldn't help grinning at that.

'I will tell you, Jack. I promise. But not now. I don't want to think about it for the moment. But thank you for finding it. And not reading it.' She let go his hand. 'If anyone else had found it! *Oh God!* Jack. I'm sorry about all this. I really am.'

'Rosemary. It's all right. It doesn't matter...'

'It does matter, Jack. Of course it matters.'

'Rose...'

'If it didn't matter it wouldn't happen.' She glared at

him defiantly. Then she relaxed and smiled again. Her smile was disarming. 'Maybe you're right...' She lay back on the pillow. After a minute she asked. 'You didn't come in last night.?'

He didn't answer for a minute. 'No.'

'What did you do, Jack...?'

'Oh. Nothing much. I went to the pictures.'

'The pictures?'

'I needed to think...'

'At the pictures...?' She gave a little laugh.

'Well I couldn't do it at home. Doc got a new stereo. He was probably playing it all night. I had to get out. The film was boring... I fell asleep.'

She looked as if she was going to say something but she decided not to. They were silent for a while. Jack was thinking about his feelings for her. And the way she would attack him one minute and then charm him the next with that bright smile of hers. He could see that she was teasing him. It always caught him off guard but she never seemed to really mean to hurt him or run him down. It was only a game she played. He would like to be sure of his feelings for her. Yesterday he was sure but now... If he could be absolutely sure he would tell her. But he was always afraid she would laugh at him.

Rosemary sighed. 'There's a lot of sadness in the world, Jack. I was lying here thinking. Last night when you didn't come and they moved me in here. When I saw all the sick people. Just look around this ward. And all the other wards. And all the hospitals. Not just here. But all over. People sick and in pain. You can tell by looking at them. They're confused by it. It's not natural. We shouldn't be sick. Even their friends and families.

They're confused too. They act differently when they come in to visit. It's false. You can see it. They put on an act. They're afraid. I watched it all last night...'

Jack looked around the ward at the patients and their visitors. He nodded. 'I know what you mean.'

'I doubt it.'

He didn't rise to her bait.

'Even you, Jack. You're different. You're different in here.'

He wasn't prepared to argue with her. He said. 'You're right.' Then he grinned. 'But so are you.' He decided not to let her away with it after all. 'You're not the same in here. I know now you feel. But you'll come out of it. When you get out you'll be back to normal.'

'You don't know how I feel, Jack. You don't know how anybody feels. You probably don't even know how you feel yourself.'

He kept his voice even. 'Rosemary that's crazy. I do know how I feel.'

'How...'

He shrugged. 'I just know. The same way everyone knows.'

'Or think they know...'

'Yeah. You're probably right.'

'We haven't a clue, Jack.'

He wanted to end this futile conversation. It was getting them nowhere. He didn't want to argue with her. Not here.

'Do you want to go, Jack...?'

'No.'

'Then what do you want?'

OK Rosemary. He thought, if this is what you want...here goes. 'I want to know...' he said flatly, underlining the words, 'what's fucking you up?'

'Hah!' She sat up, alert. 'Then why didn't you read *that*' She pointed to the letter. 'You want to know what's fucking me up? Well there it is. Open it. Read it. It's all there.' She flicked the envelope at him.

'No Rosemary.' He shook his head slowly at her. 'I want *you* to tell me.'

She folded her arms and glared at him. 'Ask yourself. What's fucking *you* up, Jack? What little secret... *fuck-ups*...' Her face darkened. He was sorry now, that he had put it so bluntly. They didn't normally use this kind of language with each other. But now he had Rosemary at it as well. 'What little *fuck-ups*...are you burying?' She was raising her voice. Jack glanced quickly about him. But nobody was paying them any attention. They had their own problems. The ward was a buzz of conversation.

'Rose. I didn't come here to argue with you.'

'Well what did you come for?'

'To see you, stupid. To see how you were. Because I wanted to. Because I was worried about you. And you don't have to be so defensive.'

'Defensive...? I'm not being defensive. I'm just asking a straight question. What has you the way you are?'

'And I'm asking you what has you the way *you* are?' He grinned. 'Stalemate!'

She didn't return his grin. She gave a little snort through her nose. Then she said, not looking at him. 'What do you want to do, Jack? Where do you want to go? What will you do when you get up tomorrow morning..? What? Why? Where? When? How?' But she wasn't really asking him. She was asking herself and she didn't have the answers either.

Jack said. 'You know all about me, Rose. I've told you everything about me. But of course I don't know everything. I mean we can give ourselves reasons. Political. Religious. Whatever... And I could go on about *that!* But we give ourselves reasons if we want - need - them. But why can't we simply accept what we are and take it from there. Accept the *what*, and then try and reason the...*why*... We always want to know *why,* before we even know what!

'That's rubbish, Jack.'

'I don't mean *simply* in that sense. I mean...quietly, or, I don't know... More, level-headed, I suppose. We don't have to go off the deep end.'

She let him finish. She was silent for a minute. Then she asked. 'Give me a reason, Jack.' It wasn't a question. It was more a statement.

'A reason?'

'Yes, a reason.'

'I don't know.' He thought for a second. Then he decided to try out that word. He said. '...Love...'

'Love...?' Rosemary gave a little laugh, which was more a sob. '...Love...?

'Yes.' He heard himself being very serious all of a sudden. 'Love.'

'You mean like the other night?'

'No. That was a mistake.'

'Mistake!' Rosemary exploded. 'Mistake. No, Jack. That wasn't a mistake.'

Jack was exasperated. He could see that all this just barging about with words. It was futile. He didn't know and Rosemary didn't know. Reasons...? So what was the point? They were both talking rubbish. The hospital was causing this. In that, Rosemary had been right. When he thought about it, his life *had* been *simple - uncomplicated*. Maybe his Mother had found it complicated. But she had made it *simple* for him. He hadn't actually ever wanted for anything. Oh, a normal home. Kids on the street. That kind of thing. *And a proper mother.* He sighed. He had had a roof over his head. A bed. Food. Companions. Education. A Job. *Yes. There had been love too.* He did know what love was. He looked at Rosemary, lying there. Didn't she know what love was, too? Her face was a blank page.

'Rosemary...?'

'Huh...?'

'Rosemary. What I'm trying to say is, if we don't like it we can change it. But - don't get mad, OK? - but the way you tried to change it the other night. That was a bit crazy.'

There was an awkward silence. Rosemary's eyes were still on the ceiling. Then she said slowly, but without any feeling. 'Sometimes, Jack, you talk a load of crap.' It was as if, not understanding him, and not trying very hard to, and him not wanting to be drawn into an argument, she had lost interest. Jack wasn't playing her game, and she had become bored. He looked at his watch. The afternoon visiting time was almost up. He didn't want to leave her in this mood.

'Rose. Let's just leave it, for now. When you get out we can talk about it.'

She continued to examine the high ceiling for a while

longer. Then she said. 'Will you be coming to-night?'

'Uh-huh.'

'I want to get out of this place. I hate it here.'

'Nobody likes it here,' He gave a short laugh. 'except the doctors and nurses.'

She dropped her eyes to his. 'I want out now, Jack.' Jack nodded sympathetically. He assumed a posh accent. 'Will Madam be requiring anything, eh, special? For the leaving? Evening wear, hmmm? Cocktail dress? The carriage...?' It brought a smile to her lips for an instant. 'Jack. Do you remember I told you about my aunt in the country? Shelagh. The one with the little cottage? Surrounded by fields and trees. I was thinking about her today. She was very good to me.' Rosemary was silent for a moment, remembering. She looked happier already, Jack thought. 'That's where I'd like to be right now.'

She reached over with a groan and took her bag out of the locker. Jack jumped to help, but she warned him off, *I can do it, I can do it...* She lay back with it clutched to her chest for a minute. The wounds on her wrists throbbed like mad. Luckily for her, the Doctor had told her, there were no tendons severed. But even that little movement had made her head swim. When the throbbing died down she took out her keys and handed them to Jack.

'Just stuff any old things into a bag. It doesn't matter what.'

'Are you sure? Will you be all right? Why don't you leave it for a day or two 'til you're a bit better. There's no hurry Rosemary. I was going to do up your flat.'

Rosemary dropped the handbag over the side of the bed. Jack picked it up and put it in the locker.

'*Bígí reidh*.' She said solemnly in her school Irish. '*Bígí reidh*'. "Be ready." She squared her shoulders.

Jack nodded, trying to recall what he had learned. '*Tá go maith*.' He replied. "Very well." 'As long as you feel up to it.' He put the keys in his pocket and stood. 'I'll see you later, then.'

'Jack.' She picked up the letter. 'I'd like you to read this.'

Jack hesitated. Rosemary shook the letter at him as if it was a nasty insect that had crawled up onto the bed and she wanted rid of it, now, disposed of, dead. He took it and held it for a second, to give her a chance to change her mind and take it back and cancel his responsibility at having to know what perhaps he didn't *have* to know. But she didn't make any move to retrieve it.

'OK.' He folded it and stuffed it in his pocket. There was a strange, hard look in Rosemary's eyes, like two cold steel doors had been shut tight. He waited another second but all she said was. 'I'll see you later. Thanks Jack. Thanks for coming.'

I'll see you to-night.' He touched her hand lightly. 'See you...'

He left the hospital with a lighter heart. On the way out he was thinking that Rosemary was a strange fish indeed. But he thought he was beginning to understand her. Her attempt at suicide was a classic case of crying for help and attention. But when you responded to that cry she build a wall of defence around herself and fought you back. But he thought he had the measure of her now. It seemed, that all Rosemary wanted was, for someone to be there. Well, he could be that someone. He told himself that he wanted to be that someone. And if they gave it time maybe they could mould their need of each other into something stronger. And who knows, it might lead to a deeper bond that both of them needed?

On the way through town he stopped and bought a small tin of white emulsion paint. It was all he could afford.

Back at Rosemary's flat he found an old paintbrush in the cupboard in the hallway and daubed on the paint with that. It didn't look so good. But it would do for the present. The new paint was very white against the older paint on the rest of the wall.

He found a holdall in the bottom of the wardrobe. He didn't know what clothes Rosemary wanted so he picked out the brightest garments he could find; he was surprised at the quality of the garments. Rosemary, he thought, could look a stunner when she had a mind to. He packed her boots. It was too cold for shoes.

When the bag was full he sat on the bed. Bedclothes? Damn! They were in the refuse bag. He picked it up. He would have to find a launderette or a dry cleaners who could do it in a hurry. He checked his watch. It was too late. It was almost five. By the time he got there it would be almost closing time. He dropped the bag. He could go back to Doc's and get some spare sheets if Rosemary didn't have any. He'd wait until he saw her later.

He was excited by the prospect of Rosemary coming back. Perhaps they could talk about getting a place together. It didn't have to be *together* together. Not in that sense. They could share a bigger flat, with two bedrooms. They could get used to each other, first, and them, later, maybe... But that could wait.

Rosemary had said once that she didn't believe in 'love'. Well not in the romantic sense that you read about in books or saw in films, anyway. She had said, that yes, she thought her parents had been 'in love' all right. But she meant it as if her parents had fallen into a hole! Jack had agreed with that on principle. But what if they decided that they wanted to be down a hole, that they wanted to be 'in' love! That it was their choice, to be in love or down a hole if both were the same thing? No, Rosemary had said, you don't understand what I mean. Nobody needs to be down a hole! Nobody makes that choice. It's more like *a need to be in love*, rather than *actual* love. Jack had agreed, although half-heartedly, with that. He hadn't seen much of it around either, laying down your life for a friend, if that was what she had meant. But then, he hadn't much - *any* - experience of parental love so he couldn't compare. He had felt it in St. Anthony's on occasions. The old Mother Superior, Sister Imelda, had *loved* them he thought. And he had loved her. Though he had hated her at times, too. But he didn't think it was the same. Then Rosemary had related a story she had been reading. Quite a gruesome story. Jack couldn't understand her reading habits at all. All her books were on *Strange Tribal Rituals*, and *Stranger Than Fiction* tales. This story was about a group of Cowboys - Mercenaries - in the Southern States of America in eighteen hundred and something. It was another *Stranger Than Fiction*, which was supposed to be based on fact. The Cowboys/Mercenaries had been attacked by a band of savage Indians. Most of them had been brutally killed. There was two survivors. They had somehow made it across the border into Mexico where they were captured this time by a band of Mexicans and dragged back to some village and there, half dead, treated to the most degrading and brutal tortures before finally being killed.

'Speaks volumes for so-called-neighbourly-love.' Rosemary had concluded.

'But that's a very extreme case,' Jack had argued. 'And anyway it was only a story. I don't know why you bothered to read it.'

'It was supposed to be based on actual facts.'

'But still, it's extreme. You hardly think they're going to write a bland story. It's morbid titillation. I don't know how you can be bothered.'

'I'm sure that some of the atrocities that are happening are probably worse, a lot worse, than anything we read in books.' Rosemary retorted.

'But that's in war, or, some other extreme case.' Jack argued.

'Not necessarily,' she shot back at him. 'What about the Park Murders? Those brutal murders. What do you call them... serial killers...?'

'But that's extreme again... What are you reading *forgodsake*?'

'And who *are* these extreme cases..?'

Jack shrugged. 'What do you mean, *who?*'

'Men.' She said. 'It's always men. Men start wars. Men are the serial killers... Men invented the concentration camps. Women don't do these things...!'

Jack shook his head. 'So what about those warrior queens, that we learned about in history. What about them? They weren't called warrior queens for nothing?'

'What warrior queens.' Rosemary asked savagely. 'Name one.'

Jack couldn't remember.

'Name me one woman who ever started a war...?'

Jack was racking his brain to remember something of

what he had learned. But History had never been one of his best subjects.

'Exactly.' Rosemary said. 'You can't... And who are the victims of the wars? Whether started by men or the women you can't remember? Women. And children. That's who. Men don't understand these things. We bring children into the world and *men* blow them right out again. They never learn. From one disastrous war to the next. They don't learn by their mistakes.'

Jack protested. 'What have you got against men? I'm a man - at least I think so - and I haven't killed anyone or opened a concentration camp, and have no intentions of ever doing so. But men are victims too. They get killed, maimed, blown to bits.'

'By their own wars.' Rosemary snapped. 'And, anyway, dead is dead! It's over. It's the women and children left behind who really suffer.' She smiled smugly at him. 'You have to be a woman to understand men.'

Jack laughed. 'And what about men understanding women? You could say the same about them. You have to be a man to understand women...'

She shook her head sharply. 'No. Women understand women.'

'And if women ruled the world there would be no wars, no killing, no fighting? Come off it Rose. Everyone's a victim of war. Even if we're not directly involved in it, we are affected by it. Any war that ever happened. It doesn't matter who or what started it. The world as a whole suffers. Most *men*, ordinary men, don't want wars, no more than you or me. The men you're talking about are *fanatics, maniacs*.'

'But we're not discussing war.' She waggled her head at him mischievously. 'We were talking about love, before you changed the subject.'

'*I* changed the subject.! Ah, c'mon now...!' Jack laughed at her tactics.

'Yes.' Rosemary set her face. 'You.'

'Now I remember.' Jack said. 'Maeve. Queen Maeve. She started a war. And if I remember correctly she started it over a cow...!'

'Probably because of men. And it was probably men who re-wrote the history books...to discredit her. Typical!'

'You don't get out of it that easy... And in that case it was men who were the victims while Good Queen Maeve sat safe and serene on her backside... And there was that Egyptian queen who's face launched a thousand ships...' Bits of what he had tried to learn at school were coming back to him.

'Just a legend,' Rosemary threw at him. 'Probably never happened.'

'So you're discounting that women ever ruled...that it was all made-up...?

'Of course not. But I doubt if the real reason your Queen Maeve had to fight, was over a cow at all. Probably something else entirely.'

'Like what...?'

'How would I know. Male oppression? I wasn't there. Was I?'

'Maybe. In another incarnation...?' He baited her.

Rosemary sniffed haughtily. 'I'm sure I *was* a queen. But I doubt if I ever killed anyone over a stupid cow. I have much more sense than that...'

Jack had to laugh. 'You're a gas woman, Rose...'

That had been one of the many frivolous bantering conversations they had had from time to time.

He came out of his reverie. It was almost time to go back to the hospital. He took the holdall and went back to his own place. He cooked the T-Bone steak which he had refused the last evening and made some tea.

When he arrived at the hospital he checked with the Receptionist to make sure Rosemary was still in the same ward.

The receptionist checked the register. 'No,' she said. 'She's been discharged.'

'Discharged!'

'So it says here.'

'But I have her clothes, here, in the bag...!'

'I'm sorry. She's left.'

'When...?'

The receptionist was non-committal. 'This afternoon. That's all I know. Sorry.'

'*Damn!*' He was incredulous. 'Can I check the ward?' But he left without waiting for a reply.

But Rosemary was not in the ward. Her bed had already been filled. He checked with the ward nurse. Her bed had been found empty shortly after visiting time this afternoon. The girl in the other bed had said Rosemary had gone to the toilet and hadn't come back. And her hand-bag was gone from her locker. They had searched the hospital. But there was no sign if her. The Gardaí had been notified. He didn't happen to have a photograph? No? Well there wasn't much she could do in a hospital dressing gown. All they could do was wait and see.

Jack rushed back to the flat. She was probably there now, having a good laugh at him. But surely not in her hospital clothes! She must have had clothes when she went to the hospital. But he didn't remember seeing any in her locker. She had her hand-bag, all right, but the ambulance men could have taken that.

There were no lights showing in her flat. He let himself in. There was no sign that she had been there. All was as he had left it. He sat on the bed and waited. An hour later there was still no sign of her.

He went out to the shop and bought an evening newspaper. He brewed some coffee in the new percolator and read the paper. By the time he had read it from cover to cover and finished the pot of coffee he was still alone. He had a feeling that Rosemary was definitely not going to appear. She must have gone to a friend. But he didn't recall her ever having mentioned any close friend that she had.

Still, he was prepared to wait. Rosemary had no clothes. She couldn't have gone far. Perhaps she was hiding in the hospital? But why would she do that?

He had her keys as well. So she would have to ring the bell.

Perhaps she didn't want to see him? Perhaps she was watching the flat right now waiting for him to leave. Maybe she wanted to be alone for a while. *Yes, Jack. She's standing out in the cold for the last few hours, in a hospital shift, watching the flat.*

He went outside and walked up and down the street and checked in the local shops. He didn't check in the pub. Rosemary didn't go there anyway. But this was ridiculous. Where the hell was she? He went back to the flat. He turned off the light and lay back on the bed.

He dozed.

When he woke up the house was quiet. He checked his watch. After midnight. He had slept for hours. There was nothing else for him to do. He decided against staying the night. He was stiff and cold. He would return in the morning. He zipped up his jacket and checked his pocket for the keys. His hand gripped the letter.

He took it out and weighed it in his hand. It was slightly crumpled now. He turned it over thoughtfully. Rosemary had said to read it. He still wasn't sure if he wanted to. His name was on the envelope but somehow it seemed alien to him. He wasn't familiar with her handwriting. He stood for a moment undecided. Would the contents explain anything to him? Would it explain Rosemary?

He sat back on the bed and slowly peeled it open. There was a wad of school exercise book pages. The writing was bold and heavy - some of it digging through the page. Parts of it were scribbled out and written in again between the lines. Other parts were barely legible. Her ball point had run out and the last few pages were written in pencil. The whole thing looked like a disaster area. He switched on the electric ring under the percolator and settled down for a long session.

It was extremely difficult to decipher. He began...

'Jack, I want to apologise...'

12

By the time Jack had left the hospital, Rosemary was determined to get out one way or the other.

After they had moved her into the public ward she had lain in bed all of the morning drained and nervous. Afraid of what yesterday had brought and today might bring. She didn't like it here. She felt trapped. The doctor had been too pleasant; the nurses too sweet. She felt they were watching her. But there was a small cold space deep inside her head that felt as if a cleansing had taken place. She clung to that feeling. *Something* had moved in her - like as if an old rotten tooth had been dug out, taking with it the pain, and leaving only the gaping hole to be covered over and the tissue to reassemble itself in the healing process. Yes, there had been a *Blood Letting* - an *Evil Spirit* had been released. She had wielded the *Sacrificial Knife* with her own hand; Had acted as her own *Physician*. All these symbolic phrases drifted through her head. And she had survived. But this old skin must be left behind. There must be a new beginning. *They* couldn't help her now. *That* she must do for herself. The thoughts floated on the surface of her mind like waves, building and dipping, as she drifted in and out of dreamless sleep.

Then Jack had come to see her. Poor Jack! He had sat there looking so awkward and confused. But it was nice to see him; his familiar face, even if it did reflect her own feelings of anguish. And then he had produced the bread knife from under his jacket - that had been yesterday - like a million years ago. She fought to bring events into perspective. Two nights ago in the flat! The wanting! The not knowing how to get what you want – need. The screwing up! Aach! But what did it matter, now. Perspectives had turned a corner. Things were different, now. But it had been funny all the same, the bread-knife wrapped under his jacket. Or had she dreamed that? Jack wouldn't be so gormless? She wondered what he had done with it. Had it really been yesterday? It had been so painful to laugh, but she couldn't help it. And the look on his face. Innocence and righteousness and then embarrassment. And then trying to hide it again...Hah! And then the letter! He was so freaked about that! Where had she put it...? She couldn't remember. Had she written it at all or was that just another twisted facet of her memory.

But now, he had come and gone with the letter. Had she been a fool to insist on him reading it? Perhaps. But even when they were arguing over it she had already made up her mind. She must get out. Not just the hospital. Out of this damn city! She pictured him sitting reading the letter. Probably on *her* bed! It gave her a flush of excitement. Poor Jack. How would he take it? Would he be able for it? Could she face him again? Then panic. Hell! She should have taken it back when she had had the chance. No. Let him read it. It was past history.

The last of the visitors had gone. Now she must act. A half formed plan was hatching in her head.

Rosemary surveyed the ward. The girl in the next bed was about her own age and height. She caught her eye.

'Hi...'

'Hello.' She seemed friendly enough.

'How are you feeling...?'

The girl made a face. 'OK...' She flicked her eyes to the ceiling and sighed. Hospitals!

Yeah. Hospitals.

Rosemary gave her a sympathetic smile. 'You been here long...?'

'A week.'

'A week! God! When do you get out?"

The girl frowned. 'Not sure. Another week...Tests and things. Y'know.'

Rosemary nodded, yeah. She dropped her voice. 'Have you any clothes..?'

'Clothes...?' The girl scanned the ward as if she expected clothes to float down from the ceiling. She turned back to Rosemary. 'Clothes...?'

'I want to borrow some clothes.' Rosemary said urgently. 'I don't have any.'

'You don't have any..?'

'No. I only had a dressing gown on when I came in. And I have to get out.'

'Out..?'

The effort was draining Rosemary. She wished this girl would stop repeating her every last word. 'Yes. I have to go out for a while...' *You stupid cow, d'you think I want to set up a second-hand stall at the foot of the bed or something?*

'Are you OK?'

Am I OK? Would I be here if I was OK? Rosemary dampened down her exasperation. 'Have you got any..?'

The girl eyed Rosemary suspiciously. 'Well...' She scanned the ward again. 'Jeans and a sweater...but...'

'Can I borrow them?'

'Borrow..?'

'Well...buy them,' Rosemary almost shouted. This girl was driving her mad, looking at her as if she had sprouted a second head. 'I'll buy them of you.'

'Buy them..?'

Rosemary rummaged in her hand bag. She had about twenty five pounds. 'Ten pounds.'

The girl didn't look too sure.

'Fifteen..? It's all I've got.'

The girl looked apprehensive 'I don't know...'

Hell! Rosemary thought. This is wearing me. 'Look.' She made a final effort, getting half out of the bed. 'I just want to borrow them.' She felt her head drain. She steadied herself on the edge of the bed. 'I have to get out of here! I have to. Look, if I don't get back you can keep the money. You can keep it anyway.'

The girl looked at her like a frightened kitten who had peed on the good carpet. 'Well...' The wide frightened eyes scanning again. 'I suppose so.'

Rosemary rolled the money up in a ball and threw it on the girl's bed. The girl's eyes darted to the door before picking it up. Then she grabbed it quickly and stuffed it behind her pillow. She turned slowly and reached into her locker and took out a pair of blue jeans and a pink sweater. She rolled them in a tight ball and handed them over. Rosemary was afraid to look towards the door, afraid a nurse might look in and try to stop her. She had no time to argue. She was getting out. She pulled on the jeans. They were a bit big. But that was to her advantage. She pulled the legs up as far as they would go under her hospital night-dress to hide them. The sweater was light enough to stuff into her handbag.

She turned to go. Hell! 'Shoes...?'

'Shoes?' The girl looked ready to bury herself under the bedclothes.

Hell! Rosemary's head whirled. If she didn't get this over with soon she would drop. She held on to the last dregs of her energy and made her way around the girl's bed. There was a pair of canvas pumps in the locker. She took them out. 'Can I borrow these?' But she didn't wait for an answer. She slipped them on. They fitted. A wee bit tight. But all right. She said to the girl. 'I'm just going to the toilet. OK? If anyone asks... OK?'

The girl watched her warily. Rosemary gave her her sweetest, conspiratorial smile. 'Just between us girls. Right.' The girl nodded. Anything to get rid of this madwoman.

Rosemary didn't think she would make it to the ward door. It was miles away. She struggled on. The corridor. A nurse. Damn. 'Should you be out of bed? ' 'Just going to the toilet.' 'Do you need any help?' 'No. Thanks.' Hold on. Hold on. Smile. Smile. Don't look as if you might hang yourself out of the toilet chain... 'Well, take it easy...' The professional concerned look. 'I'm fine. Thanks...' The nurse passed on into the nurses station. She spotted the sign for the toilets. Slowly she made her way down the corridor. It felt like miles.

When she got to the toilets she went into a cubicle and slumped on the seat. Little black dots did a dance in front of her eyes. Her stomach heaved. *God!* Would she make it? She fought against the nausea and put her head between her knees to pump some blood back into her head. Somebody went into the next cubicle. Rosemary held her breath. Then she heard a relieved sigh. It was another patient. Rosemary stood shakily and took off the hospital dressing gown and shift and put on the sweater. She took a few deep breaths to steady herself then rolled the hospital clothes into as tight a ball as she could and stuffed them out the little window. She combed her hair and tied it into a pony tail and fixed it with an elastic band she found in the pocket of the jeans. She hadn't told the girl she had taken her comb as well when she was taking the shoes from the locker. She pulled the sweater sleeves well down over her bandaged wrists. She braced herself and left the cubical.

Back out in the corridor she tried to walk as straight as she could. She was feeling better now. She was on her way. A hospital porter came out of the lift, wheeling an old woman in a wheel chair. Hold the door! Rosemary cried out in her head. For Chris'sakes, hold the door! But she was too slow. The energy wasn't there to hurry. The porter gave her only a passing glance. She came to the lift and pressed the button. It seemed to take ages to come up. When it did, luckily it was empty. Rosemary stumbled in and pressed the ground floor button, then the little reserve of energy that had got her this far evaporated and she slumped exhausted to the floor. Hot and cold flushes ran through her as the lift slowly descended. The sweat was running down her legs. Her heart was thumping against her ribs. She fought with all her might to stop herself from fainting, tightening every muscle in her body to force the blood back into her head. She sucked at the air like a fish. She had to hold on. Hold on. As the lift stopped she managed to pull herself to her feet. She was damp with sweat, but *God*, she felt like ice.

She still had to make it across the lobby and past the reception desk. It was not more than thirty feet but it looked like thirty miles. She walked as steadily as she could, hugging her handbag to her stomach for support and crossed the expanse of tiles. The receptionist was reading the evening paper. Nobody paid her any attention. The blast of cold air chilled her as she hit the street.

In the nearest coffee bar Rosemary gulped down a scalding mug of coffee. It brought a temporary relief from the shivers that played on her spine like an icy hand. She had no overcoat to guard against the cold, but she had no option now. She had to go on. She finished her coffee, revived for the time being by the warming liquid and the short rest.

She wasn't too sure of where she was. She checked the name of the street. She could smell the river close by. Something she had not been aware of before. It was unpleasantly pungent, but it gave her her bearings. If only she had an overcoat. The cold hand rattled at her bones. Keep moving. Keep moving. Don't think about it. The sooner you get to the bus depot, the better.

13

'She's a Witch, y'know...' Rosemary had told Jack once about her aunt Shelagh, that day at the end of summer when they were sitting in the window seat of the little coffee bar in a busy side street, watching the shoppers milling about with large carrier bags from the end-of-season sales. It had been a hot summer, but Rosemary was as pale as ever.

They were drinking iced tea and smoking 'Black Russian' cigarettes. Rosemary didn't often smoke, but when she did she bought what she referred to as, *exotic* brands. They were expensive and they had pooled their money to buy them. Rosemary had said that she needed something; a break, a holiday, a new wardrobe of clothes, something, anything, but as she couldn't afford much, she would settle for something cheaper. Iced tea and Balkan tobacco was what they had settled on. They were easy items to get and affordable unlike a holiday at some foreign resort. Rosemary was in a light mood that day. She had suggested it as a celebration of the end of summer sunshine and they laughed about it as they 'polluted' the atmosphere with the strong smelling Russian cigarettes. They were chatting about nothing in particular when Rosemary began talking about her aunt. It was the first time she had spoken about any of her family.

'She's my father's sister. But they never had much to do with each other. He didn't approve of what she did. Herbs and cures and things... Out in the fields gathering plants. My father was a religious man. Thought she was doing Devil's work or something. Like poking the fire. He would never let anyone poke the fire! Said it was like the Devil stoking the flames of Hell..!'

She was thoughtful for a minute. A cloud seemed to pass over her features. Then she brightened again and continued. 'But I think he just didn't like her. She was his young sister and he probably grew up *thinking* he had to dislike her! Anyway, they didn't get on.' She paused. 'I stopped believing in God after my father died.' She thought about that for a minute. 'I couldn't have done it before. Thought it had been on my mind after mammy died. I couldn't believe God could do that to me. And then my father...well...after...'

She stopped. A pained look crossed her face. She blew her nose and then continued quickly. 'But aunt Shelagh was different - a strange - no, unusual woman. Not anything like my parents. She had a look in her eye as if she knew something we didn't know. I think he was afraid of her. She came for his funeral. She was very good to me. Stayed for a week and helped me do all the things - y'know, arrangements. We got on great. I really liked her. But I'd always liked her. Even when I was small and we visited her in the country. Not that we visited her much - my father didn't like her *or* the country. But I liked her. She was like, I dunno, fresh air - like as if she spent all her times in the woods and fields.'

'She probably did,' Jack laughed. 'Gathering all her stuff for spells.'

Rosemary objected. 'She didn't do spells, Jack. She isn't that kind of Wi... Person. She's a healer. Them nuns of yours have filled your head with all kinds of rubbish and superstitions. She isn't like that at all.'

Jack raised his hands in mock defence. 'I'm only trying to get a rise out of you. Please...'

'Well, I'm trying to explain something serious to you and you're making fun of me. I don't like that, Jack.'

Jack put his hands down. 'OK. But I can't take all that talk about witches too seriously. Not in this day and age, anyway it's almost 1984. 'Big Brother' and all that...'

'Well maybe you should. Maybe you should read up about it before being so pass-remarkable. She's a good woman. And very beautiful too.'

'Like you?'

Rosemary snorted down her nose, ignoring him.

'There's a kind of glow about her. Not like you can see. But, more like you can feel it.

She was silent for a moment, a far away look in her grey eyes.

'The week after my father died we spent talking. She was lovely to talk to. I couldn't have managed without her. She helped me find a flat and move. Sort out the old house - it was just a council house - I couldn't go on living in it, even though the rent was cheap, cheaper than the flat.'

Jack watched Rosemary's face. It took on a serene look as she remembered her aunt.

'She would sit there holding my hand. Just talking together. About everything. I could feel a kind of warmth passing through her hand. Like she was giving me energy. It made me feel so calm, so happy.'

Rosemary lapsed into silence again, remembering. Her expression brought to Jack's mind that of St. Therése, in a picture which had hung in the boy' dormitory at St. Anthony's. Her eyes dreamy and virtuous and her rose-bud mouth in a half-smile as she beheld the *Beatic Vision*; the *Face of God*. She was so beautiful. So innocent. So young. And so holy. All the boys were deeply in love with her. Jack would lie in bed, staring at her for ages, enraptured, until the frame and then the wall and finally the whole room would vanish in a halo of light, as if he were staring down a long glowing tunnel, with himself at one end and St. Therèse, the love of his young life, at the other. Then she would move towards him and there would only be him and her. He was her special favourite. But later, when he was older, she stopped coming and he would have difficulty sleeping. Then it became only a picture. Then came his doubts. But Rosemary's face was real and alive and glowing - pale and beautiful here in the cafe with the sunshine streaming in the window. It was as if Rosemary saw her aunt in this way... But he didn't want to think like this. Rosemary was no saint and he was sure her aunt wasn't one either. She was flesh and blood like anyone else but the way Rosemary spoke about her, Jack was certain Shelagh was Rosemary's heroine - her saviour; the counter balance to her parents strict Roman Catholic upbringing. He had finally stopped believing in any of that religious stuff himself shortly after leaving the orphanage. It had been part of his private little rebellion at God who had deprived him of parents. That, yes, and the fact that St. Therèse had abandoned him. But it was still hard to shake off entirely. It was embedded deep in his soul even if he did deny it. A thought struck him.

'I have an idea. Seeing as the nuns have *exercised* their influence on me, maybe I should go to your aunt and have it *exorcized* out'

Rosemary flung him a look of scorn. 'Don't be stupid, Jack.'

'Why not?' He teased her, but she was having none of it.

'Because...!'

'Because...?'

'Because she's not that kind of person. And... because I wasn't brought up that way.'

Jack laughed. 'Come to think of it. Neither was I. But...'

'She's a busy woman, Jack. She wouldn't want people barging in on her. You may not have anything important to do. It makes no difference if people come barging in on you.'

'You could?'

'What?'

'Barge in on me?'

'I don't go barging in on people.'

Jack shrugged. 'Pity.'

Rosemary changed the subject. 'Let's go for a walk. It's too nice to be sitting in here. These cigarettes are making me sick. I need some fresh air.'

He took her hand. 'A stroll in the park with a lovely lady.'

She pulled her hand away. 'Don't be so flippant.' She put on her wide brimmed straw hat to shield her face from the sun and they left the cafe. Jack was wondering why Rosemary always seemed to want to attack him when he was being light-hearted. The Rosemary he saw when she was talking about her aunt was a very different Rosemary to what he was used to. He felt - suspected - knew there was another Rosemary. A wonderful Rosemary. The Rosemary that he felt sometimes he loved. But she was always brushing his amorous side away, and in the process hiding her own, too. He remembered another conversation they had had. They had been discussing the future. Their futures. Rosemary had remarked that of course he had a future. She hadn't said 'they' had a future. She had said 'you'..! Not including herself. He let it go. It was too nice a day for gloomy thoughts.

The park was full of late summer sun-worshipers. Children played and yelped on the grass or threw crumbs of bread for the ducks. Even they seemed to be having a final fling before the weather turned. It was warm and cloudless and carefree. As they strolled along Rosemary slipped her hand through Jack's arm. He looked at her askance.

'Oh. Don't worry,' She smiled. 'I'm not trying to do anything.' She wriggled her shoulders. 'I just like this...'

'So do I...' His voice took on a slight huskiness. 'You can do it as much as you like...'

'Just friends, Jack.'

'Fine by me.' But he was hopeful.

They strolled on across the grass. It was nice here away from the busy streets and the noisy traffic. To anyone they were just another happy couple walking arm-in-arm like all the others. The park had a holiday atmosphere. Children rolling on the grass; mothers dozing on the benches; glad to be outdoors away from stuffy kitchens; enjoying the last of the sunshine before autumn finally settled in. Only a few hundred yards away the city roared and buzzed, but here among the trees and flowers and green lawns it was quiet and peaceful.

They ambled across the large expanse of grass looking for somewhere to stop and sit. Dotted around were people, some with their trouser legs rolled up or skirts hitched up above their knees; couples soaking up the sun together or rolled in an intimate embrace.

But Rosemary didn't want to stop here. She led him over to the shade of a copper beech tree and taking off her hat and jacket lay down out of the glare of the sun.

Jack sat beside her. Rosemary sighed and closed her eyes. She mumbled something which Jack didn't catch. But it didn't matter. He rolled his jacket into a pillow and stretched out. He turned his head and looked at Rosemary in profile. She looked relaxed and peaceful and lovely; her long black hair and her pale skin against the green grass and the mottled patterns of the leaves dancing lightly on her bright summer dress.

He reached out and gently ran his fingertips down the length of her arm. Her skin was soft and warm. He rolled over slowly and propped himself up on his elbow so that he was looking down at her. Carefully, so as not to disturb her, he took her hand and held it lightly. He opened her fingers and gently kissed the moist skin of her palm. She mumbled something. He kissed it again, rolling his tongue softly in the hollow. A mild tang of saltiness. Rosemary stirred and slowly pulled her hand away.

'Don't... Jack...' She mumbled sleepily.

He sat gazing down at her. She appeared to be sleeping. Her eyebrows twitched now and then as if she were dreaming. He was oblivious to the others around him. There was only him and Rosemary. She looked so composed and tranquil and lovely. He wanted to wrap his arms around her and feel her warm soft body against his. He ached to hold her but she had given him no sign, no encouragement. He reached out tentatively and touched her face, feeling along the arch of her eyebrows lightly moist from the heat and then slowly down the curve of her cheek; the tips of his fingers glazing over her lips. He lowered his head and brushed her mouth with his lips. She didn't stir. Then he kissed her gently on the mouth. She moved slightly and began to return his kiss. Then as suddenly, she pulled her mouth away and pushed him aside. She sat up abruptly, glaring at him.

'Don't Jack.'

He looked at her, puzzled. 'But why...?'

'I don't know. Just don't.' But she looked puzzled herself. She pulled on her jacket.

'I just want to be friends,' she had said then.

. . .

Now, sitting in her little basement bedsit, Jack was stunned by the outpourings in Rosemary's letter. He was angry and sad and maddened by what he had just read. So this is why she had always kept him at arms length. This was why she would shrug off his attempts to touch her in a loving way. He cried to the empty walls for her to come back and together they could face up to it. Fight it. Conquer it. He went over the pages again trying to grasp the extent of her hurt. Trying to grasp at the reality of the Rosemary he did not know. The shame. The guilt. The deep buried anchors of pain. It became clearer to him now. Her rejection of him in the park. Her attack on him only two nights ago. Her reticence to talk about her family, except on that one occasion when she had talked about her aunt. Her reading of books about death and destruction and her abhorrence of war...men! Men start wars! Men kill! But it was crazy. She didn't hate men. He knew she didn't. Because she didn't hate him. It was only her hurt coming out. And she had to lash out at something. But in the end she had lashed out at herself...

He felt anger at himself. He could offer her no comfort. No respite. No solution for her dilemma. All his own years of frustration at his own deprivation, insecurity and delimitations about love, affection and even sex. His own strict religious upbringing and his rebellious denial of it. All his own anguish and pain, real or imagined, seemed frivolous after what he had just read. And, he believed, she probably had not told the whole story...

Rosemary wouldn't point the finger. She couldn't lay the blame at its rightful door. Instead, she had all but exonerated the culprit and taken all the blame and shame on herself. Jack prayed, that if there was a God, that this God would measure out punishment where it was due. Poor Rosemary, she had not struck out at her violator then, and she couldn't bring herself to strike at him, even now. Her fear and guilt had become twisted within herself and when she finally had taken revenge, she had reached within herself for the ugly solution. And it had almost been the end of her... She begged him not to hate her father and not to hate her. Well, he could not hate her. If anything, he loved her even more. At what cost had she poured out her detestable story? The degradation which had been harboured in her soul like a sunken vessel and with a great tug at its lashings raised from the murky depths. And hoping that this monster would have only to be faced one last time had she allowed it to be revealed.

Jack hated her father more than he could imagine. He hated him more for bringing all men down to that degrading level of baseness by his outrageous violation of her innocent body; his own innocent daughter. He hated that man, now, more than he knew he could hate. But even worse, it was as if he too, being a man, just as her father had been a man, was also included in that brutality. He folded the letter in a rage and, stuffing it into his pocket, headed home.

14

'Coming to the Gig...?' Doc called from the bedroom. Jack was sprawled on the sofa reading the evening paper. He didn't answer. Doc came out with his jacket in his hand. 'Well..?' He put it on and waited for an answer.

Jack lowered the paper. 'I dunno...' He looked blankly at Doc. Doc struck a pose, like Hamlet holding the skull. 'To-night,' he intoned. 'Is a night for the soul. Soul Night. Music to stir the *Inner Being*.' He dropped his hand and peered at Jack, his little black eyes squinting in mock despondency. 'Jack. *Man*!' He shook his head. 'How can you *slump* there...' He waved his hand at the sofa. 'When the greatest *soul musicians* in this *decrepit* city of ours are about to unleash their *very souls* upon us this very night. Is all you can say, I dunno...?'

Jack had to make an effort to rouse himself. Rosemary had been gone almost a week now and still no word. He had spent the last few days in a Limbo. He knew Doc was trying to help him come out of himself in the best way he could. But he was finding it difficult to respond to Doc's good humour. He wasn't sure if going gigging and drinking would do him any good. He wished Rosemary would come out of hiding, or wherever she was. He couldn't imagine what had happened to her. Died in hospital and they wouldn't tell him? Kidnapped? Murdered? Or simply run away? But why didn't she get in touch? He had mostly hung around the flat hoping that the phone in the hall would ring and it would be her.

He looked at Doc, waiting, poised, all eager to be off. He sighed, Doc was right, he couldn't sit around for ever. 'Oh. OK. I suppose so...'

Doc pointed to the door. 'Good. Right, man, let's be

gone. Lay tread. In other words. Get offa yer ass...'

Out in the street Doc flagged down a taxi, exclaiming to the world that this was no night for bussing it. In the taxi he engaged the driver in a dissertation on the roots and growth of soul music. Jack was only half listening. The driver just nodded and laughed half-heartedly as Doc incited him to abandon the taxi for the remainder of his shift and join them for the *night-of-his-life*. 'Sure,' The driver said. 'If I make my night's wages in the next hour..!'

By the time they arrived at their destination Jack was decidedly in much better form. Doc's exuberant good humour was having it's effect. Though he didn't share Doc's passionate obsession with the music, Doc's enthusiasm had him already half looking forward to the night ahead.

The support group were playing when they arrived. The venue was not crowded; a few scattered groups of mainly university students and a handful of couples hung about the bar area. A small group of girls were dancing on their own up near the stage. Jack was disappointed. He had expected the place to be buzzing with energy; jammed to the gills. Doc had been so enthusiastic in the taxi that Jack was beginning to feel that, yes, a good night out was just the tonic he needed to shake him out of his sombre mood. But the place was almost deserted and the atmosphere was cheerless. The venue and it's decor left a lot to be desired; low and long with brown walls and the once white ceiling a dirty shade of yellow from tobacco smoke. The lighting was dim and the whole effect was of a disused barn or old warehouse.

Doc pulled him across the floor to the bar and ordered pints. He waved his hand in the direction of the stage. 'Don't mind them. When the lads come on it'll be a different story...' Jack nodded. The little bit of enthusiasm he had mustered was fast disappearing. Doc continued. 'That's just the relief band.' He laughed. 'It'll be a relief when they get off. Hey! Drink up. At least we got here ahead of the posse...' He raised his pint. 'Here's to *soul*. Yours and mine, man.' He drained his pint in one long swallow and slammed his glass on the counter. 'Man, I needed that.' He raised his eyebrow at Jack. 'Ready for another...?' Jack shook his head. Doc ordered himself another pint. The place was beginning to fill up. The relief band pounded on. They didn't sound so poor now. The extra influx of punters seemed to give them extra spirit. Doc remarked that they were coming to the end of their set and had kept the 'good wine' for the big finish. He laughed. 'They only know three songs anyway! and this is them...' Jack was beginning to get his enthusiasm back and ordered another pint for himself and Doc.

He was raising the new pint to his mouth when a slap on his shoulder almost knocked him into it.

'Watch out for the bricks. HAW HAW! *Vigilance Mon Ami...!*' It was Roleston. 'Well, chaps, we seem to be a few furlongs ahead. But we'll soon remedy that.' He roared at the barman. 'A *large* brandy and two G and T's, *tout suite,* my good man.' Jack noticed that all his ss's were safely under control, for the moment. But the night was young yet. It was only Roleston's first double brandy. Roleston rattled on. 'You remember my dear spouse, Marjory, of course.' He ushered another woman into the circle who had been standing behind Marjory. 'And this *dee*-lightful lady is a very *dear* friend of ours. Maureen. Maureen Travis.' He nodded his huge head at Doc and Jack. 'And, Maureen, dear, two associates of mine, Doctor O'Sullivan, known to all and sundry as 'Doc' and ,' He paused for a second. 'Jack... em.' He lowered his bushy eyebrows at Jack. 'Hmm, I fail to remember your surname...?'

'Jack will do fine.' Jack nodded to Marjory and Maureen. Maureen smiled back a little shyly. Marjory looked at him, not remembering where she had seen him before. Her husband reminded her. 'It was at Doc's, em, unfortunate party, last week, dear...' He turned to Doc. *Mea Culpa,* once again Doc, old soldier...! And how *is* the new system?' He asked about the new stereo system. Doc raised his glass in salutation. 'Peaches and cream, man...' He grinned. They were boozing pals again.

The drinks arrived and Roleston scooped them up, at the same time ushering them all to a vacant table. 'Whilst there *is* one available before the *real* rabble, *D'après Moi,* arrive.' They seated themselves. The table was on a low raised area at the back of the hall, overlooking the dance floor, and not too far from the bar. Or as Roleston put it. 'A select vantage point, for a quick *foray* in either direction...HAW HAW...' He plonked himself down with Marjory and Maureen on either side of him and distributed the drinks.

By now the support band were leaving the stage and a young man in a red suit was bawling into the microphone ...*And a warm round of applause ladieees and gen'lemen a great bunch of lads reeeal soooul YEAH!..* This was greeted by good natured whistles and cat-calls from the bunch of students near the stage. The man in the red suit grinned down drolly at them and continued. ...*We take a short break now folks. Back in fifteen minutes with the MAIN EVENT... YEAH!* There were more whistles followed by a surge to the bar. The hall had filled up quickly in the last fifteen minutes and was now jam-packed. Roleston was on his feet and attacking. His bulk got him to the bar with the first wave and his booming and hissing order could be heard above the rest. His ss's were beginning to slip again.

Marjory and Maureen were chatting quietly together. Marjory had finished her gin and tonic, but Maureen was still sipping hers. Marjory looked much like what Jack remembered of her at Doc's party; long light floral patterned dress, worn sloppily off her thin shoulders. Maureen Travis had a dark gypsy look about her, dressed in a black satin bolero top over a tight bodice of gold and red silky material and a full skirt. She looked bright and colourful and neat as against Majory who was colourful but dowdy.

Jack wondered where the '*Inzzeperable ZZisters*' were to-night. He was about to ask Doc when Roleston arrived back triumphantly with their drinks. Doc rubbed his hands together as if he were trying to raise sparks. 'It's gonna be a great night, man.' He chortled. 'Wait'll you hear the *MAIN EVENT*. Wild..!' Roleston pushed in on the curved seat so that Marjory was now beside Jack, and Maureen was opposite him beside Roleston. Doc started to tell them about the bass player they were about to hear. 'Fretless bass, man. Plays slightly flat on the tonic. Kinda slides into it. Keeps your ear on edge. Wanting him to slide up the semi'. But he doesn't, man. Keeps you wanting...' Jack hadn't a clue what he was talking about. Roleston was just grinning with his tombstones at him and Marjory and Maureen were still chatting quietly together. But Doc was animated and nervous in anticipation of his favourite band taking the stage. As if they were *his* band. He had invited his friends to hear *his* group of lads, the best group of musicians in the city, in the country, man, and he didn't want them to be disappointed. He wanted his friends to understand that, *what they were about to hear,* was *the best, man,* so he kept up a barrage of explanations about the lads, so that they would understand all the nuances, all the traits, of each of the band members. He didn't want his friends to miss out on anything. He kept an eye on the stage. He wanted to be the first to spot the lads when they arrived on stage. He was like a kid waiting for Santa, hopping up and down and talking at a mile a minute. Roleston interrupted him. He said, with just a touch of *sang-froid* to make Doc prick up his ears. 'Met Stanley Clarke in Paris when I was passing through...' Doc put down his pint and stared in amazement at Roleston. 'You never told me, man...' Roleston continued. '...told him you were a big fan of his.' Doc shook his head slowly. '*Ho-ly Shit!* You're having me on, man. Winding me up...!' Roleston laughed loudly at the incredulous and awed expression on Doc's face. Stanley Clarke! Only the greatest bass player in the world...! Doc was still shaking his head slowly from side to side. 'Stanley Clarke, Stanley *Fucking* Clarke...'

Then the young man in the red suit was back. The ceiling lights dimmed and at the same time a number of coloured beams backlit the stage area with blues and greens. '*And Now Ladieees And Gen'lemen,*' He spoke in a low and authoritative voice. '...*Welcome Pleeease*...' his voice rising to a crescendo: '*The Main Event!*'

All eyes turned to the stage. Doc was on his feet.

Seven musicians, silhouetted in backlight, walked casually on stage, to applause and whistles from the crowd; their casualness underscored by a strong sense of purpose. After a moment's pause as they stopped in line, and then a quick nod to each other, the brass section wailed a long low mournful chord, gently augmented by the rhythm section and lifting it gradually as the front spots came on one by one illuminating each musician in turn, until the rich ring of brass reached its apex, brought it to a cutting halt so that in the split second of silence it seemed to hang in the room like a clarion... The crowd held its breath... Then in the next instant the deep pounding rhythm let loose and everybody in the room was sucked to their feet by the magic.

Except Roleston and Maureen... She obviously didn't have the same agility as Majory who had hopped over the back of the seat, and her escape was blocked by Roleston's large frame.

In the sudden upsurge created by the opening chorus of the music, Majory had vanished into the undulating bodies on the dance floor. Jack and Doc were pulled to the back of the crowd and were standing on chairs for a better view. The music throbbed through the room like an electric generator. Doc bobbed recklessly on his chair, his pint in one hand and one of Rolestons cigars in the other. Jack stood on the chair beside him, his head almost brushing the ceiling. He could feel the thump of the Bass line pounding against his solar plexus.

Meanwhile Roleston was sitting with his arm along the back of the seat behind Maureen ignoring the band and the excitement of the crowd behind him and his face bent close to her ear. What he was saying was lost in the volume of the band and the buzz of the crowd, but the closeness of his huge bulk and his breath in her ear must have been annoying, judging by the expression on her face.

The initial impact of the music settled to a steady rhythm and the crowd composed itself into an organized dancing shape. Doc and Jack came back to the table. Maureen had edged her way around away from Roleston and as Jack went to sit down they almost collided. He stood again to let her past and as she did she smiled her thanks, and with a glance back at Roleston said she was going to dance and would he, Jack, like to. Jack caught the look between herself and Roleston, who still sat with his arm along the back of the seat and his body leaning into the empty space where Maureen had been sitting just a moment before. Roleston bunched his shoulders and said something in one of his french book phrases which they didn't catch. He gave them a sort of deflated bow as if granting his Royal permission. Jack looked back at Maureen but she just tossed her head as if to say *come on*, and vanished into the crowd. Whatever it was between Roleston and herself was no concern of Jack's. He followed Maureen in among the dancers. If she was using him as a buffer well, fine. It had nothing to do with him and he was happy to dance with her.

She was a smooth dancer, and much taller than Jack had first imagined. In Roleston's company she had seemed dwarfed, but out on the dance floor among 'normal' sized people Jack discovered that she was almost as tall as he. He was reminded of Rose and Mary at the party. But he didn't check out if Maureen was wearing four inch heels. He wondered what it was about Roleston that attracted tall women, or any women! And what did Doc see in him? Jack had only met him on that one occasion at the party, and that once was enough. And what had he been saying to Maureen, trapped there in the crook of his immense frame that made her suddenly want to jump up and get away from him to the dance floor. And what about Marjory, his wife? Where did she fit into all this? Once again, Roleston had yet another beautiful woman in tow. If Marjory disapproved she seemed to lodge her protest by dancing on her own and getting drunk or stoned, as she had done at the party and now again to-night. Roleston didn't look like the type who would want to mingle on the dance floor with the, *rabble,* as he had referred to the crowd earlier. Jack imagined that if he did, some of the dancers would come of the worst from the sheer size and weight of Roleston, who was the biggest man he had ever seen. Not fat, but huge boned and at least six foot six. If he were to let loose among the dancers on this floor which was so packed some of them would as likely end up in the casualty ward. He put Roleston out of his mind and found Maureen.

She was a lovely dancer. She had a way of rippling her body up and down at the same time from the middle which was exciting to watch. Her whole body was in constant motion in a way which made Jack dizzy to look at. The floor was crowded and as they danced they kept being jostled together. It didn't disturb Maureen who didn't break her rippling flow and just smiled whenever they were thrown together. She was enjoying herself, and so was Jack.

Suddenly out of the mass of undulating bodies Marjory appeared. She seemed to materialise for a second between them. As she did so she put her arms around Maureen and kissed her full on the lips and was gone again. Jack was taken aback. Maureen simply waved after her and continued dancing as if nothing adverse had happened. She answered Jack's raised eyebrows with a broad smile and an extra accentuated wriggle of her hips. It was so powerfully sensual that Jack felt the smack of it and it checked his rhythm for a beat. The effect of Marjory's kiss and Maureen's wriggle were like a left and right hook in quick succession to his senses. If he had been in a boxing ring he would have hit the canvas, dazed and surprised. They danced on. The band didn't let up for another two numbers. Jack wasn't used to a full twenty minutes of this but Maureen seemed to be only getting her second wind by the time the band finally came to the end of the set and took a short break.

They were both flushed and sweating by the time they got back to the table. Roleston ignored them. He was locked in conversation with Doc and well into his third double brandy and his *zz*'s were back in prominence. Marjory was nowhere to be seen. Jack elbowed his way to the bar and ordered drinks. Maureen came with him as if she preferred not to sit without company while Roleston was there. While they waited for their drinks they made small talk. Jack complimented her on her dancing. He admitted that he wasn't used to it and was exhausted. Maureen laughed at his red face with beads of sweat dripping down and thanked him for saving her from Roleston whom she said was a "total pig".

She and Marjory were old friends, she explained. They had attended boarding school together. They hadn't seen each other for a few years as Roleston had been working in France and Marjory had gone with him. Though how she put up with him she couldn't imagine. Maureen had never liked him. She said that Marjory had been full of life and ideas before she married him but he had put a damper on her. Marjory was a brilliant mathematician and would have had a bright future if Roleston hadn't insisted on her playing the '*hausfrau*' for him. He had forbidden her to work after they were married. Now she was mostly suffering from hangovers and the effects of too much 'dope'. They appeared to have loads of money, but where it came from she had no idea. Roleston wasn't a professor, he was only a senior lecturer. But he had won an award in France for some special work he had done and in the press report had been mistakenly referred to as a professor.

When the drinks came they didn't go back to the table. They chatted about their lives. Maureen explained that she didn't go out much. She had a small child and her husband had died in a car crash two years ago. She was only now beginning to get over the shock. She worked for his family's firm, a small paper manufacturing business and stationers. She was an accountant and a partner in the company.

She was easy to talk to and Jack found himself telling her snatches of his own history. She listened attentively and didn't pretend pity or sympathy. Likewise she wasn't afraid to talk about herself and even seemed eager to do so. But she didn't dramatize on the sorrow she had had, or the problem of rearing her daughter alone and keeping a job at the same time.

They went back to the dance floor for another twenty minutes of jostling and sweating and then found a couple of seats away from Doc and Roleston. They spotted Marjory dancing once or twice in the crowd but she didn't come over to them. She was leaping about among the other dancers and looked drunk. She would wave at them and Maureen waved back before she disappeared again.

By the end of the night they were happy just to sit and talk when the band wasn't too loud. The rest of the time they just sat and watched the antics of the dancers and listened to the music. Jack was enjoying her company and was glad, now, he had come. Maureen seemed to be enjoying his company, too. Before the night was over they arranged to meet for a meal some night during the coming week. Maureen gave Jack her phone number and said she would try and arrange for a baby-sitter. Jack had a twinge of conscience as he wrote it down. *What about Rosemary..?* But, he shrugged away the thought, it was only an innocent dinner date. She was off somewhere doing what *she* wanted. She had made no attempt to contact him. And why shouldn't he go out and enjoy himself? Doc had been right. And where was she, anyway..? If she wanted to, she could be here to-night having a good time, too. Jack was enjoying talking to Maureen. She was good to talk to. She was easy to get on with. Nobody could object to that. There was no harm in it.

15

Rosemary's recollection of her aunt's house was far from the reality of what she found. Her memory of a rose covered cottage nestling on the edge of a mountain valley was a child's fantasy, something that her mind had mixed up with some other place in a fairy tale.

The valley was not much more than a dip in the landscape, and the cottage was a county council bungalow that was out of the same mould as a thousand other county council bungalows, except that it had a longer front than those surrounding, as if it had been originally a larger building. Yes, the garden was well tended, but the roses were suffering from the ravages of wind and rain, and the late October east wind with its biting cold was having its toll. The low, pebbled-dashed wall had not figured in her idyllic picture. The biggest shock was the council housing estate which all but obliterated any sense of isolation which she had granted to her aunt's house, and was little less than an effacement to what might have passed for *'Her Valley'*, given a little push of the imagination.

Notwithstanding, her aunt Shelagh's open-armed and big- hearted welcome was just as warm and spirited as she had remembered as she fell into it both from exhaustion and elation at having reached her destination that night she fled from the hospital.

When Shelagh opened the door she was dismayed by the sight of the bedraggled figure standing shivering in the light of her doorway, dressed only in a light sweater and jeans and pale as a ghost. As the figure staggered towards her, her initial instinct was to take a step backwards, as if from an attacker, but in that instant she recognised her niece and caught her as Rosemary fell into her arms.

'Rosemary! Rosemary! What...?' She cried out in alarm as she staggered back. But she didn't require or wait for a reply. She quickly steered her niece to a chair before the fire. She kissed and hugged her and reassured her that she was in safe hands before hurrying to fill a hot mustard bath, so that within minutes Rosemary was stripped and soaking to bring some warmth back to her chilled bones. Then wrapping her in a warm flannel dressing gown, bundled her off to bed with a steaming infusion of herbal tea. It smelled peppery and earthy, but the unfamiliar taste hardly registered on Rosemary's palate. It was warming and welcoming. Within minutes of her head touching the pillow, Rosemary was deep in sleep.

Rosemary spent the following two days in bed; the daytime in fitful sleep and the nights crowded with nightmares. Shelagh tended to her as if she were her own daughter, with tenderness and herbal drinks to redress the weakened state of her body, and fond affirmations to infuse confidence in this poor sick girl for a speedy recovery. She bathed and dressed the wounds on Rosemary's wrists, feeling along the tendons to ensure they were not severed and wondered what dreadful events had led to that desperate act. She didn't question her patient, who was in no fit state anyway. All that could be dealt with later. Her main concern was to get her back on her feet and the colour back in her pale cheeks.

On the second night Rosemary was particularly restless. Shelagh sat most of the night at her bedside, bathing her flushed forehead with a cool towel and holding her hand in her own and comforting her with soothing words. Rosemary ranted in her feverishness, meaningless phrases that made no sense to Shelagh, tossing and turning and getting wrapped up in the sheets, damp from her own perspiration. But early in the morning the fever broke and she relaxed into a deep sleep. Shelagh went wearily to her own bed, thankful that the worst was over and pondering on what the day would bring.

Rosemary did not open her eyes until lunchtime that day. She lay for some time staring at the white ceiling, not quite sure of where she was. Then, like a cobweb breaking, the events of the past week tumbled across her mind. The bread knife. The Hospital. Jack. And the crazy bus ride to Shelagh's, like some surreal episode from another world. The jolting ride through the twilight on the dimly lit bus and the fading light of the countryside as it flashed past the rain splattered window. Her mind playing tricks with reality and sleepfulness and wakefulness merging without conceivable borders like a mixed up dream and finally falling into the welcoming arms of her aunt.

Moving her head slightly from side to side she studied the room around her. White ceiling merging with white walls; the rose patterned curtains diffusing the daylight to a restful hue, and the stripped pine dressing table with a chair and wardrobe from the same wood adding a fresh, bright, homely warmth. The air was light and refreshing and for an instant she thought she caught the fragrance of roses. But when she tried to focus on the scent it evaded her nostrils, and she thought it must be something wafting up from her imagination; perhaps from a childhood memory of her aunt's cottage in the country.

Then, the full realisation that she *was* in her aunt's

cottage sprung her to full alertness. For a fraction of a second she felt a tingling of panic. She held her breath, almost afraid to breath in the formidable silence. Then, as quickly as it began, it passed, and she felt safe. Suddenly, she had an overwhelming thirst. She pulled over the bedclothes and rolled her feet onto the floor. But when she tried to stand her legs seemed to vanish from under her and she fell sprawling on her face.

Whether she lay there for minutes or seconds she wasn't aware. She felt arms lifting her and came to her full senses as Shelagh gently lifted her back onto the bed and tucked her in.

'We shouldn't try to overdo it...' Shelagh's voice was like a caress with a soft warbling laugh tucked into it. Rosemary lay back on the pillow, her eyes closed, afraid to meet her aunt's gaze. Shelagh held her hand, her fingers automatically feeling her pulse. 'So. How are we? Though I don't need to ask. You look a lot better.'

Rosemary opened her eyes. Shelagh was sitting on the edge of the bed smiling pleasantly at her. Rosemary attempted a smile to suppress her feelings of guilt and embarrassment. In the hospital she had fixed in her mind to get to her aunt's. She would be safe there. She could hide there. It would be her haven... But now, as she lay under her aunt's roof, and Shelagh sitting there smiling down at her, she felt as if she had overstepped the mark. She had no right to impose herself like this. She was an impostor. Her aunt was a busy woman...

Shelagh noticed her anxiety. She said reassuringly. 'Don't worry.' Then asked. 'You must be thirsty?' Rosemary nodded. Shelagh gave a little chuckling laugh and left the room silently and returned with a glass of water. She sat on the edge of the bed and put her hand behind Rosemary's head and lifted it and slipped another pillow behind her. Rosemary grasped the glass and drank in huge gulps. The water had a crisp metallic tang. It brought her back to those rare childhood visits to her aunt's. The clean spring water conjured up images of gurgling through rocks and stones and damp earth... She finished the last mouthful with a sigh.

Shelagh smiled. 'Be careful' She said, taking the glass from Rosemary. 'This is the real thing. It's not like what you get up in that city of yours. We don't want you getting intoxicated on it. Now, are you hungry?' She smiled and stood. 'You must be. I have a nice chicken broth. It's just about ready. Then you can try getting up again.'

Rosemary nodded. 'I'd love some. Thanks.' She felt a little more confident now. There was no hint of annoyance or recrimination in her aunt's tone. She seemed to be genuinely glad to have Rosemary tucked up in bed in her house. It was just as she remembered, warm and comforting.

'Good.' Shelagh laid her hand on Rosemary's forehead. She smiled 'Hmm. You'll be as right as rain after you've eaten.'

By the time Rosemary had finished a bowl of the delicious stew, Shelagh had the bath filled. She wrapped Rosemary in a warm dressing gown and helped her to the bathroom. She was a lot steadier now and seeing Shelagh's hesitancy in the doorway said that she would be all right on her own.

Shelagh nodded. 'Good. I have some things to do in the village. I'll be out most of the afternoon. But if you feel anyway tired you go right back to bed.' She turned to go. 'Oh. You'll need some clothes. My room is the door opposite here.' She motioned behind her. 'Help yourself to the wardrobe. I'm sure you'll find something to fit you all right.' She scanned Rosemary's thin body as she lowered herself into the steaming water. 'Don't worry about the bandages getting wet. The herbs in the water will do no harm. Just dry them off with the towel when you're finished and I'll change them when I get back.' She smiled and closed the door. When Shelagh left, Rosemary lay back in the warm relaxing bath. She was glad to be alone to gather her thoughts. The house was quiet and she could hear no sounds of any activity from the outside world. She hadn't felt so relaxed and calm for a long time.

After her bath she dressed as Shelagh had bid. She had to search among Shelagh's clothes - Shelagh was more robust than she - but she found a jumper and skirt that fitted and then wandered about the house. A small greenhouse had been added adjoining the kitchen with rows of herbs growing in clay pots lined up on long tables on either side. Through the glass she could see the little fenced off back garden with what looked like neat rows of low bushes and beyond that, the backs of a row of council houses which hadn't been there on her last visit. But that was years ago. She remembered her aunt telling her about them after her father's funeral. But Shelagh had explained that even though her little house was now all but surrounded, if you looked out of one of the windows in the sitting room, across green fields, you would still imagine you were miles from anywhere. Rosemary couldn't remember how she had found the house after getting off the bus. It had all looked so different that night. She remembered stumbling off the bus and falling into Shelagh's arms. But she could not recollect anything in between.

During dinner Rosemary felt compelled to offer an explanation as to why she had suddenly turned up on her aunts door-step. But it was a torrent of words, pouring out, mostly in a jumble and not making much sense. She seemed in a hurry to get to the end of her story and get it out of the way. But it was more *how* Rosemary talked more than *what* she actually said that interested her aunt. Shelagh could see that her niece was very unhappy and mixed up. The references to her father and a man called Jack she filed away for a later time, when she felt Rosemary would be better. In the end she indicated Rosemary's plate.

'Eat up. Your dinner will be cold,' she said, smiling. 'There's lots of time to talk.' She gave a little laugh. 'Unless you're planning to rush away again. And I hope you're not. Sure it'll be grand to have you around for a while. And I think we can dispense with calling me 'aunt'. We're both grown women. Call me Shelagh.'

At that Rosemary broke into fits of uncontrollable sobbing. Shelagh came to her and folded her arms around her, rocking her gently to and fro until the sobbing subsided. Then she led Rosemary to an armchair by the fire.

'You poor girl,' she soothed, as she dried Rosemary's tears with a napkin. 'Let it out. You'll be all the better for it.' She stood up. 'I'll go and make us a pot of coffee.'

When she came back Rosemary was still feeling somewhat exposed, having opened up her bag of troubles in front of her aunt. But it was good to be able to tell someone, especially one who didn't criticize or chide her. She couldn't have handled that at this time. She needed what her aunt was giving her; a sympathetic hearing. She wondered if Jack would have responded in the same way. But judging by his episode in the hospital with the bread knife she was doubtful. Jack had been too... dramatic. He was overbearing with his melodramatics; bringing the knife, wanting to paint the flat and arguing with her...

Shelagh handed her the coffee and sat opposite. 'It's decaff,' she explained. 'But you won't know the difference. If anything, it tastes better than the other.' They drank in silence for a while. The room was warm and cosy. The open fire was cheerful and they sat drowsily watching the flames. If a stranger had entered the room at that moment, they might have, on first glance, taken the two women for sisters, so alike were they. Rosemary was wearing a long velvet skirt in green and gold mottled colours and a dark green knitted jumper. They both had long, blue-black hair, and their faces had the same oval contours, with soft, pale blue eyes, gently sloping upwards at the edges. On closer examination, the stranger would notice that Shelagh's hair had the odd strand of grey and that her complexion was of a rosy hue compared to Rosemary's which was pale and drawn. Shelagh, too, was more robust but she expressed a healthy youthfulness that many a younger woman would have envied.

Shelagh finally broke the silence. 'You did the right thing to come...' She didn't look at Rosemary. She could sense her unease, although it was not as pronounced now, as when she had gone to make the coffee. 'And you're to be in no hurry to go. You'll stay until you feel better. Or as long as you like.' She spoke softly, taking her time with her words. 'It's good to talk out what's on your mind. It can only do you good. And we'll do all we can to get you back on your feet again. So, just take your time. There's no rush.' She smiled. 'I'm glad you came. I should have invited you anyway. But you knew you were welcome at any time.'

She let the words trail off. She had told Rosemary after her father's funeral that she was welcome to come and visit whenever she wanted. It was Rosemary's house as much as Shelagh's. Hadn't it been her Grandmother's and her father's until he abandoned it and moved to the city? If he had stayed, Rosemary would have probably been reared here, too... Now that he was dead the house belonged to Shelagh. And after Shelagh it would belong to Rosemary. There was nobody else.

She came over and knelt beside Rosemary and took her hands in her own and rubbed them gently. She said. 'Rosemary, love, there's no need to feel upset by what you've told me. It'll go no further. What you said is between you and me. As my father - your Grandfather - used to say when we were little. *"What's spoke at the table stays within walls."* ' She smiled. 'It's a pity you never met him. He was a lovely man. But he died before you were born.' She was reflective for a moment then gave a little laugh. 'We're very alike, you and me. You may not believe it, but I was a lot like you when I was younger. I didn't always live in the country like this in the peace and quiet. I lived in the city for over ten years. And I thought I liked it. But I realised, the more I lived there, the more frustrated I became. It wasn't until your Grandmother died and I moved back that I realised that everything I wanted was here in the country. The city..!' She shook her head. 'It was the city itself that was frustrating me. The concrete... The traffic... People rushing around... You could spend a whole day going from one place to another! And the pollution...' She pulled a face. 'All the things that make up a city I discovered I hated. Back here I could be myself. I re-discovered myself. All the things I ever wanted were right here. There was nothing for me in the city. Nothing at all. Here I can breathe.'

She went silent, staring into the fire. Then she laughed. 'But it did give me one thing. My livelihood. It was there

I realised that my interest in plants could give me my living. And I missed the countryside. I went to the city because I thought it had everything. But, no...' She shook her head. 'Perhaps you are a bit like me. Maybe you'll find what you want, here in the country."

Rosemary had nothing to say. But it was good to listen to her aunt. Just listening to her mellow, unhurried, words had a soothing effect. She hoped that her aunt was right. That she would find peace and fulfilment. But she didn't know how long she would stay. But it was so quiet here. Away from everything. Everything she had known. She wasn't sure how she would feel about it tomorrow, when she had to face up to why she had come in the first place. When she had to step out the door and know that she wouldn't be able to surround herself with the comfort of people and buildings and the frenzy of the city. How could you lose yourself among these small buildings and narrow streets and prying eyes?

16

'It's all in your mind. Your memory. Your psychic treasury.' Maureen said. 'All you have to do is bring it to the fore.'

She sat curled up on a large bean-bag beside the fire. Jack sat on the sofa, his coffee cup untouched and going cold on the floor at his feet. He had been trying to explain to Maureen his sense of 'loss' at not having a family; of being an orphan. His sense of isolation at not being 'connected', so-to-speak, to anyone. Yes, he realised he had some kind of connection with his mother and father. But it was so long ago, and he had never met them. He had no memories of it and couldn't grasp anything of it. That was the problem. There was nothing to remember. It wasn't as if he had known them and touched them and then they had died or gone away. It wasn't like having friends that were out of sight. There, there was the possibility that they would return. But he felt no connection with his lost parents. The link was missing. It was a void.

'Your dreams should help you,' Maureen said. 'If you could remember them in their symbolic terms, not necessarily in the pictures they present, but take the pictures and translate them into symbols and then decipher those symbols. The symbols mean more than the actual pictures.'

'I don't remember my dreams.' Jack bunched his shoulders, staring into the fire. 'And if I do, they're usually just a jumble of things. Totally disconnected. But I very rarely dream at all.'

'Oh, you do. It's just that you don't remember. That's all. But you could train yourself. It's easy.'

'Train?'

'Yes.'

'Like going to class...' He pulled a face.

'No,' Maureen laughed. 'But it wouldn't surprise me if somebody is doing it and making money out of it.'

'Like, *Learn-To-Remember-Your-Dreams* in *Ten-Easy-Lessons?*'

They both laughed. Jack added. 'For only five hundred pounds...'

'Well. Why not?' Maureen said. 'If we can't do it ourselves we have to go and find someone who can teach us.'

'If I could do it myself I could go into business.' Jack grinned wryly. 'Do you think the Industrial Development people would give me a grant? A few thousand? Set me up!'

They both laughed at the idea. 'We could draw up *The-Five-Year-Plan*,' Jack suggested. 'With your financial wizardry and my assembly line expertise ...' He drew the headline in the air. *'In Only Five Years YOU Could Be Living In Your Dreams. For Just Five Thousand Pounds..! Book Today To Avoid Disappointment.'* Maureen got a fit of the giggles and fell sideways off the bean-bag, shushing and pointing to the ceiling. 'We'll waken Aoife. Shhh...' She sat up and cocked an ear, stifling her giggles. 'She's always a light sleeper after the babysitter leaves. I think she gets her too excited.' They listened, hushed, for a few seconds, but all was quiet from above.

Maureen's daughter Aoife was a robust four year old, lively and full of games. Jack and Maureen had been out to dinner and had come back to Maureen's house for a coffee. Aoife and the babysitter were still romping around the sitting room floor when they arrived. Aoife had been too giddy to submit to bed and Maureen had to allow her to stay up a little longer to let her calm down. But instead, Aoife had become cranky with tiredness and it had taken a lot of coaxing to get her to finally submit. Aoife had insisted on a story and Maureen had placated her even though it was getting very late. The child had eyed Jack with blatant derision, as the one who was responsible for depriving her of all her mother's attention. She put on a pout until Maureen agreed to the story. 'But a short one,' Maureen had insisted, as it was late and Mummy wanted to talk to her friend, Jack. If looks could fry..! Jack felt like a sausage under the grilling of this wilful four year old's eyes.

It was a week since they had met at Doc's Soul gig, and when they had agreed to meet again for dinner, Maureen had suggested a small Hungarian restaurant in town. She had been to Hungary on holidays as a student and had fond memories of it. Whenever she could she would have a meal at this restaurant. The food and the people there, made her feel so much at home. She imagined that there must be Hungarian blood somewhere in her ancestry.

It had been an early dinner as her babysitter was studying for her Leaving Cert. exams, and anyway Aoife was at an age where she wouldn't go to bed until she came home. Maureen had suggested that she would pay for the meal as Jack was out of work, but Jack had protested. Maureen had laughed good-naturedly at his gallantry. He was somewhat abashed. But she wasn't mocking him. She convinced him that he was suffering from old-fashioned values and that it was time they were bashed. Jack had to agree. But he insisted that they take a taxi and that he would pay. She eyed him

144

apprehensively, but he assured her that he wasn't entirely broke. But she had her own car? Why go to the expense of a taxi? Jack had replied, 'Because...!' and left the rest to her imagination. She laughed at his serious face. It was as good a reason as any.

It had been a pleasant dinner. This time they could talk without having to shout in each other's ear as they had done at the gig. They dined on *Paprikscsirke*, chicken paprika, with onions and red paprika and sour cream and the dark red heady wine of Eger, *Egri bicavér*, "Bull's Blood" it was called, the waiter explained. They found it easy to talk to each other. Both had a past, hampered by misfortune. They were on a par, neither had to feign sympathy for the others adversity. Maureen found Jack a good listener. She explained how she had found difficulty talking about her husbands death, and her feelings, with her family. She didn't have a very good relationship with her mother, and her father, who was a quiet man and, she hastened to add, a lovable father whom she couldn't reproach, would only shake his head and say things like, "Time will heal..." She felt that he was as devastated as she was herself; his only daughter's life in shreds; her husband's life taken by some maniac of a drunken driver! He couldn't find the words to express his own bitter feelings. Her husband, John, had been like a son to him. The son he never had.

'And as for my best friend, Marjory,' Maureen gave a wry laugh. 'She had just married that ape Roleston and there was no getting through to her at the time. Then they went off to France. So I had really no one to talk to. John's family... Well, they were shattered completely. John was the only son, oh, he had two sisters, but they had no interest in the business. John was the heir. His father doted on him. Though at times it was more like *gloated*... After the accident he shut down completely. A changed man!' She sighed heavily. 'But business had to continue as usual. There was little time for taking stock of grief, and I had a child to real. So I had to bury mine too...'

Maureen was downcast for a few minutes. But she was grateful to have someone to open up to, who understood without having to pretend understanding. Then they both realized that the conversation had gotten a trifle morbid and had changed the subject and argued about who had been the better dancer. Jack had insisted that she was the winner 'hands down'. And he had jumped up in the restaurant and tried to demonstrate her unique way of wiggling, both up and down from the middle at the same time. The Hungarian waiter was highly amused at Jack's demonstration and had turned up the piped gypsy music and soon had them all dancing the *Csardas* awkwardly between the tables. It was a pity it had to break up. But Maureen shook her head sadly, reminding him of Aoife, waiting for her story and the baby sitter waiting to get home. It had been OK at the soul gig. That had been a week-end night and she had no play-school on the following day.

'Now. If we could chart *her* dreams,' Maureen pointed to the ceiling. 'What goes on in *her* little brain at night, it might save a lot of explaining in the future. Oh, not that she's a difficult child. Wild at times. Like most. But they live very much in the present. But I'm sure her mind is working on other things when she's asleep.'

Jack laughed. 'Probably me.'

'Oh. Don't mind that. All children are the same. They're jealous of anyone getting more attention than themselves. I'm sure it's only natural. She's probably looking for her...' She stopped abruptly. The tears welling up in her eyes. 'Oh, God. I'm sorry, Jack...' She hung her head and sobbed softly for a few minutes. Jack waited. Then she dried her eyes and heaved a long sigh. 'I'm sorry...'

Jack waved her apology aside. 'There's no need. Sometimes I wish *I* could just let it out. But... It's all right.' He said softly.

'Oh, bother!' Maureen jumped to her feet. 'Life has to go on, I suppose.' She straightened her skirt and ran her fingers through her hair, as if that would help bring her back to the reality of getting on with life. She turned and faced Jack. 'Would you like to see?'

'See...?'

'My dreams...?'

'How...?' He cocked his head to one side, not understanding.

She laughed. 'My dream book.!'

'Dream book...?'

'Yes.' She swished past him out of the room and ran upstairs. When she returned she was carrying a bundle of school exercise books. She sat on the sofa beside him and squared the copy books on her knees, placing both her hands flat on top. Jack watched her. She looked so serious and sat so still with her back straight and her hands rested on the top copy as if waiting for a signal to open the first page.

She said solemnly. 'This is the first book. It goes back to when I was thirteen. An ominous year to start. But...' She turned and faced him. When she saw the portentous expression on his face, like a child waiting for the Magician to pluck fire from the air, she couldn't contain herself, and burst out laughing, dumping the exercise books on the floor and falling back on the sofa. 'Oh, I'm sorry, Jack. It's just the expression on your face...' She rocked back and forth trying to stifle her laughter. 'I'm sorry. I sounded so solemn. And your face... You looked as if... as if you were expecting smoke to rise up...' She shook again with laughter. Jack put out his hand to steady her and she fell back against him. She lay for a minute waiting for the giggles to subside. 'I don't know why I'm so giggly tonight...' She turned her body slightly to him, making herself more comfortable against the curve of his side. He slipped his arm around her and gently pulled her closer. He slipped his other arm around her until his hands joined across her stomach. He could feel the swell of her breathing gently rising and falling against his hands.

They lay like this, enjoying the moment of closeness, neither having the inclination to bring it any further, their breathing rising and falling as one.

Jack must have dozed off. The wine had been strong. He was aware of Maureen easing herself out of his arms. He opened his eyes and saw her walking to the door and picking Aoife up in her arms. She turned back to Jack. 'I'm afraid *Little Madam* here is calling the shots...' She kissed Aoife on the side of her face, whispering soothingly to her. Aoife's eyes were locked on Jack, her little face screwed up with suspicion.

Maureen carried her over to the sofa and sat with her on her lap. Her eyes still held on to Jack's. 'You remember Jack?' Maureen said, 'Of course you do...' Aoife didn't budge. Even when Maureen bounced her gently on her knee the child's gaze never left him. Not quite hatred. Not quite disapproval. More defiance. And challenging. Jack was fascinated by the power of those young eyes. He thought, if something like an earthquake occurred at this very moment; if everything in the room were to shake, the one thing that would remain fixed would be those glaring eyes of Aoife's.

He tried a smile but the child's little mouth remained set. 'I think she's gone off me.'

'Nooo...she's just tired. Aren't you...?' Maureen crooned. Aoife didn't stir.

'Oh. This isn't like you at all,' Maureen scolded playfully. 'You remember Jack. He came home with Mummy. You were talking to him earlier. Before you went to bed.'

Suddenly Aoife broke her gaze and buried her head in Maureen's shoulder; her arms wrapped tightly around her neck.

'She's tired. She doesn't usually make strange.' She kissed Aoife and looked at Jack over the child's head. 'Yes. She's a very tired little girl. Aren't we...? I think we should go to bed now...Hmmm...?' Maureen hugged her and carried her upstairs saying to Jack as she left the room. 'Do you want to make some more coffee? I'll only be a minute.'

In the kitchen, Jack could hear Maureen crooning and talking softly to Aoife. He brought the coffee back to the sitting room. After about fifteen minutes Maureen came down. She sat on the beanbag and threw some briquettes on the fire. She noticed Jack's miffed look as she settled herself back on the beanbag. She tried to think of something to say, but the mood of earlier was now broken. She let it go. There would be other times.

The moment passed. Jack handed her the mug of coffee and she smiled her thanks. She said. 'I think she'll sleep now.'

Jack nodded. A tiny vein of envy ran through his brain.

Maureen and Aoife. He drank his coffee and stood up. He stretched, preparing to leave. It was late. He was tired. Maureen said. 'Are you off?.'

'I think so. Better let you get to bed.' He grinned diffidently. 'After all, you have to get up for work tomorrow.'

'Hmm. True.' She stood. 'I'll walk you to the door...'

As she opened the door she said. 'Thanks Jack. It was a lovely evening.' Then she reached up and brushed her lips quickly on his cheek. 'Give me a ring later in the week.'

He stood for a minute looking down at her. Then he reached out and pulled her to him. Their lips met in a long sensuous kiss. The taste of sweet saliva flowing as they explored with hot tongues. Their bodies clinging tightly, one to the other. The softness of her pushing against him. The hardness of him pushing against her. Two bodies trying to occupy the same space. Clinging. Holding. Probing. Electric excitement running through the tips of his fingers; through the palms of his hands at the slimness of her waist; the round globes of her bottom. Her hands running hard down the ridges of his back to the tight muscles of his buttocks. Moulding the softness of her breasts against the expanse of his hard chest. Oh, God. They needed this so badly. They wanted this so much. His hand pushing up under her blouse, feeling for her breast; the hard nipple. Her belly pushing against the bulge. But no! She wasn't ready for this. It had been too long. She needed to think. To think. To be sure. John..! Oh God. She needed time. Time... Then... Oh...!

Finally they broke. Panting. Heaving against each other. Jack pressed for her again. But Maureen hesitated. Time to think. Time to think. She held him off. Gently.

Carefully. No. It's too soon. I'm not ready. Slowly she pushed him away with a soft smile. They stood looking at each other for a minute, breathing deeply. Reluctant to make the next move. Wanting to make the next move. Searching each other's eyes. Can we wait? Can we pick up where we left off? The next time? Cryptic messages passing between them. Transmitted. Received. Decoded. Understood. Accepted. Agreed!

Maureen let her hands drop to her sides and swayed shyly; playfully. 'I think you'd better go, Jack...'

He took a deep quivering breath. 'Should I...?'

'Yes. No. Yes. No.' She smiled, playing with the zip of his jacket. Up. Down. Up. Down. Then finally up. Closed. 'Ring me ...'

He stroked the curve of her cheek. 'When...?'

'Not tomorrow...'

'The next day...?'

'Yes.'

Jack nodded. Understanding. 'OK. I will.'

17

Rosemary recovered quickly in the country. Shelagh fed her and tended to her and cared for her, both with personal consideration and herbal tisanes. She enjoyed doing so. Rosemary was like a daughter to her. She liked having her in the house. It gave her a sense of responsibility she hadn't been aware of in herself before. The word that came to her mind was - *motherly* - but she didn't want to admit it. So she preferred to think of it as *caring - family*. And Rosemary responded to Shelagh's attentiveness. First with an inkling of suspicion and then more readily as she gained strength.

During the day, when Shelagh was busy tending her garden, or working in her greenhouse or dealing with her 'callers', as she preferred to call her patients, Rosemary would take long walks, skirting the village as much as possible. Sometimes, when the weather was too bad to go out she would sit in her room, glancing through books from Shelagh's large collection. Anything from romantic novels to the classics to tropical diseases. Browsing rather than reading. Other times, when she was neither in the mood for walking nor reading, she would help Shelagh in the garden or the green house or take charge of the kitchen. She wasn't a great cook, but if she followed the recipes carefully from Shelagh's books, which were mostly vegetarian, they usually turned out satisfactorily. Shelagh put no pressure on her to do anything. She helped out, first from a sense of boredom and wanting something to do and then from a sense of interest and wanting to contribute.

She was beginning to feel at home. At first it worried her. She had never envisaged the country as being her home. Did she miss the bustle of the city; the sense of being among throngs of people..? Though she hadn't had much to do with many people when she lived there. But they were there. They were all around. You could feel their presence, even if you stayed in your room and never ventured out. She had been reared in the city. It was a part of her... The concrete, the shops, the car fumes, the screech of buses... But gradually she began to enjoy the country without being totally aware of it happening to her. It was as if the country was coming to her, rather than she, coming to the country. She began to lose her fear of not having a bus passing every fifteen minutes; Not having a shop within a hundred yards; The crush in the department stores; The buildings across the street... She began to delight in the sense of freedom. The sense of space. The sense of isolation. Not in a forlorn sense, but a conscious sense of detachment to herself, rather than a loneliness at being imprisoned with her own thoughts and problems in a one-room bed-sit, in the concrete block that she had called 'home'. She loved Shelagh's little house. She loved the small cosy rooms. And the garden front and back. It reminded her of her own house back in the city when she was growing up. When the city seemed more like a large village, and not the bustling monster it had become. The more she thought on it, the more she had the feeling that she had escaped. As from a prison. Perhaps Shelagh was right. She would 'find' herself in the country.

Shelagh had said a curious thing one evening during dinner. A meal that Rosemary had cooked and had been a particular success. Shelagh had complimented her on her accomplishment. There had been some small-talk then they had continued eating in silence. Then Shelagh had gone noticeably quieter, as if withdrawing into herself, and thinking deeply. Then she suddenly looked up, straight at Rosemary, but not focused on her. Her eyes had a veiled and brooding look.

She mumbled something as if talking to herself, and then,

'...and Rosemary gets her head chopped off...' she finished.

Rosemary was startled. It had come out so unexpectedly. So unnaturally. It unnerved her. She sat, rigid, staring at her aunt. Is this what happened when you lived alone for too long, she wondered, talking out loud to yourself. And what had it to do with her? But Shelagh resumed eating as if nothing had happened. Then she looked up and noticed Rosemary staring strangely at her.

'Are you all right,' Shelagh asked.

Rosemary didn't answer. She didn't know what to say. Had she imagined what Shelagh had said?

'Rose. Are you sure you're all right..? Shelagh looked anxiously at her.

'I... I thought you said something...'

'I just asked you if you were all right. You look strange?'

'No. Before that. I thought you said something about me...?'

'Did I? ' Now it was Shelagh's turn to look surprised. 'What did I say?'

Rosemary was tentative. 'I thought you said something about - heads being cut off...?'

'Heads being cut off...? Oh. I'm Sorry.' Shelagh laughed loudly, putting her hand over her mouth, embarrassed. 'I didn't realise I had said anything. I didn't mean to. What I was thinking of... Well, you know that

Rosemary is the name of an Herb. *Rosemarinus Officinalis*. It's used in all sorts of ways. In cooking. In medicines. For perfumes. Rosemary is harvested around September. There's not much of it around here. The soil is wrong. Not enough sunshine, though this year was particularly hot... Sorry. I'm wandering... What I was thinking, just then...' She gathered her thoughts. ' Rosemary is harvested around this time. The flower is cut and then distilled or dried, and the stalk is - for distillation purposes - thrown away. If it gets into the infusion it spoils it. Stinks. Like turpentine...'

Rosemary was still looking at her, somewhat bewildered. She knew what Shelagh was saying. But she couldn't understand why she had said, no, *intoned*, what she said. And the way she said it. Like an Oracle! What did she mean? She was used by now to Shelagh explaining about Herbs to her. She only half took heed, most of the time. But this time, somehow, it was directed *at* her, not to her. It was in the tone of voice. The staring. Unfocused. Uncanny..! *My aunt is a Witch!* Ridiculous...but...

'What I mean is...' Shelagh smiled at her. 'Do you feel as if you've been harvested. That's what I meant. Have you been... reaped.' She stopped at the look of sudden shock on Rosemary face. She waved her hand in the air as if to clean the board. 'No... I said reaped... *Reaped*... not... *that*!' Her nieces expression relaxed. 'I can't find the word I'm looking for.' She thought for a moment. '...Saved.' She laughed again. 'When I had the thought just then it was clear to me. Trying to explain it, is like trying to explain a Proverb.' She threw up her hands as if seeking inspiration from the air. 'But, when you did what you did, did you think you were trying to cut the flower from the stalk? The head from the body?' She shook her head. 'I was thinking about it coinciding with harvest time for your namesake...?' Her face took on a ponderous look again...

Rosemary shook her head. What was her aunt trying to say...? Oh, she knew right well what she was trying to say. But she didn't want to think about it. She didn't want to talk about it.

She said. 'I don't know...' and continued eating, avoiding Shelagh's eyes. She didn't want to discuss the subject. Not now. Not again. Shelagh hadn't broached the subject either, until now. Rosemary blocked any more discussion, keeping her head down, concentrating on her meal.

Shelagh nodded, abstractly. She spoke, but it was more to herself. 'Well, it seems to have been a good harvest.'

She continued eating again as if she had never spoken. But it played on Rosemary's mind for the remainder of the meal. Oh, it wasn't just the words, but more the associations of the words. Harvested! Reaped! ... *Raped!*

Did Shelagh have a premonition of something or was she just thinking out loud? Was Shelagh reading deep into her mind without being aware of it? She brushed the thoughts into a corner. But it crouched there, like a malevolent imp...

Another day they were walking into the village together. As they turned into the Main Street they were suddenly accosted by an old lady coming towards them leaning on a walking stick. When she spotted them she stopped and waved the stick at Shelagh, crying out. *'Belladonna. Belladonna,'* and grinning devilishly at them through her set of false teeth. Rosemary jumped with fright. The old lady barred their path. Shelagh sidestepped her, pulling Rosemary after her.

Rosemary looked back over her shoulder as they

hurried on. Shelagh laughed. 'Don't. You'll turn into a pillar of salt...!'

'What did she say...?'

'*Belladonna?* The name of an Herb - *Deadly Nightshade* - A poisonous weed. That's what she calls me. I kind of like it.' She giggled. 'That was old Missus Cavandish. One of the *Auld Shtock,* as we say around here. She and your grandmother were not what you'd call friends. In fact, if my mother had an enemy, and I doubt it, Missus Cavandish would fit the bill. A staunch Catholic family. The shape of her knees are worn into one of the church pews. One of the wealthiest families around these parts. Your grandmother was a bit of a Witch.' She laughed. 'Like me. Dabbled in herbs and cures. Took her religion to a point. But she still believed in the *Old Ways*. Taught me before I appreciated it. But Missus Cavandish hated your Granny. Accused her of doing the Devil's work...'

'But why did she call you...'

'Belladonna? Oh. That's just her name for me. The Beautiful Lady. But I doubt if she means it like that. She's a bigoted old faggot... If she only knew...!'

'Knew what..?'

'That I *am* a Witch...!

'That's what I said to Jack.'

'To Jack?'

'That you were a witch.'

Shelagh grinned a wicked grin. 'And did he believe you?'

'I don't think he took me seriously.'

'Maybe he should have...'

'But I wasn't being serious. I was only trying to annoy him.'

'Well, from what little you've told me about your Jack. You seemed to have put *him* under a spell.'

'He's not *my* Jack.' Rosemary retorted. A little annoyed at the inference.

Shelagh laughed at her, but good humouredly. 'Hah! But he could have been. If you'd wanted him to. We're all Witches in our own ways.' She winked mischievously. She was enjoying herself. 'Us Witches. We can have what we want. All we need is the right *spell* ...*HehHeh!*'

Rosemary had to laugh at her aunts antics. But all this talk about Witches was making her uneasy. With Jack it had been a joke, just to get his back up, make him wonder about her. It was a game. But Shelagh took an almost evil delight in the subject. No. She was joking too...?

A few nights later they were sitting in the Lounge of the local hotel. An old country mansion surrounded by trees and parkland. One of the old country manors, which, not a century before had been the home of Lord Birchley, R.M. The present, *local aristocracy*, as Shelagh put it, were doctors and lawyers and gentleman farmers. Most of them doubling as county councillors and politicians. It would be, what Shelagh had called a *sophisticated* drink. Mixing with the country gentry. But she didn't mean it maliciously. So they dressed up in Shelagh's finery and applied a little make-up. All natural ingredients. *Ne'er a Ha'p'orth o' Plashtic nor Animal Fat Betwixt Them.* Shelagh had joked.

Everyone in the lounge nodded or said 'hello' to Shelagh and all studied Rosemary, especially the men.

Shelagh ordered two small bottles of Guinness. Less chemicals, she explained, no gas pumped in, just a natural head from the yeast. Like two *Auld Wans* in a city pub, Rosemary had jibed. And they live to be a hundred, Shelagh riposted. Hardy *Old Dears*. Makes you as fat as a fool, Rosemary suggested. Won't do you a bit of harm, though you could do with a bit of fattening... Shelagh playful poked her in the ribs. Fat, maybe. Fool, never. Indeed Rosemary had filled out a little in the past few weeks since coming to Shelagh's. She was looking healthy and radiant. They looked more like sisters day by day.

'And how is the Dried Weed business...?' A well-dressed man in his early fifties pulled out the vacant seat beside them and sat down. He placed his glass on the table and stretched his long legs under the table with an air of boyish nonchalance.

'Hi, Doc.' Shelagh greeted him. 'Still peddling drugs...?'

'And why not. There's great money in it. Keeps me away from the Meths...' He laughed and reached for his Whiskey glass. 'How are you Shelagh?'

'Oh, I'll survive, Frank.' Shelagh introduced Rosemary. 'This is my niece, Rosemary. Frank Murray, MD.' There was a barb in the way she stressed the letters, *Emm Dee*.

Frank held out his hand and shook Rosemary's, holding on to it a little longer than necessary. He said. 'It's a pleasure.' His voice had a soft country musical lilt to it. He turned to Shelagh. 'I'm sorry, Shelagh, *a ghrá*,' he said, using the Irish word endearingly. 'I didn't think you could be surpassed for beauty. But this young lady is catching up on you.' He gave Rosemary an appraising look. Rosemary flushed. His eyes lingered on her, but it was an honest appraisal. Still, Rosemary was stung by the directness of it.

She noticed that Shelagh was a little miffed by Frank's remark. Shelagh gave him a playful punch.

'Watch your blood pressure Doc.' She threw him a raunchy look. It was another side to her that Rosemary hadn't seen before. She noticed that Shelagh and Frank were on very good terms with each other. After the initial playful exchanges they quickly changed the subject and got down to some serious talking. The County Fair, on which they were both organizers. The Arts Committee, of which they were founder members. And the Conservation Society, which was in the process of restoring the old castle and burial ground, from which the village had received its original Gaelic name, *Reilig an Chaisleáin*; The Castle of the Burial Ground – or in its Anglocised version, Cashelrelick. Rosemary listened to their animated and impassioned discussion, which they directed towards her, so as not to leave her out of the company, explaining plans and events, and at the same time showing her that country life was not all only farming and cattle. It was obvious that they were trying to influence her. More so Frank than Shelagh, she thought. But she put it down to his friendliness and good manners, not wanting to exclude her from the conversation.

But she noticed something else, much more blatant. There was much more to Frank and her aunt Shelagh than old castles and art exhibitions. Frank was not what she had expected a country doctor to be. He was rustic, all right. He was not what she would regard as good looking, but he had a hardy handsomeness and a modern sophistication mixed with country charm that took her by surprise. He also had a way of touching you with the tips of his long fingers, when he wanted to stress a point.

But not in a condescending manner. It wasn't a casual habit. It was a deliberate action. And he was a good listener too. She had an instant liking for him. She could see that he and Shelagh thrived in each other's company and she wondered about them. She wondered why her aunt had not mentioned him before.

Finally Shelagh finished her drink, which she had been sipping slowly and excused herself, saying that the lounge was getting too smoky for her and she was heading home. Frank offered to drive them but she declined, glancing quickly at Rosemary. Rosemary said she was happy to walk. Frank helped them on with their coats and walked them to the door of the hotel and wished them a good night. When he had helped Rosemary on with her coat his hands had lingered on her shoulders just for an instant. She could still feel their touch. And she didn't mind the feeling. In fact she found she liked it.

Outside, the night was clear and cool. After the stuffiness of the lounge it was a pleasure to breath the crisp bite in the air.

Rosemary wanted to ask Shelagh about Frank. But she wasn't sure how to broach the subject, not wanting her aunt to suspect that she had noticed an intimacy between them, that they appeared to hide under all their talk of committees and castle restorations. She found Frank Murray very attractive, as Shelagh was too, and she wondered why they kept this wall of committees between them. Shelagh didn't remark on Frank as they strolled home, only commenting on the freshness of the night.

Back home Shelagh lit the fire and brewed some decaff coffee. They sat quietly for some time, watching the fire as it took, and sipped their coffee. Rosemary was aware of a certain reserve in Shelagh's demeanour and reckoned it was because of her meeting with Frank. She was curious. She said, keeping her tone casual. 'Frank seems an interesting sort of man...?'

It surprised her, the way she had phrased it. She was sounding more like a country woman, day by day. Shelagh didn't reply for a while. She sipped her coffee ponderously, gazing at the flames. Then, without looking at Rosemary she said, 'Yes. An interesting man, right enough...' And seemed not to want to enlarge on the subject any further. Rosemary let it go. If her aunt didn't want to talk about it, so be it. Rosemary could understand that. But she wanted to know. Shelagh's ponderous silence was making her more curious. She suspected a story behind it all.

Then Shelagh drained her cup. She placed it on the floor and looked at Rosemary for a few seconds as if deliberating whether or not to say something. She sighed.

'We almost got married once...' She said, and sighed again as if shrugging of things past and gone. 'You could say we grew up together. We had the same interests. Art. Conservation. Life in a country town... ' She gave a little laugh. '...and of course medicine. Though from different viewpoints. Traditional versus modern. Frank is a good Doctor. He's an intelligent man. We had many a good argument about his methods and mine. We even made plans. I was going to study modern medicine also and he was going to study traditional. Together we would be a force to be reckoned with. The old and the new, side by side... We learned a lot from each other.' She shrugged. 'Well. It wasn't to be. There was one thing we could never agree on.' She paused. 'Alcohol... Drink! Franks father, old Doctor Murray was an alcoholic. Killed him in the end. And Frank is very fond of the drink... Too fond! Oh I'm not against a drink or two...but... ' She didn't finish the sentence.

Rosemary detected a sadness in her aunt. She thought, having seen them together earlier, that they would have made a great team, both professionally and personally. She wondered why Shelagh hadn't taken the risk. She felt sorry for her. Her aunt was such a wonderful woman, kind and considerate and caring. Even if she did have this tongue-in-cheek obsession with calling herself a Witch. And she had given Rosemary such a lot in the short time they had been under the same roof. She felt for her and wished her to be happy. She was dismayed at the sadness Shelagh suddenly displayed as if it was buried in the past, but could think of no comfort to offer except to mumble, 'I'm sorry...'

Shelagh shook her head resignedly. 'Oh, there's nothing to be sorry about. I didn't really see myself as the wife of a country doctor. And in these parts, even with all their modern conveniences and contraptions, that is how I would be seen. Regardless of high ideals and plans! It might work in the city, but not here. Maybe ten years down the road, but not now. Anyway, I think I'm to blame as well. I'm too independent. No. I think in the end it wouldn't have worked out... And then there was the drink...! I think that was what really put an end to it...' Shelagh allowed her thoughts to trail off. She smiled, but it was a cheerless smile.

The fire burned down and Shelagh put some more logs on. They crackled and spat as they took flame. She settled back on her heels.

'Tell me about Jack?'

Rosemary shrugged. '...Jack?'

'You didn't say very much about him. Is it serious?'

'I don't know.'

'Does he know where you are?'

'No. But he probably has guessed by now. I told him about you.'

'That I was a Witch...!' Shelagh laughed. 'He'll probably want to keep his distance.'

'I didn't tell him where you lived.' Rosemary added almost defensively. 'He won't come here.' The thought frightened her a little. What if he did turn up. She wasn't ready to face him. A twinge of the old panic fluttered in the pit of her stomach.

'Oh. I wouldn't mind.' Shelagh said. 'Though it would be interesting to see you two together. You can tell a lot from that...'

Rosemary glanced at her aunt knowingly. She couldn't help smiling. 'I know..' She was thinking of Frank and Shelagh. Shelagh read her thoughts. She picked up a cushion and threw it playfully at her. 'That's enough of that. That subject is closed.'

Rosemary threw the cushion back. Shelagh placed it behind her and leaned back against the chair.

'Why don't you ring Jack and tell him where you are. The poor lad is probably worrying about you. Running off on him like that.'

Rosemary shook her head.

'You could invite him down for the weekend...? No...?'

Rosemary didn't reply. Shelagh let it pass. Rosemary seemed reluctant to speak about Jack or her father or anything about her past since that initial jumbled explanation. They seemed to talk about anything else.

But Shelagh knew there was more to it than what Rosemary had volunteered. She was particularly keen to get Rosemary to talk more about her father. That was a deep hurt that would not go away so easily. But if Rosemary was reticent to talk about Jack it would be much harder to get her to open up about her father.

Rosemary's father. Shelagh's brother.

Oh, she knew him well enough. She had lived under the same roof with him - this roof - for many years, growing up. They fought like cats and dogs. It was *Big Brother* versus *Little Sister* all her life. John Joseph's character was something she could not fathom, and it had become more so after the death of their father, when he was fourteen and she was thirteen. Her brother had begun to resent living with these two women. His mother and sister, and his resentment took the shape of a short demon in long pants. Their mother said he was trying to take the place of the father. But she was only placating her worst fears. There was more to him than that. With his father gone, he became uncontrollable. He hated them. He hated school. He hated the country. He hated his friends. He would have nothing to do with the local girls. He despised all that the country stood for. Except for one thing; his passion for roses. During his late teens he became fanatical in his religious duties to the point of derangement. And then, finishing school, he left, abruptly, leaving a scribbled note on the kitchen table, and found a job in the city. After that he rarely appeared or contacted them. It was only after he married, that his wife cajoled him to visit his mother in her last days. Rosemary was alien to them. She was a child they knew and saw little of. It broke their mother's heart. And then to do what he did to his own daughter...! Shelagh was horrified and ashamed. He was her own brother...! It hurt her deeply that he had done such a vile thing.

Rosemary sat with eyes closed pretending to be sleeping. The mention of Jack had brought with it a twinge of fear. What if he did turn up? But he couldn't. He didn't know where she was. She wasn't ready to face him and she hoped Shelagh would forget about it. She tried to crawl back into that little clear space somewhere in the labyrinth of her mind. That clear haven which she thought she had found when she left the hospital. But it wasn't clear any more. There was something lurking there still. Fragments of the same old creature. She wanted to crawl into that space and hide herself. But it wasn't free any more. There was still a presence of something nasty. *Please God, don't let her talk about Jack again. I'm not ready. Please God, don't let her bring up my father. Please God...! Don't let her talk about what happened...! I've said all I want to say...*

'Rose...?'

Oh Jesus. Don't let her talk!

'Rose...?'

Oh God!

'Rose, love... are you feeling all right..?' Shelagh's voice was gentle. Caressing. But... 'Rose, I'm worried...'

Worried..? Oh God! What was she going to say..?

'Rose, love. This is difficult... for me. I don't know how to put it without upsetting us both. But it's hanging between us...'

Rosemary body began to tighten. *I'm not ready. I'm not ready. Please don't...!*

Shelagh could see the anguish creep over her niece. If we could only get that anguish to the surface. Up and out. Like a festered tooth. She came over and took Rosemary's hand between her own. To make contact, to help her over the brink and reassure her.

'Rose... it's not easy for either of us. I want to help you. But I need you to help me too. He was your father. But he was my brother. And I'm ashamed... You're special to me. Like a dear friend. Like a..,' she stopped herself saying *daughte*r, 'a...sister.'

She took both of Rosemary's hands in hers. 'Can we help each other to get over this.'

She could feel the tension rising in Rosemary. Rosemary was looking at her with wide, wild eyes. But she had to press on. If only they could break this wall, brick by brick, and clear the ground. She had held back purposefully until she felt Rosemary could be strong enough. Until they both had the courage to face it. And talking about her own floundered relationship with Frank had helped her to reach for the empathy she felt she needed. But the panic in Rosemary's eyes told her that she had misjudged the timing. It was too soon. *But would every time be too soon...?* It had to be faced...

'Rose. I don't want to hurt you. God knows you've been through enough already. But if we could only talk about it. Without pressure...' *God almighty! What am I saying? She's not ready to bring it to the surface. Is it myself? Is it me who wants to talk...needs to talk...? Damn that man who brought this on her... On us...!*

Rosemary bolted off the chair. Shelagh was knocked backwards with the force of her . *The beast is uncoiling! It's gnarled head rising! The eyes bulging ! The mouth twisting! And that tail..! Twitching! Groping! Hurting... hurting... hurting...*

Crashing sounds emanated from the kitchen.

Shelagh jumped to her feet. She raced from the room. Rosemary was in a fury. Plates and cups and saucers went crashing against the walls. The dresser was cleared. The table was knocked askew. Chairs flung awry. Rosemary charging around the room like a rush of wind, screaming and smashing everything in her path.

Shelagh jumped at her. Grasping. Groping. Holding. Loosing grip. Grabbing again. Holding on. Holding on.

'Rose... Rose... Please... *Please*...' She screamed. She pleaded. She sobbed.

Rosemary was not aware of her. Shelagh clung to her; dragged at her as Rosemary twisted and turned. They crashed to the floor. Shelagh hung on.

'Rose. *Oh God*. Rose. I'm sorry... I'm sorry...'

Both of them now. Rolling. Banging against the table legs; chair legs. Fragments of broken delft crunching under them, cutting into their clothes... Sobbing... Crying... Pleading... Hugging...

I'm sorry. I'm sorry. I'm sorry.

They lay there wrapped in each other's arms. Breathing together. Crying together. Clinging together. Holding on together...

...time suspended...

...The rage subsided...

They helped each other off the floor. Neither spoke. And still wrapped in each other came back to the sitting room. Then breaking apart sat in front of the dying fire. Neither wanting to break the silence. Neither wanting to make the wrong move; say the wrong word. But something had broken in Rosemary and the silence was not at peace. It hung like a vapour, then settled like a wall. Shelagh felt it but she closed her eyes against it. She had made the wrong move; had mistimed. She hated herself for it. Now they would both suffer for it. That road would have to be traversed again. She couldn't think. She was too exhausted and sat with eyes tightly closed and listened in the silence. There was no sound. She strained her ears. Silence. It was cold. She shivered and opened her eyes. Rosemary! The chair was empty. She stretched. I must have fallen asleep. The fire was dead. Rosemary must have gone to bed. She settled back.

Then bolted upright. The house was too still. She checked Rosemary's room. The bed was empty. She went into the kitchen. The table was back in place; the chairs standing, waiting around it, like skeletons for a feast that would never take place. The floor was swept. There was a note on the empty dresser.

"Shelagh. Gone for a walk. Rosemary".

She read it again. It didn't change. It was curt. It hurt. No, *Dear* Shelagh*!* No, *Love* Rosemary*!* She crumpled it in her hand. *God Almighty!* Is this where we've come to. Half a million years to get to this. That we have to break *things* - and *ourselves* - to express our pain! That we are twisted and torn apart without apology! Without explanation! She ran to the door. Outside, all was dark and quiet. *Rose... Rose...* She called. But the darkness did not answer.

Wearily, she went to her bed. She lay uneasy, her ear cocked for Rosemary's return. But sleep overcame her.

She dreamed.

Of Flower Heads

And Bubbling Broths

And the Stink of Turpentine...

18

'Let's do something crazy.'

'Like what...?' Maureen turned sleepily towards Jack. They were snuggled up together in Maureen's big bed. Their love-making had been urgent, needful. She ran her finger playfully down the bridge of his nose. 'You've got a sinister look in your eyes.'

'My eyes are closed!'

She giggled. 'So are mine. But I can imagine.' She snuggled closer to him. 'But I thought we'd just done it - something crazy.'

'That wasn't crazy. That was - beautiful, wonderful, delightful.' He opened his eyes. 'And so were you.'

'Were...?' Her eyes sprung open, feigning annoyance. 'Were?'

Jack hugged her closer. 'Are. Are. Are.'

'Are. Are. Are.' She mimicked him. 'That's only three!'

'By a million,' he said, his voice husky. He pressed against her. Maureen ran her nails down the length of his back and curling her leg around his thighs pulled him to her. They moved together, slowly and gently, clinging tightly in the long shuddering climax.

They drifted...

'So. What crazy thing did you have in mind?' She nibbled at his ear. No reply. She gave him a shake. 'Well...?' Jack was breathing deeply. 'Jack. Are you asleep?' He pulled back from her slowly, their skins pealing apart, the sweat trickling down. Reluctantly, he opened an eye.

'Hmm...' Maureen coaxed. 'What crazy thing have you planned.'

He looked at her for a second, then closed his eye again. 'I'll think of something. Surprise, surprise...!' And he pulled her against him again.

They lay, content, dozing, wrapped in the warmth of each other's embrace.

After a while, Maureen stirred.

'Jack...'

'Hmm...'

'Jack. You'll have to go soon.'

'Unfortunately,' he mumbled. He was so comfortable, so relaxed. But he knew he'd have to go.

He felt Maureen unfurling. Her warm stickiness peeling away, letting a draft of cold air shiver down the length of his body. He reached out to pull her back but she slipped out of the bed. He rolled after her but she dodged him and catching the duvet, snatched it off him. He sat up smartly.

'O.K! O.K.! I get the hint,' he chuckled, and rolled onto the edge of the bed and pretended to shiver. Maureen came and sat beside him and wrapped the duvet around them both.

Jack hugged her inside the cover. 'If you're trying to get rid of me,' He grinned. 'You're going the wrong way about it.'

'I know. But you have to.' She pouted, a little girl pout, just like Aoife.

'I know...but..'

'Aoife.' Maureen reminded him and whipped the duvet

from around him as she jumped up.

Jack reached for his clothes. 'Aoife. Yeah. Kids Rule O.K.'

Maureen slipped on her dressing gown. 'They sure do...' She sat back on the bed and watched Jack as he pulled on his clothes.

'Jack...?'

'Yes Ma'am.' He buckled his belt, assuming a Cowboy drawl.

'Jack. It's probably none of my business...' Maureen hesitated, watching him, her head cocked to one side. 'But...' She waved the thought away. 'It doesn't matter.'

'Say what's on your mind Ma'am.' He mimed reaching for his *six-gun*. 'Well...' Maureen started. 'Tell me to shut up if it's none of my business. But...do you always...What I mean is. Do you always wear that jeans and jacket...?'

'I reckon so, beggin' yer pard'n Ma'am.' He put the *six-gun* away. 'Why.?'

'Oh. I was just wondering. That's all.'

'You don't like them?' He turned and faced her.

Maureen shrugged apologetically. 'I knew it was none of my business. But do you have any other...I mean...are you all right for...' She stopped. 'I'm sorry. I shouldn't have said anything.'

Jack looked at himself in the wardrobe mirror. 'Looks like me.' He said. 'That's the way I look. I suppose. Never thought much about it. But if you don't like it...'

Maureen stood, undecided, embarrassed now. She wished she hadn't said anything. But it bothered her. On the three occasions she had met Jack he was wearing the same denim jeans and jacket. They were clean. Well washed. Almost washed away. But she suspected that he didn't have any other clothes.

'I'm not very good at buying clothes, ' Jack said, noticing her discomfort. He didn't mind at all, her referring to his denim 'suit'. 'I never give it much thought. I just buy jeans and jackets. Saves me a lot of hassle... You women are better at it than us men.'

Maureen went over to the wardrobe and slid back the second door. Then she quickly slammed it shut again. But in the half-second it was open, Jack saw the neat array of crisp business suits displayed. *His suits. Her husband's suits. Her dead husband's suits...Oh God...!*

Maureen slumped against the door, every muscle in her body straining. Forcing it shut. As if it might burst open of its own accord and *those suits*, take on shape and substance and mock her in some devilish dance. *What am I doing..? Good God! What am I thinking of..?* She was afraid to turn and face Jack. *What must he be thinking of me. What mad idea took hold of me..?* She moaned. *Stupid! Stupid! Stupid!*

Jack froze, not knowing what to do. Maureen lay bunched against the wardrobe door. Suddenly there was miles between them. A chasm opened across the expanse of carpet. Opened between them and how they had been, only minutes before, enjoying the mysteries of each other's sexuality. *And those suits had been a witness, hanging there, silent, listening, holding their breath, behind the louvered doors!* The wrong action now, or the wrong syllable, would widen that gulf, deepen it... make it unforgivable.

Jack stood like a statue, listening to Maureen's stifled sobbing. He wanted to go to her. Touch her. Tell her he understood. Reassure her that it didn't matter. But he was afraid to cross that gorge. *Afraid of the suits!* Afraid to interfere. In her blunder. In her grief.

Gradually her sobbing came under control. The chasm narrowed. Jack breathed again. She didn't turn around. He heard her say, softly. 'I'm sorry...' To him? To the suits? What could he say to her? What could he offer? She was trapped, caught in the middle, between the suits, and what they had been, and Jack, and what they had done.

'It's all right.' He mumbled. To break the silence. To fill the air between them.

'I'll be fine in a minute.' She didn't turn.

Jack hesitated a moment. 'I'll go and make some coffee...' He wasn't running away. He checked himself. He wanted to give her space.

Maureen understood.

'Thanks Jack.'

As he passed her he touched her lightly on the shoulder. She turned her head slightly. She didn't look at him. But it was enough to convey that she understood.

'I'll be down in a minute.'

'OK.'

While Jack busied himself in the kitchen, Maureen locked herself in the shower and wept. Her mind playing over and over that moment, that unredeemable moment of opening that *damned* door. *Why. Oh why. Oh why...? Why had she kept them? Why hadn't she thrown them away?* But no amount of 'whys' could throw back that moment of opening. That moment of seeing them uselessly hanging there. The line of suits. *Her husband's suits. John's suits. Hanging. Useless! Lifeless! Oh, but when they had been alive...* But those moments had already skimmed past on the stream of time, like the hot streams of water washing over her. They were gone. Past. And they could not be retrieved. *Why had they no chance? Why had they no chance together? Why were they cut apart before they had time to do anything together? Why were they denied that ordinary, simple, common, pleasure? Dear God. Why..? To have a life together. To raise their child together...!*

Aoife.

She jolted back to reality.

She turned off the water. If only it were that easy, like turning the knob of the shower.

The coffee was cold when she finally came down. Jack was sitting with his back to the door, staring into the fire. It was obvious from the hunched set of his shoulders that he had been thinking too. He turned with a start when he heard her come in.

'I think the coffee's cold. ' He half rose. 'I'll make some more...'

She slumped down on the sofa, her eyes avoiding his, her mouth tight. 'Don't bother. It doesn't matter.'

A thin wall between them. Fragile.

He had been asking himself. *Am I attracted to tragedy? Rosemary? Now Maureen? Or do I attract it to me? Is it me that's tragic? "Mea Culpa. Mea Culpa. Mea Maxima Culpa". Through my fault. Through my fault. Through my most grievous fault!* Have the nuns done this to me? With their prayers? With their breast thumping? With their *"mourning and weeping in this valley of tears."* In their acceptance of this *"purgatory on earth..?" "Oh Lord, graciously hear us, Poor Sinners."* Progressive in their ideals. Medieval in their beliefs.

Jack stood to go. He was feeling the strain. 'I think I'd better hit the road.'

Maureen didn't respond. He waited, feeling awkward, like a spare piece of furniture, as yet without its designated place in the room, the other pieces eying his suspiciously. Would one of them be discarded to make space?

'Sit down for a minute.'

He sat.

'I'm sorry about upstairs. Jack,' she said.

He was thinking there were two parts to upstairs, and the first part was wonderful. But he didn't voice the thought. He knew what she meant. Maureen continued. 'I couldn't help it. I thought I had all that under control.' She paused. Grasping for that control. 'I thought it was all buried. You try to forget. You try to get on with life. Then sometimes it just bursts through.' She focused somewhere in the distance.

'I know.'

'Do you Jack?' Her voice sounded hopeful.

Jack nodded. 'It's different. But I know. I'm just sorry I was of no help. Upstairs.'

'No.' She looked at him now. 'You were...'

'I didn't know what...' he began.

'You couldn't have done anything...You...' But she let it hang.

'Well.' He stood again. He needed space. Maureen needed space. 'I'd better go.'

'Yes.' Maureen stood too. Paused. Took a step towards him. 'I'll see you out.'

Jack made a face. 'Throw me out. More likely.'

Maureen accepted his little joke. She smiled. 'If necessary.' She slipped her arm through his as they went to the door. 'Thanks Jack.' But a part of the wall was still there.

Outside it was raining. Jack scanned the sky, playing for time. 'This blasted rain. I'll have to get a coat.' He said it without thinking. Then mentally kicked himself, zipping up his jacket as if zipping his lips. If Maureen noticed his *faux pas* she didn't let on.

She held the door. 'Do you have a birthday coming up. I could get you one.' She said. It was as if they were purposely talking about the coat to show they weren't afraid to mention clothes.

'A Birthday? I suppose I have...' Jack gave a dismissive shrug. 'I have a *date* all right. If you know what I mean. But there's no need to buy me anything. I'll sort something out. Have to live within my means.'

He stepped out into the night. 'Well. Here goes...' He turned back to her, unsure how to ask about tomorrow. He wanted to dismantle the remainder of the wall that had sprung up between them. 'Will I give you a ring?' Better to get it out in one go.

Maureen hesitated. 'Yes. All right.' But she didn't sound so sure.

'A few days..?'

'Yes, in a few days...'

'Right.' He stood for a second. 'Right,' then he turned and walked down the path. The door didn't close until he got to the gate. That's a good sign he thought, hopefully.

Behind the door Maureen stood with her hand still holding the latch. She leaned her forehead against the dark wood. Her mind was a cold forest.

What to do now? How to get out of this dark eerie miasma? Plod on. Plough upward. To the light. To the light.

Automatically she bolted the door. Automatically she checked and locked the back door. Turned on the alarm. Banked the fire. Listened for a moment at the foot of the stairs.

All was quiet. She opened the cupboard under the stairs and pulled out a large cardboard box and carried it up to her room. She opened the wardrobe door. A wall of defence wrapped itself around her mind; her heart.

But it must be done. It had to be done.

She could smell the material. The stale whiff of un-use mingled with the faint smell of dry-cleaning. *The warm aroma of his body...Oh God!* She cut the thought dead. She had to.

She reached in and took out the first suit. Slipped it from the hanger. Turning her mind away. Folded it into the box. Took out the next and the next until they were all in the box. The wardrobe looked so bare. But...

She carried the box downstairs and stuck down the flaps. She would drop it off at the Charity shop in the morning. *The voice in head accusing. So this is it..! So this is the end..! A coffin of suits..!* She fought the voice. *What else can I do..? What..? Someone else can give them life. Give life back to them! But not me! NOT ME...!*

Aoife thrashed in her sleep.

A muffled scream.

Maureen shivered. A cold hand on the back of her neck. She ran to the foot of the stairs. Listened. Every nerve stretching... Not a sound.

The house was eerily quiet again.

19

When Maureen answered the phone two nights later, she had to check herself. She had thought a lot about Jack and the suits and their night of love and she was unsure. Uncertain about the whole thing. She secretly hoped he would have been put off. Not for ever. But for a... well, a week or so. To give her time to come to terms with her feelings. About him, about John, her life, her work and what she needed and wanted and... and now, here he was on the phone and she sensed his merriment as soon as she picked up the receiver. She had been preparing to get Aoife off to bed and have a quiet night to herself. She wasn't prepared for Jack's call. She wasn't prepared for Jack at all.

'I'm on my way. Can you get a baby-sitter?'

'Jack? At this short notice...?'

'Oh...! Never thought of that.'

Of course he didn't. 'I was just putting Aoife to bed.' She hadn't expected his call so soon. But if she put him off... 'I suppose I could phone her and find out. But I doubt it.'

'Well, if you can. I'm on my way...and...' He chuckled.

'What...?' *What?*

'Oh. Surprise.' She heard his suppressed laugh.

'Jack...?' She wasn't ready for surprises. She'd had had a busy day. Work. Aoife. Shopping. Dinner. Jack didn't understand. She couldn't just drop everything. And it was Aoife's bedtime.

'Jack...' She needed more time to think. About Jack. About herself. This relationship. What to do. She had a house to run, a job to do, a child to rear. But at the same time it *was* exciting. The attention. The courtship. The unexpected. But there were 'buts' too.

'Jack. What are you up to...?'

'Oh. You'll see.'

'Jack.' She felt pressured but tried not to show it. She needed space. Jack, she wanted to say. Don't expect too much. To prepare him. But at the same time she didn't want to put him off completely. She said instead. 'I'll try the baby-sitter...'

'Good. See you in half an hour.' She heard him chuckle again as he rang off.

Maureen stood with the 'phone in her hand for a few minutes. Was this mad? Is this what she wanted? It was perplexing. Oh yes. She wanted Jack. Or did she want Jack? Or was it 'A Jack'?. A man? A lover? Any man? Any lover? No! Don't be ridiculous...! She hadn't thought about it for two years. But the meetings with Jack had been fun. But not with pressure... She didn't need the pressure. Not now. That was fine when you were single and carefree...! But now... There were responsibilities... And where did Jack fit into all this? But you can't cocoon yourself. You can't hide away...? I know. I know. But I'm not ready... *Damn!* Jack was on his way.

She phoned the baby-sitter. It rang for a few minutes. No reply. She hung up, then dialled again. Nothing.

Aoife was in her pyjamas, playing on the sitting room floor with her dolls. Maureen picked her up and hugged her.

'Time for a story, sleepyhead.' She tried to sound normal.

Aoife didn't resist. The heat of the room had her drowsy. Maureen had lit a fire. Not because it was needed, the central heating was adequate to keep the house warm, but the open fire added a more cheerful cosiness to the room. Maureen enjoyed the open fire and it had done it's work on Aoife.

Upstairs she tucked Aoife into her bed.

'Dolly' the child said sleepily. Maureen picked up the doll from the bedside chair and tucked it in beside her. This was her special sleeping doll. Not to be played with downstairs. This was the doll, the only doll, that shared Aoife's bed! And it had no name. Dolly, was all she had ever called it.

'And what story would we like...?'

Aoife gave a huge parody of a grown-ups sigh, as if a monstrous problem had to be solved. 'Well... I want Peter an' the Wo'f. And... Dolly wants... emm, The T'ree Lickle Lams...' Her expression was calculating and hopeful.

Maureen cocked her head to one side. 'Hmmm...' She could see that Aoife was measuring her tolerance in anticipation of being left to the devises of a baby-sitter. Aoife was thinking that maybe that friend of Mummy's was coming again, so soon! She didn't like him. She didn't know why. The little voice in her head told her and that was good enough. If she had to give into her mother's whims - then her mother would have to play tit-for-tat.

'Two stories is it.?'

'One fo' Dolly. One fo' me.' The tone was childish, but the expression on her cute little face warned: 'Or else!'

Maureen was aware of the challenge as she began to read. She knew Aoife didn't like Jack. That had been made plain to her from the start. And now the child was playing power games with her! But she needn't have worried. Before she was half way through the first story Aoife was already struggling to keep her eyes open. Her eyes, just like John's. Every time the child looked at her it was as if John shone out of them. And more so in the last few days. She shook the thought away. Don't think that. Don't think it. By the start of the second story, Aoife was asleep. Maureen stopped reading and waited for a few seconds to see if Aoife would notice. But the child was into her night's sleep.

She put the book on the chair and crept downstairs, pulling Aoife's door almost closed. She rang the baby-sitter again. But there was no answer. Just then the doorbell rang.

Jack! Maureen opened the door quickly so that he wouldn't ring again and disturb Aoife.

Jack stood on the step dressed in a black suit and a priest's dog-collar.

'Hello. I'm Father Jack. I was in the neighbourhood and wondering if you could spare a few moments of your time to help us with the depleted parish funds.'

Maureen stood, shocked. 'Jack... *For Godsake*...!'

'Yes.' He grinned. 'You could say that.'

'Jack...! This is...' She wanted to slam the door in his face.

'Yeah. Crazy. I know. But well...' He grinned half-heartedly, seeing the dismay on Maureen's face. He almost said - You wanted me to wear a suit - but he caught himself just in time.

Maureen was rooted to the spot. This was awful! Not what she had expected. Not what she wanted. She hadn't known *what* to expect. But she would never have guessed... *This*...! This was out of the question...!

'It's only a joke...' Jack ventured. He was deflated by the look of horror on Maureen's face. The joke had backfired. He could see that plainly.

Maureen stood back and ushered him in. He followed her into the sitting room. He stood awkwardly in his shapeless black suit and clutching a large carrier bag that Maureen hadn't noticed until now. What was in *that*...? She didn't want to think. Didn't want to know! She motioned him to a chair and sat herself on the sofa. Jack sat and placed the carrier bag on the floor at the side of the chair, half hidden. Maureen stared at the floor, her face pinched, her hands restless on her lap. Jack sat, tensed. At last she looked up at him.

'Jack. I'm sorry. But this is ridiculous.' Her tone was sharp like a slap in the face. She stopped, looked away, her fingers restless on her lap again. 'I don't know... the suit... I know it was supposed to be a joke...' She broke off.

Jack spread his hands in a gesture of wordless explanation. What could he say? He was taken aback by Maureen's sudden rancour. The acre of carpet unfolding between them again. He took off the dog-collar and put it in his pocket. He didn't feel so dressed-up now. Now, it was only a suit, but the gesture didn't ease the agitation on Maureen's face. She stood up as if to leave the room but sat down again. He could see that she was struggling with inner thoughts, but he couldn't fathom why she was *so* worked up. It was only a *suit..! For Chris'sake!*

'It was a mistake,' he offered, limply. 'A stupid mistake. It was crazy...' But he could see it was more than that to Maureen. But what? Now he was baffled. He had apologised. He had taken off the collar. But now they were both embarrassed and confused, sitting opposite each other waiting for the right 'something' to be said, to be done. He was tempted to go to her. Kneel before her. Take her in his arms. Beg her. Tell her it didn't mean anything. Cry with her. Laugh with her. Anything. *Anything*. To make it all right. Not like the last night in the bedroom. This had to be said. *But not in this goddamn, sonofabitch suit!*

Jack said, softly, hoping to reason with her. 'Maureen. I did the wrong thing. I'm sorry. I realise the problem I've created... The suit...' But he didn't see why it should be such a big problem to her. He struggled with the words. 'But it's only a suit. We don't have to take it seriously. It was only a joke. A prank...' He pointed to his open shirt neck. 'It's gone. I thought we could...well...after the other night...face it. As a joke. Then let it go.'

He didn't mention the trouble he had gone through getting the costumes. He didn't tell her what was in the other bag - nun's outfit for her. There was a fancy dress party at the Collage in Doc's department. Just the excuse he needed when he was trying to rack his brains for the something 'crazy'. He had thought it would be a gas to turn up with Maureen. Father Jack and Sister Maureen. And it was one of the short modern nun's outfits, not the old '*High Nelly*' model. He had had to go to Aisling, through Paul, to get them from the Theatre Company's wardrobe. A special favour. Paul had been the go-between. Aisling had almost chopped him up. But he had gotten the costumes, fair play to him. But it had happened so fast and he had forgotten that Maureen would need a baby-sitter. Stupid! And they were going as guests of Doc's and it had been tricky, but Doc had fixed it. He didn't want to ring and ask in case she was reticent about the idea, or the fancy dress... He wanted to surprise her...

Now. Sitting opposite her... and facing her chagrin... across this chasm! He had thought it would have been a great night out. Father Jack and Sister Maureen. But the wall was erecting itself between them again. He felt deflated. But now they were even. They had both made mistakes with suits!

Maureen said. 'It's not your fault. You couldn't have known.'

Known! Known what? Jack waited.

'Oh...' She shook her head in little sharp exasperated movements, 'it doesn't matter. I'd prefer not to talk about it.' Her tone was brusque. Dismissive.

Jack thought for a second. Now she was being absurd. Evasive. And mysterious. She was clamming up. The wall was getting higher. He decided, one way or the other, to have a go at it. Chip it away.

He grinned knavishly at her. But it only made her clam up more. 'Maureen.' He said quietly and leaned forward to get her attention. 'We're even...'

He waited for her reaction. She didn't budge.

'Let's face it. We both made a mistake with the suits.' He remained leaning towards her, to try to cut down the space that hung between them, hoping she would accept his attempt. He could see that she was struggling. If she would only say what was on her mind.

Maureen took a few deep breaths.

'Jack...' she began. 'I don't know how to put this. I don't actually want to talk about it...but...' She sighed. 'You seem to want an explanation. Well, all right, I'll give you an explanation and then... I'll have to ask you to go...'

He couldn't believe this. Over a stupid suit!

'I'm sorry. I'm not ready...for...this... ' She stared at the ceiling for a minute. Was this what she wanted? Was this the right thing? She was putting an end to Jack. An end to their relationship before they really had one. She took a deep breath.

'I met my husband, John, when we were at school. We didn't go to the same school. John was a Catholic. I'm not. But the schools were quite close. We met in fourth year. We had to meet secretly. His parents would disapprove of him going out with a Protestant girl, even in those days. It was ridiculous. But of course they found out. Not that it stopped us. They absolutely forbid it... but we found ways. We became very devious. And clever. It became a great game for us. We were in love. We recognised no barriers. Parents were old fashioned. What did they know? Outdated values.' She stopped.

Jack thought. So that's what it's about. Religion! Damn! She read his thoughts, shook her head. 'But that wasn't it all. Just before his last year. They sent him away to a Seminary, to complete his studies.' Maureen laughed, but it had a bitter edge. 'Some priest,' she all but spat the word, 'a friend of the family, had gotten to him. Convinced him that he might have a vocation... Yes. I know. It's hard to believe. But it's easy to convince someone who's been under a strain. Exams! Parents! Religion! Duties! All that. Anyway, this Priest, it appears, had been on to him before, about me and mixed marriages! All that old stuff! I believe he was put up to it by my John's parents. Before we even thought about getting married ourselves. We had other plans. Collage. Degrees. Work. Marriage, yes. But that was a long way off... The last thing on our minds... Anyway...' She clasped her hands into a tight fist. 'The rest is immaterial... But when you arrived in the suit. *That suit.*' Maureen grimaced. 'It was too much. I couldn't take it. It brought all that trouble back.'

She broke off, almost in tears. Jack was floored.

'But...you did get married.? And you work for their company.? You told me... and there's Aoife.'

'Yes. But that was later. After...' She stopped, her words caught. She swallowed and hung her head for a minute.

'I'm sorry.' Jack shook his head, baffled. 'I didn't know.'

'Of course. How could you. You're not to blame.'

'But...' But he didn't know what.

'I'm not ready, Jack.' She spread her hands resignedly. 'Not ready for... this... yet. I'm sorry.'

It was a dismissal. She stood. Jack fought for time.

'But, Maureen. We can talk about it... surely...'

Maureen sighed. A mournful sound. 'I can't Jack. It's too much for me. Too soon.'

'But, Maureen...?'

She shook her head, fighting her tears. 'It's too hard to explain. You wouldn't understand. I hardly understand myself.'

Jack squeezed his eyes closed in frustration. He tilted his head back until his neck hurt then opened his eyes. The ceiling was white. The wallpaper stopped at the exact edge where the wall and the white ceiling joined. The chandelier, with all its little bulbs threw patterns on the white ceiling and no answer came. He continued to study the whiteness. Not a flaw. Not a crack. Nothing for his eyes to follow. Just the patterns of light thrown by the little bulbs. Maureen was silent. Shut down. Jack realized it was no use. He couldn't fathom what Maureen had just told him. It was too complicated. He stood up.

He couldn't believe it was all over so soon. Just like that..! Before it had gotten a chance to start. He looked at Maureen. But she just stood there, like a block of stone. And only the other night she had been a pool of warmth and love. A Gypsy. A hope. A future. How could he have dared think it... He bit his lips, trying to make some sense, trying to figure out what he felt besides this confusion...this nothing...

'Well. It's a pity.' He picked up the carrier bag hoping she wouldn't ask what was in it. He held it, trying to make it invisible and wishing he could make himself invisible, too.

'Well.' He shook his head again in disbelief and turned to go. Maureen didn't move. He hesitated, hoping..? But nothing. He could see Maureen was close to tears, battling with herself, waiting until he was gone. He turned and faced her. She didn't look at him. He thought, this could be cancelled if you would only give me a line. Anything...a straw...? But she remained shut tight. She was right. He didn't understand. And without her help he would never understand...

'Well...I just want to say...I admire you.' He said, sincerely. 'You've kept it all together. It couldn't have been easy for you. All that's happened.'

Maureen hung her head, not looking at him. Jack continued. 'I hope it works out for you. You're a brave woman.' He was almost in tears himself. He was thinking. If only my mother had had half the courage Maureen had. Religion, priests, parents, opposition, exams, marriage, mortgages, bills, work, *and a child!* And didn't opt out.

He turned quickly and left, letting himself out. He closed the door quietly behind him. *God! What an idiot you are, Jack-in-the-Box-Weasel. You blew it. You blew it again. You damnwell blew it. First Rosemary. Now Maureen. What next? Huh..? What next...?*

He wanted to tear the damned suit off and hurl it away. As far away from him as possible. And the carrier bag after it. See the black material skitter across the street. He wished it was raining so that he could trample it in the gutter. But how would he explain it to Aisling?

Ah, fuck Aisling!

He pulled the dog collar out of his pocket and flung it across the street in frustration.

Fuck them all!

20

'I mean, what kind of a job was it? Minding a machine that puts caps on jam jars? Paid a wage at the end of the week. That's about it! A dead end job. And where did it get me? On the fecking dole queue. That's where.'

Doc was finishing his dinner. Jack was sprawled on the sofa. Doc had never seen Jack so agitated. 'But, Jesus, I know I can do better! But what...? The opportunities aren't exactly leaping up in front of me! I'm twenty seven and where am I? Queuing up every week to sign on the dotted line and get the hand-out. No training. No papers to show I can do anything. No qualifications. Out of school at sixteen into a nowhere job. Feck it! It'd make you want to get out... But why should I? I like living here. I don't want to leave. I want to... Am I afraid. Am I afraid to go away? I don't know. I know millions do it. So why don't I just feck off... Ach, what's the point...? I don't know what I want. And nobody can tell me!

He held up the 'paper for Doc to see.

'Look! Look at this. "Six hundred and eighty jobs to go at Tyre Factory." And that's only this week. Practically every week it's the same. The way things are going, by the end of the Century only the people behind the hatches in the dole office will be in work...! ' He rattled the 'paper and read off more headlines. '"Crime rises by nine percent." "Seven shot by Gunmen" "Porno films blamed for increase in Rape" And so on. Is it any better anywhere else...? No...!'

He threw the 'paper on the floor in disgust.

'Oh, I check the 'papers all right. Qualifications for this. Qualifications for that. Experienced this. Experienced the other. And all the rest. But nobody wants an experienced jam-jar-cap-putter-oner. No *Papers*. No *Qualifications*. No *Degrees*. No Job! Maybe I should apply for a job at the dole office...' He laughed wryly. 'By the looks of things they'll never be out of work!'

Doc peered at Jack through his round glasses from the dinner table. He had not seen Jack since the previous night when he had set out in high spirits for Maureen's, with the fancy dresses. He had wondered what had happened when he hadn't turned up later at the dance. Jack told him about the episode with Maureen and the suits. Then he had been unable to stop himself and poured out the rest of it.

Doc finished his dinner and lit a cigarette. 'Fuck, man. I didn't realise...! It's a bad situation, all right. But something has to turn up...' But he didn't sound as if he was convinced himself. He knew the economic situation as well as Jack. He read the 'papers too. Cut-backs seemed to be rampant. And the university departments suffered like everywhere else. With unemployment rising all the time. The Common Market was supposed to solve all those problems. But would it? The situation in other European countries wasn't much better.

'You thought of London...' He ventured, limply. He knew Jack's thoughts on emigration. 'Why should I? Why should I have to? I like my *own* country. I want to work *here!*'

Jack waved the question aside. Doc grunted. Jack continued grimly. 'I thought it was going to be all right with Maureen. It was like... magic. Until last night. *Jesus!* I still can't believe it! I should have checked. I shouldn't have been so damned impulsive... I really screwed that one up good...!'

Jack's predicament circled around in his head and

came back to the same place before starting out on its unresolved journey once more.

'And all this has happened in the last nine months. Since I started signing on... Makes you wonder...!'

'Well, man,' Doc thought for a second. 'It's an interesting theory...' He blew some smoke. 'My Ma used to say, y'know, *"Tragedy comes in threes"*. Not exactly scientific. But... Well, man, I think you've had yours...'

Jack wasn't listening. 'I almost wish Rosemary would come back...'

'Almost, man? I thought you were...y'know...stuck on her...?

Jack nodded. 'I was I suppose. Well. Oh, I dunno. Since she vanished... Fell into a *black hole* or something... But she was...stable. Y'know. In an unstable sort of way...' He grunted.

'Are you serious, man?' Doc shook his head. One encounter with Rosemary had been enough for him.

'Yeah. Rosemary was unreliable. But *that* was reliable.' He laughed. 'Hey Doc. D'you think they'd give me a job at the Uni, teaching bullshit...?'

'I've heard worse. You should look up that book by that Zen guy. What's his name..' He screwed up his face. 'Ehh... Laotzu, or something. You might get it in the Library. But I doubt it, man. It's not a great Library. Though you could try the one at the Uni. What was it he said. "The way that can be counted cannot be the constant way". Something like that. Makes more sense than you think. Even the atoms aren't constant. Only a few of them are. "Cesium" is one of the few. The use it in atomic clocks. Most of the others are irregular in their revolutions. Fact of life, man.'

193

'So why the hell are we all trying to be...stable? Regular?'

'Order out of chaos...' Doc intoned. 'We search for the root. Everything springs from there.'

'That scientific...?'

Doc shrugged. 'You have to go back before you go forward. Check the past, compare it to the present and put it to work for the future.'

'Thanks Doc.'

Doc blinked. 'Sorry man...'

'I feel as if I'm going in circles.'

'Works that way sometimes.' Doc lit another cigarette. He offered the packet to Jack. Jack shook his head. 'I'll have a rolley.' He took out his tobacco and rolled himself a cigarette.

'You ever go back to the root?' Doc asked.

'My roots...? Jack frowned. 'You mean St. Anthony's?'

'Well, yeah.'

'A few years ago.'

'And...?'

Jack shrugged. 'Didn't find anything I didn't know already. New Mother Superior. That's about it.'

He recalled the trip for Doc. It had been strange going back. He had promised himself, the day he left, that he wouldn't. But after a few years he had felt guilty about not keeping in contact.

The building seemed smaller than he had remembered. Or maybe he had grown. It's former rural setting was slowly being gobbled up by rows of semi-detached middle income estates of two storied houses, pretending to blend into the countryside behind clumps of trees, that the developers in their wisdom had not obliterated, completely. The wrought iron gates to the drive-way of what had been his home for sixteen years now stood at the edge of a four-lane dual carriage-way. It wouldn't be long before the gates themselves would be shaved away to allow for more houses. And probably the whole of St. Anthony's as well! As he stood again at the gates he had a vision of giant bulldozers churning across the well-kept lawns. He vowed to himself, that if the day ever came, he would be one of the first to throw himself down in their path! *This had been his home Godammit!*

As he made his way up the drive memories threatened to crowd his mind, but he fought them back. He didn't want to get emotional. He wanted to appear calm and composed. A *man-of-the-world!* Making it *'Out there in the big bad metropolis!'*

The front door! He had never used the front door. Well only once. He grinned sardonically to himself. Twice actually. Once coming and once going. Ironic?

He rang the bell and waited, suddenly nervous.

A young novice answered the door. Yes. He was expected. Would he wait in the parlour. The parlour! This *was* a first! The parlour was a revelation. It was surprisingly spacious. It was beautiful. High walls, painted in apple green. A large circular oak table with heavy carved legs and high-backed chairs of the same wood and design, stood majestically in the center of the room. On its polished surface sat a crystal glass vase filled with roses of all colours, from the nun's own garden. A garden he had often worked in. Along one wall an ornate oak dresser with a set of silver dishes sparkled, as did the surface of the table and everything else in the room. The thick linoleum around the edge of the red and gold rose-patterned carpet gleamed. Gold tasseled curtains framed the high window which looked out onto the well-tended garden. And above the carved marbled fireplace a gold framed painting of *'Christ the King'*, gazed down benignly over it all.

The house was quiet. Serenely still. As if no activity was happening within miles. But he knew there was lots of activity at the back of the house where the orphanage and school was situated. He strained his ears, but he could hear nothing, only the silence. He felt strange. He was - had been - part of it, but from where he sat, now, it was as if he had never been here at all. This part of St. Anthony's was alien to him. Like another world.

The young novice crept in like a ghost and was standing inside the door informing him that Mother Superior would see him now, before he was aware of her entering the room. Her hushed voice startled him from his reverie.

A knot of tension caught at his stomach muscles. Mother Imelda! That lovely old lady. How had he stayed away so long? How would he explain? He wanted to turn and run. Not from fear, but from shame at having turned his back on this loving woman who had been a mother and father to him. To all of them for all those years.

But the novice had already knocked and was showing him into the office. What confronted him took him by surprise. Not what he had expected at all. He was standing in a bright, streamlined, modern office. The only hint that he was in a convent was the picture of the *"Holy Family"* hanging on the wall behind the desk. And rising to greet him, from behind the desk, one side of which held a small computer, was, not the old nun, but a much younger woman with a shock of thick black hair, bursting out of her new, neat, short veil. Her smile was wide and welcoming. Her hand extended. He shook it. A strong grasp. She noticed his look of surprise and motioned him to sit.

'I'm delighted to see you, John,' She said, pleasantly, using his old name, which nobody had called him since he had left. She smiled and settled back in her chair with a hint of amusement in her eyes. 'You look surprised.'

Jack blinked, disorientated.

'Yes,' Mother Superior continued. 'Most people expect something out of a Dickensian novel. But even we must keep up with the times.' She indicated the room with a wave of her hand. 'So, John, what can I do for you? Anything we can do to help one of our past pupils, if it's in our power, will be a pleasure.'

Jack was tongue-tied. The modern office. The youthful Mother Superior. Her welcoming smile. The shock of black hair sticking out. Her business-like manner and straight-forwardness. He had been prepared for a tentative and uneasy preamble with saintly old Mother Imelda.

She noticed his confusion. She hadn't been here during Jack's time. 'I'm sorry,' she said, her tone modified. 'You must have been here when Mother Imelda was mother superior. I'm sure you must have been saddened, as we all were, when she passed on. The Lord have mercy on her.'

Jack found his tongue. 'Yes, well, no. I didn't know. I'm sorry to hear it...' He was taken aback by the news. 'You see... well, I haven't been back... haven't kept in touch, since... since I left.'

Mother Superior nodded. 'Yes. I understand.'

Jack was uneasy about the admission about his long absence. He realised now that there was no real need for it. It was simply bravado on his part. And he felt a deep sadness that he had neglected Mother Imelda. But the new Mother Superior's look held no admonishment. She continued quickly to put him at his ease. 'She was a saintly woman, an example to us all. God rest her.' She sat back in her seat, was quiet for a moment, then smiled. 'Now, John, what can I do for you?'

Jack took a deep breath. Even though Mother Superior was friendly and doing her best to make him feel at home, he still felt like a small child. All six feet of him. It had been eight years. Eight years! Was it really that long? He missed Mother Imelda. He wanted to leave. He didn't belong here anymore. Why had he come back? To see..? Or to show them..? He didn't know which.

Mother Superior sat, waiting patiently for him to explain his visit.

Jack started. 'I...' His voice faltered. 'I was curious... to know if... if there was anything more about my... parents.' He shifted uneasily in his seat. Was that why he had come? 'I, well... I realise there wasn't any... much information at the time. But I...' He stopped, confused, stared at the ceiling for inspiration. This was going all wrong. He had been prepared for a bit of a ramble about old times with Mother Imelda and then a casual question about the *improbable possibility* of his parents. This was going all wrong. It was too clean-cut. Too modern. Too business-like.

The Mother Superior saw his dilemma. She said kindly. 'It's all right, John.' She opened a drawer and flicked through for a minute and took out a disc and put it in the computer, quickly tapping a few keys. She read off the screen.

Weasel. John.

She didn't look at Jack. She tapped another key.

Admission...Hmmm...Yes...

Another key.

Comments...Hmm...

It was too much for Jack, too impersonal. Mother Imelda would have known. She wouldn't have fiddled with computer keys. She would have known. But she was gone, and he realized there was nothing for him here, nows

Mother Superior looked up. 'I'm sorry, John. She spoke slowly, gently, she was trying her best. 'I'm afraid there's nothing new to go on. I hope you're not too disappointed?' Her eyes were sympathetic. She knew his difficulty. She wanted to help him, but she, too, was at a loss. She sat back and folded her hands in her lap and waited for Jack to respond. The details were already known to him. He knew them off by heart. Mother Imelda had told him so long ago, as she had told them all. She had treated all her children in her saintly old manner. Nothing was kept back from them. She felt they had a right to know. But Jack had dared hope that there might be something new... *After all these years?*

He said hesitantly. 'I wonder... if it would be possible to have...' He wanted to get out of here. But he wanted something, anything! He indicated the computer. 'I realise they're probably confidential... but...' He broke off. Mother Superior pursed her lips and leaned forward, placing her hands on the desk between them. She wished she could tell him something more positive. But she had nothing to offer him. She said. 'I'm afraid so.'

'I realise,' He started again. 'I realise that the... eh, files are private... but I was hoping that...' He left the sentence unfinished.

Mother Superior raised her eyebrows. 'Hoping...?'

Jack let out his breath. He braced himself. 'Would it be possible to have,' He hesitated, unsure if he had the right to ask. '...the note...?'

'The note...?' She looked at him quizzically. Then she tapped the keys again. 'Hmm. Yes. The note...' She said it more to herself than to Jack, keeping her eyes on the screen for a few moments more, thinking. 'Hmmm...' She nodded her head slowly, several times. Jack waited. Then she reached for a sheet of paper. 'Give me your address, John. I can't promise anything, but I'll see what I can do.'

Jack nodded. 'Thanks.'

A week later an envelope had arrived at his flat. Inside it was a letter from the Mother Superior and enfolded in it a small slip of faded yellowed paper in a little plastic cover. Scratched on it, in almost illegible pencil was the solitary word:

WEASEL

Jack's proof of existence! An old, almost disintegrated, faded piece of jotter-book paper. He had turned it over and over in his hands and cried uncontrollably. This tiny, worn, slip of paper was the only thing he had that his mother had touched. His only connection to his - so long ago - lost mother.

He finished his story. Doc was silent for a few minutes, then he took off his glasses and gave them a vigorous rub with his jumper and squinted through them at the light before replacing them. He whistled softly. Jack lay staring at the crack running across the ceiling. But like himself it went nowhere. Just stopped at the blank wall opposite.

'And that's my claim to fame.' He sighed gloomily.

Doc shook his head. 'Right...'

'Yeah. I've been back to my roots. Stood on the spot. Brought back to evidence.' He took out his wallet and fished out a small plastic envelope. He handed it over to Doc, who took it gingerly and stared at it for some minutes, holding it up to the light. He handed it back to Jack.

'Right.' Was all he said. 'Right, man.' Jack could see that even his flat mate was moved by the little slip of paper and its significance. Doc stood up abruptly to cover the twinge of emotion he had felt then. 'You want some coffee...?'

'Yeah. OK.'

Doc disappeared into the kitchen. When he returned with the coffee some minutes later they sat and drank in silence. Doc toyed with his cup. He didn't know what to say to Jack. There was nothing he *could* say. He thought. 'Poor bastard...' Then checked himself. He stood up from the table and went back to the kitchen with his cup. 'Poor bastard, right enough.'

Jack closed his eyes on the crack on the ceiling. In the retelling of the story he had exposed his old anxieties once more, and it left him with raw feelings of the same old doubts about his capacity to come to terms with it. Doc returned from the kitchen.

'Hey, man...?' He stood inside the door, uneasy.

'...Yeah...'

'You want to do something...?'

'Do something.' Jack opened his eyes.

'Or d'you need some space...?'

'...Huh...'

Doc pointed his thumb in the direction of the door.

'You up to a pint?'

'...A pint...?'

'Yeah.?'

Jack blew out a breath. 'I dunno...' He looked at Doc shifting from foot to foot, restless to be gone. He was undecided. He could see that Doc was eager to change the subject and get out of the flat. He was offering the same opportunity to Jack.

Doc was right. He pushed himself up off the sofa and grabbed his jacket from the back of the chair. 'Yeah. Why the hell not...'

21

Rosemary thought she had finally fallen in love. It hit her like a brick. She wanted to scream and roar; laugh and cry; all at the same time. She wanted to race up Main Street and tell all the Village. She wanted to broadcast it to the countryside. She wanted to hug her aunt and dance around the kitchen. But she didn't do any of these things. She kept the news tightly clenched in her breast, for how was she to break the news? There was a problem! She had fallen in love with Doctor Frank Murray! She remembered asking her mother, once, when she was a little girl, how she would know if she was in love? Her mother had just laughed and replied; Oh you'll know... It'll hit you like a brick! Well, that brick had finally found its mark.

If only it had been anyone else, other than Frank!

It happened on the night she had smashed Shelagh's crockery and stormed out of the house. She walked, away from the village, away from the lights, into the darkness. It surrounded her like a cloak, and she was glad, for her head was full of dark thoughts. How could she betray the love she should have felt for her father? How could she deny his love for her? He had loved her, surely? Hadn't she loved him? So why did this cause her so much pain? Why did it harbour in her soul like a sunken rock? Of all the moments in her life. *God, oh God,* she prayed silently, *That that episode in their lives had never happened!* If only he had lived, there would have been forgiveness. If only he had lived, there could have been reconciliation. Why did Shelagh want to talk about it? Why did she want to drag it to the surface? Why couldn't she just let it be! Why did she have to say that she was ashamed, too? And why did there have to be this turmoil, this burning *anger*, tearing her apart?

She wasn't aware of the car coming up the road behind her. She hardly noticed it slowing down and pulling up beside her. She hurried on, deep in thought, the headlights causing her long shadow to dance like a giant spectre on the road ahead of her. She didn't heed the voice that called out to her. Then footsteps coming after her. Then a hand on her arm. She struggled free and stumbled on after her shadow.

'Rosemary...?'

And then again. 'Rosemary...?' This time more urgent. It had a vague familiarity. Who knew her? Who did she know? It wasn't her aunt's voice. It was a man's. She stopped and turned, blinded by the headlights, annoyed at the intrusion. That's all she needed; some blasted man following her...

'Rosemary...' The man approached her. 'I'm right, it is Rosemary.' What was she doing out on this cold night without a warm coat. Was she mad; was she trying to get pneumonia? 'It's me. Frank. Frank Murray. Are you all right...?' Now she recognised him; his silhouette against the light. The remembrance of his voice in the lounge. 'You'll catch your death... Let me give you a lift?'

Suddenly she was aware of the cold. She shivered, hugging herself. She had rushed out so fast she hadn't thought of a coat. Frank came up to her. He put out his hand and took her arm. 'Let me give you a lift,' He said gently, as he led her to the car and helped her in. The car was warm. Her teeth began to chatter. 'I'll take you back.'

Back? He had been sent out to find her by Shelagh. She almost shouted, 'No...' She couldn't face going back. Anywhere, anywhere, but not back!

Frank touched her hand. Her skin was cold. He could

see the wild glare in her eyes in the reflection of light from the dashboard. He could see she was in shock of some kind. He could feel it radiating from her. She was very agitated. And she didn't want to go back to Shelagh's. There must have been a row. He couldn't imagine what. They had seemed in good form in the Lounge. There didn't appear to be any arguments between them then. So, she didn't want to go back and she wasn't a hospital case, and anyway the nearest hospital was thirty miles away and the hotel was closed. The best thing to do would be to take her out to his own house let her warm up with a hot drink and then when she had calmed down take her back to Shelagh's. But he knew that there was more to it than that for him. He was secretly thrilled that he had encountered Rosemary again so soon. He had been thinking about her only then, as he drove home. How he would get to see her again. This accidental meeting out on the road was not what he had had in mind but it was fortunate all the same. And there wasn't much wrong with her that a hot drink and a couple of aspirins wouldn't deal with. There couldn't be much wrong with her if she was living with Shelagh. Shelagh was one of the best around. He slipped the car into gear and they started to move forward. He said. 'You'll freeze out there without a coat.' She couldn't reply. Her jaw was locked tight to stop her teeth from rattling. 'Would you like to come up to the house and have a warm drink of something?'

She nodded, staring ahead, glad to be in the warmth of the car. Glad to be with someone who wasn't arguing with her, probing her thoughts.

Frank bundled her into the warm sitting-room and wrapped a heavy knitted woollen shawl around her shoulders. He left the room for a moment and came back with two tablets and a glass of warm water.

'Take these. I'll make you a coffee in a minute. I'll just check on Mother - won't be a second...' The room was a clutter of old stuffed couches and armchairs, and everywhere there were piles of books and stacks of classical records. It had an air of *Olde Worlde* comfort mixed with the untidiness of a bachelor's neglect. It was untidy, but even though she didn't like untidiness, somehow this untidiness didn't bother her. It had a *devil-may-care* atmosphere to it that was somewhat pleasing. It was a cluttered world unto itself. It was a man's room, but a man who wanted to know things, the books, the record albums, the paintings. A country house, yes, the shape, the furnishings, the feel... but, also, a certain *sophistication*... Rosemary sensed in her bones the solid stone walls, steeped in family history, surrounding her, almost enfolding her.

Frank arrived back with a tray of coffee and sat in a stuffed armchair opposite her. He reached behind him and took a small bottle from the dresser and poured some into his coffee. He proffered it to Rosemary, but she quickly shook her head. Frank screwed the cap on again and replaced it on the dresser. He settled back and stretched out his legs to the fire. He spoke quietly. 'Mother is confined to bed.' He nodded his head towards the ceiling. 'Old age finally got her in the end. She's eighty one and tough as nails. Fought tooth and claw, but she had to give in in the end. Doctor's orders...' He chuckled to himself and settled deeper in his chair.

Rosemary nodded and sipped her coffee. It was warming and she began to feel better. Frank closed his eyes. He seemed to doze for a while. Rosemary studied him. In repose, his face lost some of its animation. In the hotel lounge, earlier, it had been mobile and almost boyish as he talked about things that concerned him. Here, at home, it seemed to take on the demeanour of the surroundings; relaxed, sagging a little at the edges. But there was strength in the structure of the bones. He looked older, but at ease. Like the old house.

He opened his eyes and sat up. He indicated the coffee pot. 'Would you like some more...?' Like he hadn't dozed at all.

'Yes. Please.' He poured.

'Well.' He smiled self-consciously. 'I didn't expect to see you again, so soon.' He didn't make any comment on the fact that he had encountered her rushing along, alone, like a frightened rabbit, on a dark country road in the middle of the night. Rosemary was relieved.

'You seem to be enjoying the country?' There was a bemused gleam in his eyes, but he wasn't being sarcastic.

'Yes. It's a change.' Rosemary checked herself. Why am I being so formal? 'Well, I didn't think I'd like it at first, but, it's different...'

'You don't miss the hustle and bustle...?'

Rosemary shook her head. 'No. I'm getting used to it.' She smiled.

Frank settled back again. 'I love it here. I don't know how anyone can live up there. Medical collage was enough for me. Then back to the 'sticks'. I think you have to grow up in the countryside to really appreciate it. Were you reared in the city?'

'All my life.'

He chuckled. 'You poor girl...'

'It wasn't so bad.' She couldn't help smiling at the mock concerned look on his face.

Her smile took Frank again by surprise. A young Shelagh smiling at him. Radiant. He let out a little sigh, remembering. Then said, to cover it. 'This used to be a small village. When I was growing up. Only two doctors. My Dad and Doctor Kidney...'

'Doctor Kidney...?' Rosemary couldn't help laughing.

Frank sat up, his face coming back to life again. She had a wonderful laugh; it seemed to warble up through her throat like bubbles. He wanted to hear her laugh again. He went on quickly. 'Yes. Doctor Kidney. I suppose it is funny. I've never thought about it like that. I've known it all my life. But you'd be surprised how many doctors have names like that. When I was at collage... In my class alone there were three. Young Doctor Kidney, old Kidney's son, John Foot and Phelim Headd.' He laughed. 'Yes, I suppose it is funny. And yes... we had a Professor Harte, too.' He laughed long and loud slapping the arm of the old chair and rising dust out of it. Rosemary found herself laughing along with him. But she didn't really believe his stories, thinking he had made it up to amuse her. He pointed a warning finger at the ceiling, *Mother!* And they brought their merriment under control.

When the laughing subsided Rosemary indicated the room. 'Is this where you work?'

'Here? Oh no. Not even in the house. I have a surgery in town. My father. Now he was a tyrant.' He laughed again. 'No. I'm joking. But he had his surgery here. He believed that if the patients could make it this far - it's not even a mile from the main street - that they were already half cured. But I prefer to work out of the house. So I keep a surgery in the village. Three doctors now - and a herbalist! We can't forget your aunt.' He smiled. A great boyish smile. 'It's hard to believe she's your aunt, that you're her niece. You're more like sisters...' An expression of boyish glee lit up his face.

'Yes, we are a bit...' Rosemary smiled. She was enjoying his talk. She liked his attention; his boyish charm when he talked and the way his eyes appraised her almost caressingly. He was almost twice her age but he didn't act it. She sat back in the old comfortable couch, relaxed and happy. 'It's nice here...'

'It is indeed.' He patted the stuffed arm of his chair. 'Good old solid furniture. Has been here since my parents were married. Hard to believe. Must be nearly fifty years old. It has certainly stood the test. I grew up on this furniture. Myself and my brother played cowboys and indians on it. It was our horses, our covered wagons and our train. Relations have slept on it. Cats have had their kittens on it and people...' He was going to say 'made love on it', but stopped himself. '...done everything you could imagine.' He gave her a knowing look. 'When it finally gives up the ghost, I dread to think what will replace it. Some imitation, I suspect...!'

Rosemary closed her eyes. She felt warm now and tired, but happy. *Happier!* She could hear Frank's voice as he chatted on about the house and the surrounding country and then she heard nothing at all... She was cosy and she felt... safe. Cocooned by those solid old walls. Content to just sit here in this cluttered old room with all its relations and cowboys and indians and cats having kittens and it's covered wagons and trains... and Frank...

'Rosemary...' She heard her name being called as if from far away. 'Rosemary...' A light touch on her shoulder. 'Rosemary...'

She opened her eyes, for a moment not sure where she was. Then she saw Frank standing over her smiling.

'Rosemary. I'd better drop you home.'

'Oh. ' She sat up. Her head fuzzy.

'We must have fallen asleep.'

'Sorry...'

'Oh, don't let it bother you. It's my fault, really.'

She stood up. The shawl fell from her shoulders. Frank picked it up and replaced it around her. That light touch of his hands, lingering again, for a moment. The cold night air hit them as they came out to the car.

'Not a good night to be out in this east wind.' Frank remarked as he started the engine.

'Does that go for patients only.' Rosemary noticed that Frank hadn't put on an overcoat. But he had insisted that she wrap herself up in the shawl.

'Hah! Caught me there. If mother saw me she's box my ears.' He laughed heartily, glancing back and up at the bedroom windows as if expecting his mother to be peeping through the curtains. Conjuring up a vision of his eighty-one year old mother tottering down the stairs to clip him on the ear!

They drove in silence to Shelagh's. As they approached the house Rosemary asked Frank to stop some hundred yards from the gate. He agreed. 'Yes, you're right. Of course.' Out of consideration for Shelagh, he thought. He stopped the car, letting the engine idle. He cleared his throat.

'I'm going up to the city tomorrow.' He glanced across at her. 'If you'd like the trip...?'

Rosemary grimaced. The city! The idea didn't appeal to her. 'No. No thanks. I...' She shook her head violently..

'Well. I'll be home by eight...' Frank ventured. 'You wouldn't like to have dinner - at the hotel. Nothing fancy, mind you. But the food is good.?' He thought for a second. 'I could meet you there. Say about half past eight...?' Consideration for Shelagh again, Rosemary thought for a moment. He continued. 'I could ring first thing. Before I go. To reserve a table. Just to be sure...'

Rosemary studied his profile in the dimness. She liked it. The strength in the set of his jaw. His strong hands on the wheel. Yes, was her first thought, then, uncertainty.

Frank waited.

'OK,' she said, but it was neither yes nor no, then finally, 'OK, I'd like that.'

'Right,' Frank said. 'I'll book then.'

But neither of them made a move. Rosemary was thinking that she didn't want to get out of the car just yet, enjoying Frank's company, but not sure what to do about it, whether to show it or not. In fact it was the first time she had felt this way with any man, even Jack. But she didn't want to think about Jack at this moment. She felt no pressure from Frank, either, although they were at her destination, and he had to drive to the city in a few hours, she was content to sit in the car with him. She was content not to go into the house. She wasn't sure about facing Shelagh. What to say to her? How to explain. She had run out. She had been out for hours. With Frank! What would Shelagh be thinking. Had she phoned the police? Was she waiting up? She looked towards the house. There were no lights to be seen. Had Shelagh gone to bed? She felt a light touch on the back of her hand. Only then did she realise that her hands were clasped tightly together on her lap. And then, also, she realized how much she enjoyed that gentle touch.

Frank said. 'You must be tired. I know I am.'

She nodded. 'Yes.' But she still did not want to go. The old fears rising up once more. Frank's hand still covering hers. It was warm. It was firm. It was reassuring. She wanted to clasp it in her own. But she was afraid. She didn't move. She was in a quandary. She turned to look at Frank to see what he was thinking, and as she did so, he reached over with his free hand and drawing her to him, kissed her warmly on the mouth. It took her by surprise. A twinge of panic rising up for an instant, but she pushed it back and didn't pull away.

Frank said. 'Until later...' He got out of the car and came around and opened her door.

As he drove off she stood and watched until the little tail-lights vanished out of sight before letting herself in. She shivered again. Frank had tried to get her to keep the shawl but she had refused. He had also told her to go straight into the house out of the cold, but she had stopped at the door to watch him drive away. But she wasn't being defiant. She didn't want to keep the shawl because she would have to explain to Shelagh. And she wanted to share as long a time with him as possible, even if it was only watching his tail-lights vanish down the road.

. . .

The following day she rose late and left the house without breakfast. She was afraid to face Shelagh. But Shelagh was not about. Rosemary walked about the village, browsing in shops all afternoon and then took the long way home.

Sheila was in the kitchen preparing dinner and made no comment when Rosemary came in, just 'hello'. But there was a coolness. Rosemary asked if she could help and Shelagh gave her some vegetables to chop. They didn't chat like they used to. Rosemary couldn't help but notice the new array of delft on the dresser, but didn't say anything. She didn't want to refer to that episode again. They sat down to dinner. Rosemary found she couldn't eat. Her stomach was in a knot. Shelagh watched her picking at the food. 'I hope you didn't catch a chill out last night. You shouldn't go out without a coat.' Matter-of-fact tone. Still no admonishment. But there was a certain tension beginning to stretch across the table.

'Are you all right?'

'I'm...not very hungry...'

Shelagh stopped and studied her. 'Have you eaten anything today? Are you sure you're all right? You look a little pale.'

'I had something in the village...' She didn't say what, that it had been a feed of fish and chips from the little take-away. She had felt the urge to fill herself with *gunge* after all the healthy meals she had had with Shelagh. Now she felt trapped. She didn't want to eat at all. She had thought she would get away with picking and saying she wasn't hungry. But to be off your food in Shelagh's was a sign that something was amiss. And the greasy fish and chips were still mucking their way through her intestines. And because she was going out to dinner later. She should have said... but couldn't face telling her aunt. The knot in her stomach tightened.

'I'm all right. Actually...I...' She had to say something. She swallowed. 'Actually...I'm going out. Later. I should have said.'

'Going out?'

'Yes.' She hesitated. 'To dinner.'

'Dinner? Rosemary. Why didn't you say...?' Still Shelagh's tone was neutral, under the circumstances. But a little *too* neutral. 'Dinner?'

'Yes. At the...hotel...'

Shelagh looked up, this time sharply. It reminded Rosemary of the way her father would look at her sometimes, when she had been bold as a child. 'At the hotel?'

'Well, Frank...he..'

'Frank!' Shelagh started. Frank! Not, Frank *Murray*. Not *Doctor Murray,* but, Frank. 'Frank Murray...?'

Rosemary nodded.

Shelagh's fork froze half way to her mouth. 'Frank Murray! Rosemary!' She stared wide eyed at her niece. 'He's old enough to be... *my God Rose...!*

'It's only dinner...' Rosemary blanched under her aunt's glare.

'Only dinner...? Shelagh exploded. 'When did this happen?'

'Well...last night. He gave me a lift...'

'A lift? Where?'

'We...' *Jesus!* She felt like a bold child again. Why did she have to go through this? You're not my father! She battened down her rising anger and continued. 'He gave me a lift. We went out to his house. We had coffee. Then he dropped me back.'

Shelagh's look darkened. 'My God! He's a fast worker and no mistake...' Her mouth tightened into a knot. She shook her head slowly from side to side. 'I don't believe this... I just don't believe this...'

Rosemary blanched. 'But...what...?

Shelagh jumped up from the table and stormed out.

Rosemary sat, astounded. *You're very alike!* Her thoughts raced around in her skull. Her heart pounded up against her breast-bone. She wanted to scream. She wanted to smash something. She wanted to cry out. But she wouldn't. She wouldn't allow herself. She clamped down tight. *This has nothing to do with you. I didn't plan this. It happened. It just happened. I'm not a fortune teller. I didn't foresee this. I'm not responsible. You... dumped him! You didn't want him! Well I do! He may be old enough to be my...Jesus, yes...my father. But I don't care. So what? He made me feel good. He made me feel wanted. He made me feel special. He made me feel... ALIVE! And that counts! That's what counts!*

She left the table and went to her room, refusing to rush, walking purposefully, head up, shoulders back, face set, stamping on her temper. She was in no hurry. She had time to kill, but she would fill that time, heedfully. First she would get herself ready, with care and attention. After all, she was *invited* to dinner in the *hotel,* with *Docter* Frank Murray. What mattered now, was, that she was doing exactly what she wanted to do. And it didn't matter what anybody thought or didn't think. And whatever problems *that* flung in her face she was prepared to tackle, head on if need be. She felt strong, yes, felt a strength she didn't realise was there before. She could also feel the tears and the temper lining up like a band of *desperadoes* in the background. But that is where she would keep them, that is where they would stay. Holding them at bay would be her new strength. Yes, she knew what she wanted, at last, she knew what she wanted and she knew how to get it. Against the odds. Against the city. Against Jack. Against Shelagh. And against her father...

22

The three lads, Jack, Doc and Paul, had been on a pub crawl. Or as Doc had put it, a pub *trawl,* for as the night wore on he had to almost drag both Jack and Paul along behind him. Doc was in his usual high spirits, and traveling at the speed of light. Jack and Paul were lagging behind, fast running out of steam. In the last pub of the night, both Paul and Jack were contemplating calling it a night, and they had just got a round of drinks and were looking for somewhere to sit, when a small, bird-like, girl, with dark, deep-set eyes and a smile that took up half her face, suddenly burst out of the crowd, and flung herself around Doc's neck, almost flattening him.

'Doc.! Heeey...!

'Aud! *Jee-Sus!* Audrey! Aud. Wow! What are you doing in town...*Man!*'

'Back to straighten you out...'*man*',' Audrey mimicked him and let out another whoop.

Jack and Paul gaped.

Doc was jumping up and down with excitement. 'This calls for a celebration. *Yeehaa!*' he roared and sent Paul to the bar, '*Fuck the expense, man!*' to buy a bottle of Southern Comfort.

Audrey introduced them to her companion, Jean, a tall slim woman, with short blond hair stylishly dressed in a neat, business-like trouser-suit, whom she introduced as her 'boss'. Jean, laughed heartily and admitted that it was true, and that the occasion was in effect an office party, and as it was a small office - just the two of them - well, here they were! Audrey had only arrived back in town that day. She had been away, for almost two years, working in London as a beautician. Jean had been looking for an assistant to help her expand her little business in natural cosmetics in Dublin, and Audrey had jumped at the opportunity to get back home. It had been a chance meeting with Jean, who was in London on a business trip, and they had hit it off, instantly. And now she was back in the city. 'For good,' she proclaimed and gave Doc a resounding thump on the shoulder. When Paul arrived back with the bottle Jack was amazed to see her matching Doc, drink for drink! When they were eventually ejected from the pub, way past closing, Doc had insisted they all come back to the flat and continue the party.

Audrey came out of the kitchen with a tray of coffee. Doc followed her, singing an old Beatles song in his tuneless voice, *"All ya need is love..."* He pranced around in Audrey's wake topping up everyone's cup from another bottle of Southern Comfort, which he had inveigled the garrulous barman into selling him 'around' the counter, twenty minutes after the bar had closed! Jack had never seen him so ecstatic. On his way round he picked up the stereo handset and zapped on the music. *"Return to forever"*. An appropriate album, matching Doc's euphoric mood, featuring Chic Corea, with Stanly Clarke (*Stanley-Fucking-Clarke, Man!*) on bass. Wild and furious Jazz-Rock. Doc zapped the bass booster. The floor shook.

'Yeeeaaaw...! *Man!* Gig that baaassmaaan! Dig that baaass..! He roared and leaped around in a frenzy. Jean and Audrey jumped up and began to dance with him, frenetically. Paul and Jack were slumped on the sofa watching in amazement as Doc and the girls ricocheted off one and other in their excitement. Paul topped a bottle of beer and proffered it to Jack. Jack shook his head and waved it away. He couldn't handle another drop. He would stick with the coffee. It might sober him up. Doc danced over with the bottle and tried to top up his coffee. Jack pushed him away. Audrey joined Doc and grabbed at Jack and tried to get him on his feet to dance with them. He couldn't make it: his body felt like a lump of lead. Jean joined in and got Paul to his feet. Just then there was a loud pounding on the door.

'Oooh Ssshit!'

Doc fiddled with the handset and the music came down to an acceptable volume. 'It's the nightshift guy from downstairs. *Shit!* He must have a night off. *Shit!*' He went over and flung open the door. 'Sorry, man. Just having a bit of a, eh, celebration. Come in. Come in!' The man was little bigger than Doc, but he was wide and stocky. He filled the doorway.

'Can you keep that fucking noise down,' the man barked, his fists bunched at his sides. He looked ready to kill. Doc held up the bottle and pulled him by the sleeve. 'C'm'on in, man. Have a drink, man...' The man didn't budge from the door frame. But Doc insisted and almost dragged him into the room. The man's glare was a neon sign which read, "*Keep your maulers offa me, you freak.*" But Doc's welcoming good-nature and the sight of the girls seemed to disarm him for an instant. Audrey pushed a glass into his hand and Doc filled it. Doc waved his hand around at the others. 'This is Aud...and Jean. Jack. Paul. Call me Doc, OK, man?' The man glared around at them for a second. 'Sit down, man. Relax. Yeah. Too loud. You're right. Too loud, man. Just a celebration. No harm done, man. OK...?' Doc pointed to the full glass in the man's hand. 'Don't let it go to waste...'

'Tom,' the man said between clenched teeth and

nodded at them.

'Tom.? Glad to meet you, man...seen you on the stairs a couple of times. Yeah...' Doc grinned at him. 'Like I said, man, no harm meant. OK?

Tom nodded, it read, "*I'll let you off this time, freak!*", then downed the drink in one long gulp, before turning on his heel without another word and stomping out. Doc grimaced and closed the door behind him.

'*Shh-it.*' Doc turned to the others. 'Doesn't pay to fuck with the *drinking classes*, man. Damn shop-keepers.' He waved the bottle accusingly at the closed door, then turned off the music altogether and slumped down on the floor. 'Yeah. Shop-keepers, man. No...' He glanced around at the others. '...sensitivity. They're a primitive order, man.'

Audrey plopped down beside him. 'What do you mean? How do you know he's a shop-keeper. I thought you said he was a night watchman?' She jostled against Doc and playfully pushed him over.

'Hey, man. Watch the liquor. OK...!' He held the bottle aloft as he fell on his side. He was visibly miffed at not being allowed to play his records at his usual deafening volume. Audrey grabbed the bottle from his hand and took a swig.

Doc righted himself and took the bottle back and took a drink. 'Don't mean it literally, man. How the fuck would I know...what he does for an existence. I only see him on the stairs, going out when I'm coming in. OK! But it's the mentality. No appreciation of good music, man!

Jean giggled. 'You got off lightly, I think. I thought for a minute he was going to flatten you! *And* us! He probably thought his roof was caving in.'

Paul stuck his finger in his ear and wiggled it about. 'Sometimes you forget.'

Doc ignored his gesture. 'Good sounds is good sounds, man.'

Audrey gave him a dig. 'Give us a break, Mike. He was probable just trying to get some sleep. And suddenly his roof is attacked...'

'Mike..! Mike..!' Paul guffawed. 'I never knew! Is that your real name?'

Doc glared at Audrey and then at Paul. 'Yeah. A good shop-keeper's name'

'Same as his Dad...' Audrey grinned.

'So...?' Doc made a face. 'Gave me a good old behind-the-counter name.' He mimicked his Father's deep country accent. '*A haffa pound o' tay and a cupple o' dem sawsidges, Missus? Right ye be. Tanks very much. I'll be wit you in a minnit, Missus MaCafferty....Oh, I'm not in any hurry, MIKE. No hurry a tall. MIKE...*'

Audrey mimed a serious face at the others and said, 'He loved his Dad!' She nudged Doc. 'Didn't you, Michael.!' She took a swig out of the bottle with Doc still holding on to it. Doc pulled the bottle back. He waved it in the air.

'Yeah! Man! Fucking shop-keepers.' He exclaimed. 'No appreciation of good sounds.'

'Who?' Audrey challenged him. 'Night-watchmen, or shop-keepers?'

Doc waved the bottle disdainfully. 'There's only two things of any value... Science and Art. No! Three... Science, Art and S.E.X. in this world...'

'...man,' Audrey finished for him.

'Right!'

'And all the rest are shop-keepers.' Paul said.

'Yeah.' Doc took a swig.

Audrey beamed a gloriously mocking smile. 'Oh. He's on his old nag again. Giddy up there, Mike.' She took the bottle from him and waved it in front of his face. 'All he needs is his carrot...!

Doc made a grab for the bottle, but Audrey held it out of his reach.

'She has you well taped.' Jean laughed. 'Michael, me boy! I can see, now that Audrey is back in town, you'll have to watch your step.'

'But I'm no shop-keeper. A shop-keeper I am not...!' He jumped up and retrieved the bottle from Audrey. 'Somebody'll have to keep a weather eye on li'le old Aud, here.' He turned the bottle upside-down and shook it. 'Who's drained the last of the liquor? Huh? This little alcoholic here.' He shook the empty bottle in Audrey's face. Both of them seemed to be fully enjoying the charade.

Audrey sneered good-humouredly at him. 'If you don't stow it I'll spill the beans and tell them where you're from.'

Jean clapped her hands in glee. 'She's got you there, Mike. Tell! Tell!'

Doc got on to his hands and knees and pretended to grovel. 'Not that. Anything but that. You'll ruin me... please...!'

'Where are you from, anyway.' Paul asked.

Doc jumped to his feet.' Saturn, man. Saturn! The planet of artists and... alcoholics. That's from where, man!'

'...and scientists...?'

'Yeah. And scientists. It's the big 'A'. The big 'A'. Turns you inward and outward at the same time. From the infinite to the finite. From the mundane to the sub-*feicin'*-blime.' He held his fingers up, a millimetre apart and then threw his arms wide. 'What do you think, Jack.?'

There was no reply.

'He's asleep!'

'Well wake him, man. He's wastin' good drinkin' time.'

'He's missing nothing but you're big mouth...'

Jean stood up and headed for the kitchen. 'Anyone else for coffee, before Round Two begins.' She wasn't sure how far Audrey would go, goading Doc.

'Right.'

'Please.'

'No thanks. I have to go.' Paul stretched.

'Don't go yet, man. I might be able to rustle up something...'

Audrey frowned. 'Our mad scientist is going to conjure up another spirit brew in the Lab. *Hubbley Bubbley...*'

'No. Honestly. I have to go. Aisling will be wondering.'

'Hah! Under the thumb already, man.' Doc wagged a finger at him. 'You've got to fight it, man. Oppose the oppression. Don't let the women rule you, man. Basically, man, hang around a bit...' He mimed a pantomime witch, wringing his hands together. '...see what we can spirit up in the Lab. *Hey. Hey!*' He disappeared into his bedroom.

Audrey sat on the sofa beside Jack. 'C'm'on, Jack. Wake up. The doctor is about to do some magicky...' She shook him by the shoulder. Jack opened his eyes. He peered at Audrey, not recognising her for a second. 'Sorry...I was dreaming...'

'Good for you...' She shook him again and a joint materialised in her hands. 'Here, have a whiff of this. Wake you up...Ho. Ho!'

Jack took a long drag and fell back on the sofa, his eyes glazed. He felt very happy.

Paul stood in the center of the floor. 'Well, I've really got to be going...' Nobody paid him any heed.

Audrey said to Jack, who's eyes were closing again.

'Coffee's on its way. And God knows what else. The Doc is in the Lab with his cauldron.'

'Huh...?'

'Brewing up a little something to enhance the coffee.'

'Yeah...?' He blinked. He didn't know what she was on about.

Jean arrived back with the coffee. Paul was still standing, a little sheepishly, in the middle of the room.

'Are you off. Will you have a coffee first?'

'Well...'

'You might as well. It's all here, ready. I have to go myself after a cup. I could give you a lift. Which way do you go...?'

'West.'

'No problem.' She poured him a cup.

Doc emerged from the bedroom with a gleeful but subdued whoop. He held up a half filled bottle for all to see.

'Twelve year old vintage moon juice.'

'Looks like a hundred and twelve...'

'It's OK.' He unscrewed the cap and took a sniff. 'Hmm... Mature...!'

'...Manure...'

'...Tractor fuel...'

'...Rocket juice...'

'Not exactly. But close.' Doc held out the bottle to Audrey.

She shook her head at him. 'Oh, no way. You first!'

Jean handed them all a cup of coffee. Doc held the bottle aloft. 'For what we are about to receive...'

'Keep religion out of it.' Audrey said. 'Just pour.'

Jean eyed the bottle suspiciously. 'There's no label.'

Doc poured a drop into her coffee. 'Drink this and you won't need to buy petrol for your wheels for a week.'

Jean sniffed at her cup.

'Don't worry.' Doc assured her. 'You've drank worse and paid good money for it.'

'But at least there was a label on it. I knew what I was paying for.'

'Label. Hah! That's *exactly* what you paid for. The label!' Doc sniggered contemptuously. 'Label. Huh!'

'Well, at least I had some comeback if it poisoned me.'

'There'll be no comeback with this.' He held the bottle aloft reverently. 'Next...'

Jack held out his cup. 'Why not. I can only die once

and it might as well be tonight.'

Paul refused. 'I'll stay alive and write the obituary.' He grinned. He refused the joint as it was passed around again.

Audrey took the bottle and tasted a mouthful before letting Doc ruin her coffee. She swirled it around her mouth, before swallowing it. She let out a stream of breath.

'*Jeee-Suss*....!' I can feel my back teeth disintegrating.'

Jean downed her drink. 'Well I'm still standing. And I've got to be off. Are you coming Aud...?'

'No... I'll hang on a bit...' She glanced at Doc. Doc shrugged.

'OK. See you bright and early at the office... You ready, Paul?'

'Sure.'

When they were gone Audrey threw herself on the sofa beside Jack. 'God, I'm zonked.'

Doc indicated the bedroom with a nod. 'You want to hit the sack...?' You can have my room. I can manage on the sofa...?'

'No. I'll be all right in a minute.'

Jack looked at her curling up on the sofa beside him. She was so tiny and hardly a pick on her bones. But this little woman had the personality of a firecracker. He was looking forward to seeing herself and Doc together in the future. Together they were a two-man Circus.

Jack' eyes were threatening to close again. Doc touched him on the shoulder. 'You OK, man?'

'Yeah. Fine. I'm wide awake now.'

'Want another drop?'

'OK. Just a drop.'

Doc poured him a finger measure. 'Take it easy, man, this is lethal juice if you're not used to it.' He turned to Audrey, 'You want a drop. Aud..?' But she was already fast asleep. Doc regarded her for a few seconds, contemplatively; her small bird-like frame curled up on the sofa beside Jack. She hardly took up any space at all.

Jack watched Doc, and raised his eyebrows inquisitively. 'You never told me...' He nodded at Audrey beside him.

'One of those things, man,' he said quietly.

'She's a gas woman!'

Doc was reflective for a minute. 'Yeah. A gas woman. We had something going a few years back. Before she went away...' He drained his cup. '...we decided not to make a 'thing' of it. Y'know...'

Jack grinned. 'And now she's back...'

'Yeah.' Doc wagged his head, grinning. 'With a vengeance...!'

'Well,' Jack wagged a finger at him, mockingly. 'Don't let her rule you, OK?'

Doc pretended to take a swipe at him. 'Hey, watch it, man, OK.'

Jack feigned terror. Doc was about half his size and weight. He cowered and poked a finger at Doc. 'Don't have me to call the night-watchman... *Man*...'

'Night-watchman, *shit*...' Doc growled.

Jack got up off the sofa. 'Well I'm... Oooh...' His head swam. Doc steadied him 'Hey. Wooa! Take it easy, man...'

'I'll be OK... I think...'

Doc helped him to his bedroom. Jack gripped the door frame. The walls spun. The floor was coming up to meet him.

'Take it easy, man.'

'Yeah... Hold the floor... Hold the floor..!' The pints earlier and then Doc's unlabelled *rocket fuel*, followed by the joint were taking their toll with a vengeance.

Doc steered him towards the bed. Then the lights went out. Jack didn't even remember hitting the bed.

23

Shelagh could not believe she had so much fury left in her. Her thoughts clouded around in her head. This fling with Rosemary and Frank was threatening to consume her. She had to fight hard with herself to contain it.

Damn Rosemary! Within weeks of welcoming her into her house, tending her, feeding her, encouraging her, befriending her; this girl had turned her world - the world she had shaped with her own thoughts, words and hands to her own requirements - on its head. All the underlying violence of the city, which she herself had lived with for so many years and turned her back on, to carve out a life and livelihood, away from that madness, in the peace and quiet of the country-side she loved, Rosemary had carried back with her to her doorstep; into her living room and into her very heart. And the violence and hate of her own brother, which had had its foundation in this very house, had now come full circle, in the shape of his daughter, to be visited upon her once more.

And damn Frank Murray! What galled her most of all was, that her niece's meeting with him was like a re-enactment of her own first date. But without the violence. Without the broken crockery. Out for a walk. Frank pulls up. Out to his house for coffee. Back home and then dinner the following night. It was too much for her to accept. It was like she was reliving her own life through Rosemary.

And that she could do without!

And yes. Her own affair was over with Frank; had been for years. There was nothing between them now. They had each gone their own ways; avoiding each other for a while; hurt, disappointed, withdrawing, rebuilding, and finally compromising. And then learning to live in the same small community with a former lover, whom you couldn't avoid. And finally blocking the past so that they could maintain their separateness and their dignity. And, as they were continually been thrown together, because of their mutual interests, then having to find a new footing as friends. It had not come so easily.

But it hurt. Rosemary resembled her so much; just like what she had been herself twenty years ago. In looks and the general frustration of youth, yes. *But never this violence...!* And, to cap it all, Rosemary had been wearing *her* clothes when Frank picked her up...!

Jealousy! Was she jealous? No, she reasoned, it was shock and annoyance at the sudden turn of events; at the people involved. She didn't want it to be any of her business. But it had imposed itself on her. She was involved. She felt responsible for her niece's welfare and future. In her own mind she had all but adopted Rosemary in the past few weeks. That, she decided, was a grave mistake. She could not be a surrogate mother to Rosemary. Rosemary wouldn't accept it. And if she continued to think this way it could only lead to deeper trouble. More to herself than to Rosemary. After all, all Rosemary was doing was having dinner. Going on a date. Quite natural. It was what any young girl of her age needed and wanted. It would help to build up her confidence. *And what if it was with Frank..?* She had put Frank to one side many years ago. *But they had been so close to being married...!* It was something she had had to give a lot of thought to, at the time. If only Frank had not pushed so hard for marriage. If only he had left their open-ended relationship as it was... But in this community...? It wasn't possible. And maybe not even now!

She stamped on the thoughts. She could not allow a rift between herself and Rosemary. This was *Family!* What was needed now, was action, before this went any further. First, she would have to get back into Rosemary's confidence; then talk to Frank. And then, if she could only find that Jack...! But first, Rosemary. She left the kitchen and went to Rosemary's room.

The door was ajar, but she knocked to assuage the tension. Rosemary was sitting at the dressing table brushing her hair. She glanced at the door as if she was wondering who it could be, then stood and pulled the door open. Shelagh stood in the door frame, waiting. Rosemary stood back and motioned her to come in. They stood, facing each other awkwardly for a few seconds, then Rosemary continued with her hair. A brief twinge of anger shot through Shelagh. She wanted to slap Rosemary across the face. It was the attitude of her stance; the weight on one leg, the other stuck out, her arms raised to her hair and her head cocked to one side. But the expression on her face was sullen, arrogant, defiant! *You little vixen, this is my roof you're under. Watch your step!* Then Rosemary moved and her attitude went with it. Shelagh checked herself. She forced herself into pleasantness.

'I'm sorry, Rosemary. For what happened at dinner...' She made an aimless gesture with her hands. But she felt small. Belittled. Betrayed.

Rosemary continued with her hair without looking up. She seemed at a loss as to what reply to make. Shelagh accepted the silence. She continued. '...It's not any if my business. I don't want to interfere.' *It is my business. But I wish it weren't!*

'You're not.'

'I don't want to. It's just... I've been thinking...' She

sighed.

'I know. I've thought about it too.' Rosemary put the brush down without looking at Shelagh. 'I'm aware it's Frank.' *How easily the name rolled off her tongue.* 'You told me. About you and him. But it just happened. I didn't plan it. Nothing may come of it. I... It's just... I like him. That's all.'

Shelagh's thoughts raced. *That's all? Is it? But you don't know Frank...! You bitch..!*

Rosemary continued. 'I don't know what else to say ...'

Shelagh nodded. 'I understand.' *I understand all too well!*

Rosemary turned towards her. She looked her straight in the eyes. 'I realise what you've done for me. I realise you've put your home and your...time...at my disposal.' It wasn't what she wanted to say. She heard the words coming out of her mouth before she could stop them. She wanted her aunt to take her in her arms and hug her. She wanted to hug her back. She didn't want to fight, but she blundered on, hoping that she would hit on the right things to say. 'I've eaten your food. You've given me your clothes...and I've accepted your...hospitality... And I don't want to fight with you. Or anybody. I don't want to talk about it. I...'

Shelagh took a step towards her and slapped her across the face before she could stop herself.

'How dare you. How dare you throw that in my face. How dare you flaunt my hospitality. Anything I have given I've given freely. I'm asking you for nothing in return. Yes. You've eaten my food. Had the free run of my wardrobe. The free run of my home... But to stand there and fling them back at me... *How dare you...!*'

Rosemary's face smarted. She could feel the rage boiling up in her, wanting to strike back. But no, she fought it down. 'It's not what I meant,' she cried out. The tears welled up behind her eyes, but she fought them back too. No more of this breaking into tears. 'I didn't mean it that way...'

Shelagh clamped down on her own rage. She hadn't meant to let it out like that either. She hadn't meant to strike out. She was angry at herself that the rage was still fuming inside her. She had lost control and knew that if she didn't leave the room now..!

She turned quickly to go.

Rosemary shouted at her back. 'I'll go...'

Shelagh snapped around. 'What..?'

'I'll go...leave...'

'You'll do *no* such thing,' her aunt commanded.

'Well...what...?'

'You'll stay right here.' Shelagh's rage suddenly dropped from her. Her control returned. 'We're not running anywhere...' She was surprised at the sharpness in her tone. She took a secret delight in its cutting edge. *I'll sort this out. But to do so, you will have to stay where I can keep an eye on you!*

Rosemary nodded. Where could she go? Better to stay here and face it. She was the little girl again being chided by those eyes; her father's eyes that Shelagh had too, when she got mad. 'I didn't mean it like that. I'm sorry. It came out all wrong.' She swallowed and rushed on. 'I've enjoyed it here. I probably have no place to go back to in the city. And all my stuff is probably gone as well... But I have...lived off you. I should be more help. I'm sorry, I haven't given it much thought. It's my fault. I know I've helped you a little and I know it's not enough. I should get a place of my own. I could get my dole transferred... I'll...' She stopped, confused. The positive feeling that she had enjoyed earlier began to slip. The d*esperadoes* were lining up for the attack again. She wasn't sure now what she wanted, except that she wanted to see Frank. But she didn't want to cause Shelagh any annoyance. She didn't want to lose her, as a friend, as family. 'I'm not sure what I want to do. I don't mean just about staying here, or...' She stopped herself, had said enough, better not to say any more. She would have to give it a lot more thought.

Shelagh came over to her and laid her hand on her shoulder. Rosemary stiffened at the touch. 'We'll talk more about it, later...' She turned and left the room.

Rosemary sat and studied herself in the mirror. She was happy here. That, she could not deny. Happier than she could remember. Except for those two moments, last night and now again to-night, when the anger had overtaken her. But she would not let that happen again, not if she was to win this through. She would rebuild her trust with Shelagh. That was the first thing. She would decide about whether to stay living here or get a place of her own. That could wait. She wasn't going back to the city, there was nothing there for her, now, not even Jack. That had been a passing phase. She could recognize that, now. She had managed to put that into the back of her mind. It was now in the past, as if it had happened in another age. She was glad Jack didn't know of her whereabouts. Even though he was a part of why she had come here to her aunt's house. That was something she had not told Shelagh. She had told her about the row with him. But she hadn't said why and all that was connected back to her father; back to her hurt. Back to this house. Maybe even back to this room! Was she strong enough yet, to say it out loud...? *If she could say it out loud...* She surveyed her face in the mirror, trying to look behind the mask of her expression. What was in there? Was there enough strength? Enough courage? How could she test it? She sat for some time deliberating then she went and sought out Shelagh.

She found her in the small green-house attached to the kitchen. Shelagh looked up, surprised to see her. Rosemary looked miserable. She wanted to go to her and hug her; take her under her wing again, but instead she motioned her to come in. Rosemary took a few steps inside the door and stood staring at the floor. Shelagh continued with her potting. She waited for Rosemary to say whatever it was on her mind. She could see there was something.

'Shelagh...'

'Uh-huh...' She carried on with her work.

'There's something I want to tell you...'

Shelagh looked towards her. 'You don't have to. Not if you really don't want to.' Her tone was non-committal.

Rosemary was silent for some seconds. Shelagh carried on with what she was doing. 'You remember I told you about the row with Jack...'

'Jack? Yes.'

'Well, there was something else.'

Shelagh raised an eyebrow. Whatever it was it couldn't be so bad. Jack didn't seem the type to do much harm from the little she had heard about him. But if this led to an opening about Rosemary's father, well... 'You don't have to say if you don't want to.'

'I know. But you might as well know it. You know the rest.'

Shelagh nodded. 'Go on.'

'Well. That night. The night Jack and me had the row. I asked Jack to stay with me...'

'You told me.'

'Not really. I told you I asked him to stay... But what I really wanted him to do was... Well, stay for a while.'

'A while...?'

'...Live with me...'

'Live with you. It a bed-sit? But surely there wouldn't have been enough room.?' Shelagh knew well what Rosemary was trying to say, but she wanted to draw it out to make Rosemary say it herself.

'No, not like that. I mean...not just for that...'

'For what?'

'For...' But she couldn't say it. *To help me get over my problem with men!*

'I didn't think you felt that way about him...? From what you told me you weren't in love with him or anything...?'

'I wasn't. But... He was the only one I could trust. He might have understood... We could have made an a... arrangement. But... well you know what happened.'

Shelagh laughed. *You poor girl. Was that all!* She saw the hurt look on Rosemary's face. 'Oh, I'm not laughing at you. But poor Jack. I can imagine the look on his face. What he must have been thinking. The poor lad! I shouldn't be laughing. But you can imagine. Coming out straight to him like that. Men have such egos. You probably scared the daylights out of him. Upset his instincts. They can't handle that. Shatters their... Oh I don't know... their hunting instincts, I suppose, their superiority... and God knows what else.' She came to Rosemary, still smiling. 'Oh. Poor Jack.'

'It was stupid, I suppose, but it was all I could think off...at the time.'

'Oh, don't worry about it. He'll get over it.' She put her arm around Rosemary and led her back down to her room. 'Though he'll probably never get a better offer.' She laughed again. 'Now if you don't put a move on, you'll be late.'

When she had put her arm around Rosemary, she had felt her stiffen, just a little. But she pretended not to notice. Her mood and her feelings had tempered. Pottering around with her plants had been her tonic. She wondered what Rosemary's tonic might be. It wasn't Jack... But it might be Frank... Time would tell. But whatever the outcome she had decided to have a hand in it. One way or the other...

When Rosemary had gone out for her dinner date, Shelagh had continued working in her green-house. It was the place in which she functioned best; where her thoughts were clearer. She cautioned herself against over-protecting Rosemary. I am not her mother; nor even her guardian. I must give her her head. One way or the other she will sort this out for herself. But she will need guidance, and she will need me. And Frank? Well what man could avoid having a handsome young lady on his arm. She had seen him in the hotel lounge. She could see it in his eyes. A younger version of his lost love! How could he resist. She had noticed all eyes turn in their direction when they presented themselves. And even the women! Yes, even the women, her contemporaries, and at one stage her rivals. But Frank had not bothered with them. Not even after they finished together. Well, maybe for a short time. After all he had had to prove to himself that he wasn't finished. Just because Shelagh Carr jilts you does not mean you are at the wall. Rosemary was a new face in town, and a very attractive face at that. Frank's ego would be boosted with this nubile young woman on his arm. But she was being unfair to Frank. *Dammit, she was jealous!* That Frank saw Rosemary as a younger version of herself rattled her to the core! She hoped that that was not the case.

It had taken Frank some time to get over her rejection of him. She had had to do most of the work to bring them back to friendship again. And it was not only the fact that they had been thrown together on committees. No. Frank had been badly hurt by her refusal to marry him and it had shown. She did not regret it. She knew it had been the right thing for her at the time and it was still true for her now. It had not only been his drinking. If she had been really sure that she loved him; prepared to give up everything for him, if necessary, then nothing else would have mattered. But her right to lead her own life as she saw fit was more important to her. So, she had had to face the consequences. And it had been the right decision for her. Rosemary's affair with Frank was only picking at old wounds in her. It would pass. It would heel. But she honestly thought Rosemary was on the wrong course and she felt it was her duty to guide her through it without scars.

And what of Jack? Was he frantically searching for her niece? At one stage Rosemary had been prepared to take him as a lover; whatever her motives. So there must had been a solid bond between them. Rosemary had made a mistake there. She could have had Jack if she had played her cards properly. But in her dilemma she had misjudged the situation. That was all. But at the bottom, Shelagh had a genuine affection for her niece and she didn't want to lose her. If Rosemary was on the wrong course, and Shelagh was certain she was, then she would have to be careful with her. But whatever the outcome she was resolved to stick by her. She would not abandon her.

24

Jack went on a binge of drinking after that night in the flat, the night Doc had produced the mysterious bottle without a label.

He awoke the following morning, surprisingly early. He opened his eyes and felt great, but only for that second, then a blinding pain shot up through the back of his neck and pierced his eyes like an arrow. The slightest movement was agony. His stomach churned and when he tried to turn over to alleviate the feeling it set the hammers in his head pounding. He groaned. The only solution was to remain as motionless as possible. But he needed something to quell the throbbing and he desperately needed to empty his bladder.

He lay for a long time without moving, trying to decide what to do. If he stayed motionless he didn't feel too bad. He knew if he tried to move he would throw up. But he couldn't stay like this all day. And he couldn't get back to sleep. And his bladder was at bursting point.

He inched his body carefully to the edge of the bed. Slowly he raised himself on his elbows and shifted himself into a sitting position. The hammering increased with every little movement, but he was getting there. Then as soon as his feet touched the floor, and he tried to stand, his stomach heaved and his head exploded with a thousand hammers inside the echo chamber of his skull. But, heaving or not, pounding or not, reverberating or not, he had to make a dash for the bathroom, where he spewed up the contents of the night before.

He thought he was dying. His heart beat a yammering tattoo up against his sternum, threatening to burst its way out. He wished he were dead. He lay on the floor in the cold and every muscle in his body fought for independence and pulled at his joints in every direction. His head swirled like a whirlpool. He lost all sense of up from down and when he tried to raise himself he kept slipping sideways. The only thing to do was to remain motionless and wait for it to pass. But he wasn't to be allowed even that little luxury. *Achhhhh!* His stomach fought against it and began churning again and he groped desperately for the edge of the toilet bowl and heaved himself over the rim. *Oh God! Never again. Never again. Never again!*

He picked himself up painfully and it seemed as if his flesh and his bones were having difficulty holding together. They held out long enough for him to turn on the tap and fill the sink basin and plunge his head into the cold waters. It helped. But not much. He groped his way to the kitchen, every part of him aching. The *Dangers of Alcohol!* Like all the other kids he had taken the p*ledge* against the d*emon drink* at his Confirmation when he was twelve. My God! What must sweet Jesus, looking down on him now, be thinking...??? The light coming through the kitchen window cut his eyes like a razor and he quickly swallowed four aspirin and downed them with a glass of water. It tasted like it had been dredged up from the river. Back in bed he lay exhausted, limp, waiting for the aspirin to take effect. *God! Had he overdosed! Would he be meeting sweet Jesus sooner than he thought...?* No. Not four. They were only aspirin. Calm down. He drifted into a half sleep. *Sweet Jesus. Never again, never again!*

At some stage he heard Doc grumbling and swearing in the bathroom. Jesus! The stink in there must be woeful. He panicked. Had he flushed the toilet? He couldn't recall. *God!* He couldn't go through this again. How was Doc's head this morning? Probably clear as a crystal... *How did he do it...!* Blast him anyway! Later he heard dishes rattling and music from the stereo and voices. Audrey. He hadn't even noticed her asleep on the sofa. How was she going to face work this morning in her new job? Jack was never so glad at that moment to be unemployed. *Jesus!* How could they face it in that inebriated condition?

When he woke later the flat was quiet. He lay still and listened to the soft hum of traffic filtering through from the front of the house. His head didn't feel too bad, now, and his stomach felt calm, calmer, but empty, but he didn't think he could eat anything. Maybe just a hot cup of tea. He got out of bed and dressed. Except for a slight queasiness he was OK.

He plugged in the kettle and went to the bathroom. The air stank. After his cup of tea he would clean up the mess, in the meantime he opened a window to let in some fresh air. He took two more Aspirin with his cup of tea and rolled a cigarette. The smoke stung the back of his throat and made his head swim. His mouth tasted like a drain. He stubbed out the cigarette, swilled out his mouth with the tea and crawled back to bed. *What was in that bottle of Doc's?* Never again! Not after a rake of pints and Southern Comfort. Doc should be shot! Well, he *had* warned him...

Doc arrived home that evening in great form. 'Get your glad rags on, Jack, man, we're going to a party.' Jack protested. He didn't feel up to it. Not another night of boozing. He couldn't take it. 'Hair-of-the-dog, man, hair-of-the-dog...! Sort you out.' So he went, but unwillingly. One of the lads at the lab was having a stag party in a private room in the college bar.

It was a wild session. The pints flowed - the host was footing the bill - and much to Jack's surprise, he began to feel the life creep back into him. Later in the night, when they were all rightly plastered, the groom-to-be was ceremoniously stripped of his clothes, right down to the skin and 'baptised' in pints of Guinness. He was a large hairy fellow and the beer matted the hair on his body and made him look like a drowned ape. It was grotesque. But he seemed to enjoy every minute of it, slipping and sliding on the slops on the floor and licking the beer of his arms and throwing himself around in a wild frenzy, while his friends, *friends!*, clapped and jeered and sang and shouted and danced, *danced!*, bumping and pulling and shoving until all ended in a drunken heap on the floor. While this was going on some of the less agile, *soberer!*, lads deposited his clothes in a litter bin down the street. And the poor, sticky, stinking ape, unable to borrow a coat, had to streak down the street to retrieve them, followed by a jeering, hooting, mob of drunken mates. Then they all piled into taxis, *Oh the stink!*, and headed for a disco, only getting in by the skin of their teeth, having to hide the reeking groom-to-be in their midst and because one of them knew the bouncer. The groom-to-be had to sit it out for the remainder of the night because nobody could come near him with the stink of beery sweat and god knew what else. Luckily he fell asleep in a dark corner and was left alone. Jack's memory of the nights events were hazy. He stayed in bed most of the following day. Doc went to work in his usual high spirits, and when he came home that evening, insisted on going out again, dragging Jack with him. 'You got to get in training, man... Once you've taken the course, you'll be fine. Be able to take it or leave it, as you want...' Jack wasn't so sure about that. But it seemed to work for Doc and he was enjoying himself. It kept his mind off his recent romantic *screw-ups* and Doc and his mates were great company, so long as the pints were flowing. Luckily they didn't encounter Roleston too often, so Jack was happy enough to tag along. He wondered about Audrey, but as Doc didn't mention her, Jack didn't question him.

Surprisingly enough he woke in good form with a clear head on dole day. After a big breakfast he sauntered into town with time to spare. He intended to stay in town most of the day. His shoes were letting in and he intended to spend the day searching for a good stout pair of brogues to get him through the winter. After the dole he went to the bank to get some of his savings. He had only fifty pounds left in his account. He was surprised. He thought he should have more. He shrugged. That's the way it goes, he would have to be more careful. He withdrew twenty five. That should be enough to get the shoes if he shopped around. He could try some of the second-hand shops.

He was lucky. In the back-street second-hand markets he found a pair of almost new brogues for five pounds. Wasn't it amazing what some people could afford to throw out! He tried them on. They were a size too big, but otherwise they were just what he wanted. The stall-holder looked him up and down and told him with a roguish grin that "*he'd grow inta dem before he was twice married*", and threw in two-for-a-pound pair of heavy '*woolen*' socks. The shoes were light tan in colour. Not what Jack would have normally preferred, but for five pounds...! With a lick of dark brown polish he would soon fix that! And they were already '*broken-in*'. He threw his old shoes on the heap, but the stall-holder told him droll-fully to take they away with him and not be "'*tryin' t' ruin me trade...*" and pointed him in the direction of the nearest litter-bin.

After a coffee, with time to spare, he walked to

Rosemary's street. He didn't expect much, but he still had her keys in his pocket and decided to give it a shot. As he approached the door his heart began to race. Maybe. Maybe. Maybe...! He put the key in the lock but it wouldn't turn. Of course it had been changed. The orange curtain was gone and in its place was one of a floral design. His hopes dwindled. He rang the bell, on the off chance... But there was no reply. He went back into town and had a bowl of soup and a roll. He missed Rosemary! Why hadn't she contacted him...?

During lunch he had an idea. He gulped down the remainder of the meal and hurried to the General Post Office. Why hadn't he thought of it before. But he had expected Rosemary to contact him all along. And it had been weeks, now, and no message. He hunted through the Golden Pages;

Acupuncture.	Homeopathy.
Alternative Medicines.	Naturopaths.
Aromatherapy.	Macrobiotics.
Herbalists.	Holistic Medicines.

He hadn't realised there were so many alternatives. But no Shelagh Carr among them. His heart sank. He thought, perhaps her name wasn't Carr, the same as Rosemary's, after all. She could be married, or, she was Rosemary's mother's sister? Or she was listed under a Company name? Jack didn't know. He realised how much Rosemary *hadn't* told him. All she had really said was, that her aunt Shelagh was a Witch and lived in the country. The phone directories didn't list Witches, *HawHaw!* And neither the phone numbers nor the addresses were of any help, either. He didn't know where she lived. Not even which part of the country; North, South, East, West or Midlands...! He tried all the books for all the postal codes. It had taken him most of the afternoon. But nothing! Had Rosemary made it all up? Did her aunt exist at all? Was the cottage in the country with the resident Witch a Fairy Tale in Rosemary's imagination. It must be. It had to be. This was crazy. He went home dejected. Rosemary had certainly made a good job of disappearing. But, he brightened, there was one other possibility...! Yes, it was only a possibility, but it was as good as any other. Audrey! Or rather Audrey's boss, Jean... It was a long shot. He hurried home and threw on some dinner while he waited for Doc to come home.

Doc came in excited. 'Get your boots, man, we have a match to-night. Five-a-side, at the college gym. We're a man short. Hang-overs... would you believe it...!' He threw up his hands to the ceiling and threw himself down on the sofa as if to say. *Those guys, man, can't hold their drink. What kind of imbeciles am I dealing with atall atall...one little Stag party and they're relegated to the sidelines...!*

'Doc.' Jack stopped him short. 'Will you be seeing Audrey...?

'Audrey...?' Doc rubbed his nose with his finger and squinted at Jack as if he didn't know an Audrey. He shrugged. 'I dunno.'

'I need to ask her something.'

'You going into the cosmetics business?'

'No. No. But Audrey's boss, Jean, might be able to help me. Y'know... The natural cosmetics. She might know about Rosemary's aunt.'

'Her aunt?'

'Yeah. She's an Herbalist, or something. Well, some

kind of alternative medicine. I'm not sure. But Rosemary said something about going to see her. When she was in the hospital. It's a possibility.'

Doc looked askance at Jack as if to say, You still carrying that torch for that crazy woman, who ruined my night out..! But he said. 'Oh. Sure, man... Yeah. I see...' He fished in his wallet and gave Jack Jean's number.

'So who's playing...?'

'Oh yeah. The match.' Doc lit up again. He bounced up off the sofa, now that he had the possibility of filling his team. 'Your old team, man. The *Jammy Dodgers*. They want a friendly. But you're playing for us, the *Microbes*. You'll have a chance to 'crease' a couple of your old teammates.'

'But...'

'No buts, man. It's a friendly and we can tell them you're taking a degree or something. That'll shake them. Anyway, what's it to them. They're gonna lose anyway. You were their best full-back. But if they ask, and the stupid sons of bitches won't if they have any sense, tell them you're in *Mycology*, that'll shut them up. Anyway, they won't display their ignorance, they won't even ask you what it is.'

'What is it...?'

'Mycology, *Your-cology, Their-cology*!' He laughed at his little joke.' No seriously, man. Mushrooms, man. *Fungi.*'

'Right.' Jack laughed too. Now that he had Jean's number and there was a possibly she would find out something about Rosemary's aunt, he was game for anything. 'Right. You're on. From now on I'm a Mycologist.'

'Great, man. There'll be an almighty *piss-up* after...' Doc rubbed his hands gleefully in anticipation.

Jack was jubilant. He was sure that, somehow, Jean would be able to help him find Rosemary. Nothing like having a contact on the inside. And a re-union with some of his old workmates, with him playing for the University... *Mycology, Yourcology... Pure Codology...!* Hah! He felt as if he had been swimming under water in the dark for the past few weeks. Swimming in the darkness of pints of Guinness, more likely! But now with Jean's help, there was a glimmer of light shimmering on the surface up ahead.

'Right.' He served up the dinner. 'Dig into this...*Man*!'

25

Shelagh rang Frank at his surgery. He was busy, but his Receptionist said she would get him to ring her as soon as he was free. Shortly after, he rang back.

'Hello, Shelagh, what can I do for you.'

'Could we meet for lunch?'

'Just a moment... Yes. That would be fine. The hotel. One 'o clockish?'

'Yes.'

'Everything all right?'

'I'll talk to you then, Frank.' Her tone was edgy. Frank didn't convey that he noticed.

'Fine. Looking forward to it.' He rang off.

Shelagh pottered around for the rest of the morning. She had to get her thoughts straight. She went to her little green-house and took stock. She didn't relish the idea of confronting Frank, but she felt it had to be done.

The hotel dining-room wasn't crowded. It was well past the tourist season. Only a few local business men and commercial travelers. Shelagh insisted on paying and Frank acquiesced graciously. They found a table where they wouldn't be disturbed. They made some committee small talk during the soup. When the main course arrived Shelagh came to the point.

'Frank, I'm worried about Rosemary.'

'Oh...?'

'Yes. I'm worried that she might be getting into something that she's not ready for...yet.'

'I see.' He chewed for a time. He knew what she was

hinting at. Shelagh always came straight to the point.

'You mean with me, of course.'

'Well, yes, in a way. But not only that. Rosemary is... well, she's not quite herself yet.'

Frank nodded. 'How do you mean...?'

Shelagh dropped her voice and leaned towards him. 'Frank. When Rosemary appeared on my door-step she had just come out of hospital... She literally fell at my feet I wouldn't be telling you this, except you're a friend. As a Doctor you'd have been obliged to bundle her back...!

Frank ignored the taunt. 'Not necessarily... She didn't mention that. Nothing serious, I hope.' He tried to hide his alarm.

'When I say, 'she had just 'come out', I mean she had discharged herself.' Shelagh paused. 'Run off...'

Frank's look was grave. 'I see. Would you like me to look into it?'

'No. That won't be necessary. It might only complicate matters. She came to me...' Did he detect a note of triumph?

Frank smiled. 'And you've done a good job...' He saw Shelagh's sharp look. 'No. I mean that sincerely. Rosemary seems quite radiant.' He laughed. 'Better than some of mine.'

They continued eating in silence for a few minutes. Shelagh asked. 'Did you notice anything... about Rose...?' She nodded to her wrists.

'Well. Yes. You mean the scars?'

'Yes.'

'Hmm.' He was thoughtful for a minute. Shelagh could not be so naive as to imagine that he hadn't noticed the scars on Rosemary's wrists, and that they were recent. And of course he was concerned, but more for her mental well-being than her wrists. She couldn't have thought that he wouldn't be. Both as a doctor *and* as a man. He deduced that they weren't as serious as imagined. They had healed quickly with Shelagh's care and Rosemary still had the full use of her hands and fingers. But Rosemary was not his patient. And he was not being flippant in that respect. Rosemary was in capable hands with Shelagh's care and attention. And as a doctor he was aware of the statistics regarding suicide attempts, and was a member of the National Lobby, which was preparing a deputation to the High Court to have suicide decriminalised. But, was Shelagh using this as a wedge between himself and Rosemary? Did Shelagh already suspect a deeper relationship between himself and Rosemary than they had even admitted to themselves? Shelagh was very astute. Her intuition was finely honed. But he was not a dullard either. When he had encountered Rosemary striding headlong, without a coat, in the middle of the night, he was not ignorant of her state of mind. He had suspected a row. Family quarrels and storming out of houses was not uncommon, either. And in Rosemary's case a warm drink, a couple of aspirin, and a friendly chat had sorted that out. But whether he would allow himself to be influenced by the undertow of Shelagh's alarm, concern, panic or jealousy, was something he would have to make an instant decision on, now. Shelagh was trying to influence his *Em De* side. But he wanted to keep his interest in Rosemary as a man, foremost. In this case he removed his doctor's hat and donned that of a man under the influence of *Cupid's arrows*... Nobody could accuse him of not being concerned for Rosemary's well-being, both mentally and physically. Not to be so, would be sheer stupidity. But, he reminded himself, Rosemary had come to him as a woman and not as a patient. So, at the risk of appearing nonchalant and unprofessional he responded calmly to Shelagh's reference to the scars. 'They've healed well. And there's no sign of infection. But I take it, that was you, and not the hospital.'

Shelagh ignored his compliment and his appearance of easy unconcern. 'But the other scars, Frank? The ones we can't see.'

Frank nodded. 'Yes. Of course. But she couldn't have come to a better place. The country will do her all the good in the world and she couldn't be better cared for, than in your own hands.' He wasn't sure how Shelagh would react to that, coming from him, a registered M.D. There was still a lot of animosity between the registered profession and alternative healers. But Frank respected Shelagh and her methods as did many others, both professional and non-professional.

Shelagh said. 'I'll do all I can for her. But I'm still worried, that before she has fully recovered, she might rush into things..!' She eyed Frank closely.

He bent to his dinner. Had Shelagh read his thoughts. Could she know what he had already decided that Rosemary was not just a passing fancy. That it was more than a man's infatuation for a beautiful young woman. Frank had already courted the most beautiful woman around and she was sitting right here in front of him, until now, he thought guiltily. If another woman had, after all this time, brushed her out of his mind, and if he could sit here and be sure, under the scrutiny of the woman who had meant more to him than anything else in the world then it was time to admit, that yes, he was in love with Rosemary, and let's be honest with ourselves, he wanted to marry her. He had already decided that. He hadn't fully admitted it to himself. But he knew in his heart.

That night, in his house, when they had chatted, and Rosemary had relaxed, Frank was captivated by her. When they were alone, away from the hotel lounge and Shelagh, he was able to see Rosemary as she was, by herself. In the hotel Lounge she had been a passive audience to the conversation. But he had tried to draw her into it as much as possible, asking her opinion - he smiled when he thought back on it, asking her opinion on things that she couldn't have known anything about. But he wanted to look at her and touch her, and that was his only way of doing it. He was disappointed when Shelagh had taken her home early. He would have loved for Rosemary to stay. But how could she? But later in his house, when they had dozed by the fire, he hadn't slept as much as Rosemary - he was used to cat-naps - and had spent most of the time awake, just looking at her, sleeping, sitting back straight on the big old couch with the knitted shawl around her; the last thing his Mother had knitted, for she was renowned for her knitting, before she finally took to her bed; the wools, in the muted colours of bog earth and heather with light touches of soft blue, like the morning sky reflecting on pale cornflowers. Like Rosemary's eyes. Beautiful! And Rosemary...! Exquisite...!

He was smitten. Yes! She reminded him of Shelagh, and all the times they had had together, and then, disconsolately, all the time they didn't have, after she had turned him down. But Rosemary was not Shelagh. Granted, she was younger. Almost a younger replica. But she was different. There was an energy emanating from her; not the kind of energy that one senses from an athlete or a dynamic worker, such as Shelagh had, but an almost violent deep-rooted energy - a vibrant restlessness, even as she sat there sleeping. He loved her. He knew it. *God! I'm a raving old lunatic,* he warned himself, old enough to be her father. He remembered her father! A desperate boy! They had been in the old school at the bottom of the village until they were ten or eleven, before Frank had been sent off to boarding school. But he wanted to be father and brother and lover and - dare he think it - husband...! to this beautiful girl, sleeping quietly, the pale stark face, with its catlike eyes, wrapped in the shawl like a madonna, within arm's reach... He had shook himself, thinking he had better take her home before... before his imagination ran away with him...!

Then later in the car, parked outside Shelagh's, he hadn't wanted her to go. And he sensed Rosemary didn't want to go either. He was sure of that. He could almost touch the atmosphere in the car. It would leave a space when she was gone. And then he had kissed her, nervously, not knowing how she would react. But yet, hoping, that she wanted to as much as he did. He sensed a moment of resistance in her and then it broke and he was certain. He wanted to drive with her... back to his house... to his bed! And then, the following day in the city; he hardly remembered what he was doing. He drove home like a man possessed. And the empty space in the passenger seat where she had been sitting, only hours before, still had the presence of her...and he hadn't picked up any hitch-hikers, because he didn't want anyone else to sit there, in Rosemary's space. Yes. He was possessed! He had only met her for the first time, not twenty four hours before and already he felt as if they had been together for a lifetime and that they would be together for the rest of his lifetime and he didn't want to be out of reach of her for longer than necessary. Yes, he was perhaps twice her age. And yes, it was madness. And yes, he was a doctor and a respected member of the community, but he was smitten. But one thing he must do, he warned himself – curb the drinking. That was one of the things that had ruined his relationship with Shelagh. He would give it much thought...

Shelagh was saying. '...and I don't want to tell you what to do. Frank...'

He hadn't been listening to a word. '...Yes. Of course...' He came out of his dreaming '...and you're right. I'm glad you spoke your mind. It's better that way. For all of us. But I'm very fond of Rosemary...and I appreciate, well, the difference in our ages. But...' He stopped. What was there to say. I'm a doctor. An up-standing member of my community. Chairman of the Restoration Committee. Member of the Arts Club, the Golf Club, and maybe next year a County Councillor. And I'm not a man who is inclined to rush headlong into things. But I have waited, waited for many years, waited for half a lifetime for something like this to come and transform me. He was in no hurry. *Was he in a hurry..?*

He said. 'Don't worry. I'll give it time, and thought...' But he knew it wasn't the whole truth. He ate in silence for a while. *What was he saying? Surely he could do as he wished? He didn't have to make any compromises, did he? Shelagh was being too cautious. Or Jealous. Was she jealous? She had no right to be!*

He said, reflectively but pointedly, 'Shelagh, you are one of my oldest and dearest friends. I would hate to be the cause of any anguish to you. I realise what you are saying and I appreciate your concern. But what can I say. How can I put it... I realise that we have had a...' He searched for the right word. '...a relationship... a rewarding relationship, and a long friendship building out of that. That, we can't brush aside. And I wouldn't want to. But, and forgive me for being blunt.' He paused, searching her eyes. 'When we...went our separate ways, we...well. I went through a, for want of a better word, a...debriefing, of myself. It was necessary, given the circumstances. And allow me to be blunt again...' He smiled to soften what he was about to say. '...You turned me down. And, I'll admit, it took me some time to accept that your decision was final. And unchangeable.' He chose his words carefully and continued slowly. 'That was your decision and your right. We're still friends. I'm glad of that. You're very special to me. I would be saddened to lose that. But I must make up my own mind about Rosemary.' He paused. 'And she must be allowed to do the same. I'm sure you appreciate that.'

Shelagh was thoughtful for a moment. 'Yes Frank. I do. But my main concern now, is for Rose and her welfare.'

'Absolutely. I think we both agree on that.'

Shelagh looked at him solemnly. 'I hope so.'

He glanced at his watch. 'Well, I'm afraid I have to go.' He pushed back his chair. 'I'm glad we talked. But I must get back...'

The following Sunday he drove Rosemary out to see the Castle. It stood on the top of a small knoll overlooking the town. They climbed the winding stone staircase to the battlements which were still intact along one wall. The view was magnificent.

'Thirty miles in either direction,' Frank explained. 'From here you can look into three counties. They knew where to build in those days. And how to build! Can you imagine any of those *botháns* down there...' He waved at the little houses in the distance. '...lasting as long as this? Seven hundred years and still standing. And when we're

finished with it, it will stand for another seven hundred!'
He looked at Rosemary, the wind streaming through her hair, and her coat hugged tightly around her. *God!* She was divine!

'Are you cold?' He was aching to put his arms around her. It was a clean crisp, November day, but there was a bite in the wind, especially at this height. Rosemary shook her head.

'No. It's wonderful. It's like flying.' And she opened her coat like great black wings to catch the wind. Her coat billowed and she staggered for a second with the strength of it, then leaned into the stiff breeze. Frank started. It was a risky game to play. A sudden gust could knock you off your feet and send you hurtling to the stone courtyard, sixty feet below. Rosemary closed her eyes and leaned still further, resembling a great black gargoyle against the sky. Frank grasped her arm in alarm.

'We'd better go before you get cold.' He spoke as gently as he could. But he was frightened. He kept his voice steady. '...Or before you really do fly away. Then I'd have to learn to fly, too...'

Rosemary laughed. 'Yes, let's flyeee...' And she held the wings of her coat still higher. Frank could feel the wind tugging at them both. Then Rosemary let out a long cry, and jumped out of his grasp. Frank almost fell back with the suddenness of losing her support, the wind whipping at him. Rosemary wrapped her coat around her and ran along the battlements. Frank was startled. This was dangerous play. Rosemary turned and faced him, her face lit up like a child's, taunting him. *Come and get me! Catch me if you can!* His legs felt like jelly. What if she lost her balance? There was only a hastily erected builder's balustrade between them and the drop to the flag-stones below. *God! Stop it, Rosemary!* He tried not to show his alarm and walked as casually and as quickly as he could towards her. This was no place for a game of 'catch-as-catch-can'.

'It's not the safest place in the world for a game of chase...' He warned, keeping the alarm out of his voice. But Rosemary suddenly began spinning around and around and laughing in glee. Frank caught her and they both had to struggle to keep their footing.

'That's enough...' He said sharply, holding on to her tightly. She turned towards him and buried herself against him.

'Scaredycat...' She pretended to sulk.

'Scaredycat my eye.' He scolded. 'I don't want to be the one to have to scrape you up off the courtyard. Doctor or no Doctor. My job it to save lives. And *you* can consider yourself saved... Now let's go...'

He led her down. Frank shivered. It had been a close one! They returned to the car. He sat for a few minutes, pretending to search for something in the glove compartment, but really, waiting for his hands to stop shaking. Rosemary's antics had rattled him.

Then they drove in silence. Rosemary seemed to be wrapped in her own thoughts. Frank still had a mental picture of her spinning, sixty feet up, in the wind. The slightest slip...! The merest shift in the direction of the gust of wind...! He shook the picture out of his head. But he had to admit to himself that he was excited by the danger of it. It had been a long time since he had been so close to danger. In a way it was thrilling. *My God!* She was a thrilling woman! He pulled over and stopped the car. Rosemary remained huddled in her coat.

'Rosemary.'

'Uh-huh.'

Blast her aunt. This was the moment!

He blurted out. 'Rosemary. I want to marry you!'

She giggled.

He waited. 'Rosemary...?'

'Yes Frank... I heard you...'

Don't put me through this agony!

She turned and faced him. 'You said you wanted to marry me...' She bit the collar of her coat between her teeth,, grinning at him. But the look in her eyes read volumes...!

'And...?' *Was she taunting him again? Did he have to snatch her from the wind again?*

'And...' she mimicked him playfully.

'Will you...? Rose. Will you...?

'I will. I will. I will.' She chanted, turning away and snuggling back into her coat, thinking, *'I must be mad. But it's wonderful, wonderful.'*

Frank sighed with relief. If she had said no, like Shelagh had so many years ago, he would have wanted to drive back to the castle and throw *himself* into the wind... *Oh God! You love sick old man...!* He put the car into gear and drove on. It wasn't how he had visualised proposing to her. But then he hadn't visualised proposing to anyone ever again until just a week ago. They didn't talk until they were approaching the Village. He didn't want to let her go.

'Rosemary.' He loved saying her name. It had a magic ring to it for him. 'Rosemary. Come home with me...?'

She giggled again. 'Yes.' She wasn't thinking what he

meant. She just knew that she wanted not to go back to Shelagh's. That she wanted to be with Frank. She was still whirling on the battlements in the wind.

Frank thought, is this the same girl? The same girl I saw one cold night charging down the road like a frightened rabbit...? The same girl who had fallen into her aunt's arms in distress...? The same girl who tried to put an end... He stopped himself.

Back at his house, after a drink to warm them up, they had settled together on the big old couch.

His attempt at making love to her started off well enough, but by the time they had discarded most of their clothes Rosemary began to panic and the atmosphere between them shifted. It was a disaster. Rosemary was as frightened as a mouse in a corner. Frank was nervous too. Her tension pricked into his skin like millions of little needles and then, his nervousness became a taut wire and it encircled them both and switched them around as though they were clutched body to body so that not even a breath of air separated them, neither of them knew how to go about unravelling the chords of dissonance, and both desperately wanting to, and pull them back to harmony.

'What is it, Róisín, a ghrá.' *Little rose, my lov*e, he asked soothingly, desperately. She only shook her head. Oh! She wanted him. She wanted him. But it was the other thing. The thing she couldn't say. What was she to do? She felt his warm body on top of hers. The touch of his smooth skin. The feel of his caressing hands. The warmth of his mouth on hers. But... *Oh, God! what was she to do...? It was as if a fiend was watching her... It's little black eyes bulging... It's scrawny throat throbbing... Dear God, please let it go away...* She cried softly to herself. Frank rested his head on her breast and she gripped it in her hands, and held on tightly, digging her fingers into the sides of his head. It hurt; her nails digging into his skin, but he didn't pull away. What was hurting him more was the quiet sobbing pulsating from her chest. What could he say? *Rose! Rose! Rose!* Presently the sobbing calmed and her breathing eased and she seemed to be sleeping. Frank could feel the cold seeping into his back and legs. He shivered but Rosemary held on tightly to him. He eased himself up off her and wrapped the shawl around her and, lifting her carefully, as one would a sleeping child, carried her upstairs to his bed. Her eyes remained closed. She reached up and wrapped her arms around his neck. The sheets were like ice and they clung together for warmth. Gradually they transmitted their heat to each other and their bodies merged together and Rosemary opened to him and they clung together in joy and love; the juices of their love-making mingling as one. Then they drifted together on a warm soft cloud.

Frank woke her early the following morning with a cup of tea. He grinned sheepishly at her.

'Frank...?'

'Hmm...?

'Can we get engaged...?'

It took him by surprise. 'Engaged!' He laughed softly. 'Is that still popular?'

'I don't know. But I want to...' She looked at him over the rim of her cup. He was slim in his silk dressing gown and she could make out the outlines of his muscles against the fine material. She had touched all those sinewy strong muscles, and they had touched her. She felt as if they were a part of her now. And she loved the feeling. Was that all there was to it...? That you only had to love a man? That he enters you with love and becomes a part of you and you of him? Love him enough to simply want him? Oh, she had loved the way he carried her up the stairs to his bed, wrapped in the woollen shawl. And how they had clung together for warmth between the cold sheets. Was that all there was to it. That you needed to keep warm...? She smiled to herself. It had been so beautiful... and yes so fulfilling... so real and so natural. Not like...not like... She stamped on the remembrance. *The lizard retreated and cowered in a corner...* Now she knew about love! Just like her mother had said?

'Yes. Of course we can get engaged. When...?'

'Soon.'

He raised his eyebrows. 'To-day. If you like.'

'No. Not to-day.' Her eyes danced. ' Next Sunday.'

'Next Sunday?'

'Yes. We'll have a small party. I'll make a cake. I'm learning to cook.'

Frank eyed her quizzically. She was like a child who couldn't be refused because she wouldn't accept refusal. He murmured. 'Is that wise...?' He was thinking of Shelagh. But he was committed. He had proposed! Their night together... And she had accepted...

She giggled. 'It won't poison you.'

He laughed too. 'I wasn't referring to the cake.'

'I want to...and...' The little girl's face again.

'And what...'

'And a ring...?

'Well. Why not.'

'Good. Next Sunday.'

He thought for a moment. She was flying in the wind again. They were both flying! Oh well! But it was reckless... and exciting at the same time! And wasn't this what he had always wanted.

'But why, if I may inquire, next Sunday?

'Because...' Rosemary giggled and the tea slurped from the cup. Frank made a grab for it and missed. The hot tea seeped through the bedclothes. Rosemary jumped and giggled hysterically. '...Because it's my Birthday!'

26

The city sky was overcast, but the day was dry and had the look of brightening later. Jack was in good spirits as he walked into town. He had cut down on the regular boozing with Doc and his friends, the hang-overs and his depleted bank balance helped his decision, and he was all the better for it. Once a week was enough, he had decided. Doc had treated him in the early stages, but Jack was feeling guilty about not paying his own share and eventually he had to do what was best for his little deposit account and his head.

But to-day he hoped to have some news about Rosemary. He had contacted Jean and she said she would make enquiries for him. She told him not to hold out much hope, as there were probably thousands of herbalists in the country, and as she didn't deal with any of them - most of her products were imported - she could only ring around and hope that somebody knew Shelagh Carr. That was almost a week ago, now, and she had said to give her a few days. Well, it was more than a few days, now. And he was keeping everything crossed.

What was it Mother Imelda used to say..? *'Ask, and you shall receive.'* If Mother Imelda was a saint in heaven, and Jack was sure that if anyone was, then certainly she was, he hoped she had heard his silent prayer. He smiled to himself. Was he putting too much faith in his hope? Was that a charitable thought? He laughed to himself at his little joke. But he did feel positive to-day. To-day something constructive was going to happen. You only had to keep your eyes open! You only had to ask! Was he being stupid? Was his good feeling simply that he had cut down on boozing and staying out late? Was it simply the fact that his head was clear? Was he putting too much hope in Jean? But he had a feeling...! It was a good feeling. A positive feeling. May as well hold on to it while the going was good...

A young ragged kid was drawing with chalks on the pavement in front of a jeweller's. Jack stopped to watch. Now this kid had the right idea. A little entrepreneur, and no mistake. A cheap box of chalks, a pavement, and he was in business! There was a chalk circle on one side of the drawing with a few coppers in it. Jack fished in his pocket and threw in a ten pence coin. The kid was good. He didn't look more than five or six, but he was probably much older. He had a natural flair. The picture showed a large, two storied, house with a huge tree to one side. On top of the tree an oversized blackbird was perched, ready for flight. A winding driveway snaked away from the front door. It reminded Jack of St. Anthony's. He crouched down beside the kid.

'Good drawing.'

The kid made no reply; didn't even look up. He was engrossed in his work. Jack tried again. 'You like drawing?'

The kid continued colouring in a window. 'Yeah.' But he didn't look at Jack.

'Where did you learn to draw like that?'

The kid stopped drawing for a few seconds and scrutinised Jack. His expression said; what a dumb question! And he bent to his work once more.

'What's your name?'

The little artist moved to another window. 'Jack.' He mumbled.

'Jack? Same as mine.' *A good omen?* Jack fished out another ten pence and threw it in the chalk circle. The kid turned and stared at him. A puzzled look. Two ten p's! What did this guy want? He had a strong little face, dirty, with matted curly hair hanging in his eyes. He brushed the hair aside with his free hand. He had small slit eyes with dark lines underneath. His skin had a greyish pallor. He looked older than six or seven, but he was very small and thin. He looked past Jack down the street and hastily bent back to his colouring.

'Here's me brudder comin'.'

Jack looked down the street. Standing about five shops away was another scruffy lad of about twelve. But he, too, could have been older. He wasn't very tall, but he looked sharp. He was wearing a tight little grubby suit and he had a mangy dog attached to a piece of string. He was watching Jack and the little pavement artist, but without looking in their direction. But both knew he was watching.

'Is that your brother?' Jack didn't believe him. Little Jack made no reply. 'Does he look after you?' Little Jack continued with his work. He mumbled something which Jack didn't catch. He placed another ten pence in the circle.

'What did you say?'

Little Jack hesitated for a moment. "E takes th' money.' He mumbled, under his breath.

Jack glanced at *Big Brother*. 'And if you don't want to give it to him.?'

Little Jack added a few flowers to his garden. "E's godda dog.'

Jack doubted that Little Jack and Big Brother were related. They certainly didn't resemble each other in any way, except that they were both scrawny and dirty and undernourished and desperate.

'Where do you live?'

Little Jack remained silent. He pretended not to hear. He studiously coloured in a purple flower.

'And where's your mother.'

Little Jack shrugged. Jack guessed as much. He stood up.

'Well, I'll see you...'

Little Jack continued with another flower. Jack waited for a moment, but he got no more response. He shrugged and continued on his way. *Big Brother* was crossing the street, dragging his scraggy mongrel behind him. Jack glanced over across the street. There was another emaciated pavement artist working in front of a chic little boutique. They certainly picked their spots! Jack watched *Big Brother* on the traffic island waiting for a gap in the cars so that he could cross. He felt like following him and giving him and his dog, a boot up the arse. *Fecking little gangster.* Then he changed his mind. 'Well, maybe not. At least he's there...'

Suddenly there was a loud screaming. Jack turned and looked back. Two Gardaí were standing, one on either side of Little Jack. They were looking down at him and one of them was saying something and moving the few coins in the chalk circle around with his foot. Little Jack stood between then, rigid, his mouth open in a wide circle and screaming at the top of his lungs and rubbing his eyes with the back of his hands. He looked like a little black beetle that they could crush with one of their big feet if the fancy took them. Jack stared openmouthed. *The bastards!* He looked across the street, but there was no sign of *Big Brother,* of the other little artist or the dog! They had vanished into the concrete. Jack was enraged. The feckin' cops! Garda Síochana, *Guardians of the peace* how are ye ...! *Jesus*!

The Gardaí sauntered away. Little Jack stopped his wailing instantly. Jack watched the Gardaí walk on down the street. He approached Little Jack, who had gone back to colouring as if nothing had happened.

'What happened...?' Jack was furious.

Little Jack shrugged. 'Nut'in'.'

'What did they say...?'

'Dey'd take th' money if dey cot me ag'in.' He gave Jack a big toothy grin. 'Dey say dat ev'ry day.' There was no sign of tears in his eyes.

Jack couldn't help laughing. This was all a game.

'Good trick, Jack. Good trick.' He gave him another ten pence. He deserved it. He was a great little actor as well. Paul's girlfriend, Aisling, was going to the wrong classes!

Jack went for a coffee. Yesterday had been dole day so he had a few pounds in his pocket. He sat and thought about the kids. Tough little kids. And street wise, too. Organised as well! He hadn't paid them much attention before. But there they were! He rolled a cigarette and wondered where they lived. He should try to find out more about them. But where to start? They certainly weren't giving away much information. And why should they? It was part of their protection! But there must be someone or some organisation who looks out for them? The Gardaí? Hah! He didn't think so. Probably the Social Welfare? But then wouldn't they be at school or in a home? Well he didn't want to go to the cops and he didn't want to approach the Social Welfare officer. But where else? Perhaps City Hall? It was worth a try. And at least it was neutral ground.

The receptionist at City Hall shook her head. She was a middle aged, motherly looking, woman. 'But, no. It's not any of our departments. Not that I'm aware of... I've noticed them, right enough. Given them the odd few pence, the poor little mites...' She shook her head stoically.

Jack turned to leave.

'Just a moment,' the receptionist called him back. 'I just thought of something...' She motioned him to wait and picked up the 'phone and pressed a button. 'Hello, Maria. Joan here, at reception. There was a girl in your department, she went off about a year ago... something to do with child care? Yes... That's it. Yes. There's a young man here at the desk, enquiring... Yes... Thanks Marie.'

She replaced the 'phone and beamed at Jack. 'Well, you seem to be in luck. One of our girls left last year to do something in Child Care.' She closed her eyes and nodded her head as if to say, I knew there was something, I'm not the Receptionist for nothing. 'And I've just been told she's working at this new drop-in Center. I'll write the address down for you...' She handed the slip of paper to Jack. 'Ask for Helen.'

'Thanks. You're very helpful.'

Joan beamed at him. 'You're welcome.'

The address she had written was the street directly behind the dole office. He'd have no problems finding that.

The house was a narrow three storied building, wedged at the rear of the dole building. It had a new coat of fresh white paint. The door was open. He went in. There was a long hallway, with a stairs in one side and a door on the other. At the end of the corridor was another door and what looked like a kitchen. The whole house both inside and out was painted white. It was spotless. He hadn't expected that. There was the sound of someone hopping a ball on the wall in the room on the right. Otherwise the house was quiet. Jack headed for the kitchen. The door was open. He knocked and a woman came into view. She was a stocky woman of about his own age with a round face and a shock of fuzzy ginger hair, and a wide smile.

'Come in. Come in.' She called.

Jack went in. 'Are you Helen?'

'That's me.'

'Jack...' He introduced himself.

She motioned him to sit. 'Would you like a coffee? I was just about to make some.'

Jack nodded. 'Thanks.'

'So, What can I do for you...?'

'I was talking to the people in the City Hall. They told me I'd find you here. It's about the kids. The ones on the street. I was interested.'

'Yes?'

'Well. I was wondering... I'd like to help. If I could...?'

Helen nodded. 'What do you do?'

'Do...?' *I used to put lids on jam-jars! He couldn't very well tell her that!* He shrugged. 'I'm unemployed at the moment.'

'Signing...?'

'Yes.'

Helen handed him his coffee. 'Just instant. Our budget doesn't run to fancy brands, yet.' She laughed. 'Well,' She settled herself and took a sip of her coffee. 'If you're signing-on you could start off by becoming a Volunteer. All you have to do is sign a form. I'll get you one in a minute.'

Jack looked surprised. Helen laughed. 'It's one of the little perks of being unemployed. Of course they don't tell you about it. You have to find out the hard way.'

Jack asked her what they did here at the Center. She explained about the kids. Some were runaways from broken homes. Others were local inner-city kids who used the Center because they couldn't stick it at home, for various reasons. Cruelty. Fathers out of work. Drink. Violence. General poverty. A whole bunch of reasons. Some families were too big and the flats too small and the kids needed space and shelter. They were free to come and go at the Center as they wished. Between ten and five. She laughed. Just like an office job!

'We have three other Volunteers. Just like yourself. Unemployed. We're not goody-goodies here. It's mostly all work and little pay! We're here because we want to be. We're not a charity. There's a possibility of a Social Welfare Employment Scheme. But we haven't got confirmation yet. When it comes through we'll be able to employ some of the Volunteers. Maybe two or three.' She finished her coffee. 'If you come down to the office I'll get you the form.'

She led the way down the hall and into the front room, where the ball hopping was coming from. A small girl of about ten was throwing a ball against the wall.

Helen said. 'This is Jack. And this is Mags.'

Mags continued to hop her ball. There was a boy and

girl sitting on the sofa looking at comics. 'This is Johnny and Maria.' They glanced up and went back to their comics. Jack nodded to them. He followed Helen through a door at the back of the room, marked office. It was kept locked.

Jack took the form. 'Fill it in now if you don't mind, it'll save you coming back.' Helen gave him a ballpoint. As he was filling it in Helen continued.

'It's all *on-the-job-training* here.' She laughed. 'We're not here to ask questions. We don't put pressure on the kids. We're here to offer them a shelter during the day. It's not the perfect solution. But then what is? We help as much as possible and refer when we think it necessary. Unfortunately it's only a Day Center. We have no authority after that. The kids have to fend for themselves then.' She saw Jack's bewildered expression. 'Oh. Most of them have homes to go to. But there are those who have to sleep rough... Some of the volunteers know where they are. They do a night shift of sorts. They're good. Some of them were reared on the streets themselves. You'll meet them. But the kids... they're crafty little buggers. They shift around. Derelict sites, abandoned buildings... But we keep on their trail...'

She explained about the problems with drinking, shop lifting, glue sniffing, hand-bag snatching and prostitution...

Jack was stunned. He had thought that the kids he saw begging on the streets were from itinerant families. He was amazed at the vastness of the problem. Children from the whole gambit of society. 'Rich as well as poor. You'd be amazed. It's not only the poor kids... And they come in from the country too, stowaways on the train. They're not all city kids.' Helen pointed out. *God!* He had a lot to learn...

'When can I start?

Helen laughed. 'Right now. You just did!'

Jack laughed, too. *So easy to get a job when the pay is zero.* 'So, what do I do?'

'Well... you can sit in the sitting-room for a while and see who comes in. But don't be surprised if you're ignored. It takes them a while to accept you.' They went back into the front room. Helen locked the office door, explaining that it was the only door ever locked in the house, except for the front door at night. Johnny and Maria were gone. But Mags was still hopping her ball. Helen left him and returned to the office. Jack sat on the sofa and watched her. She was a skinny little one with straight black hair caught up in a ribbon. Her little dress was a dirty white torn First Communion dress that was probably a hand-me-down from an older sister. She didn't look at him nor stop her ball hopping. She just hopped it and caught it and hopped it and caught it without a break.

Well, Jack thought. At least she didn't run away from me. That's a start.

By the time he got home he was elated. He felt at last as if his life was taking on some shape and meaning. What a lucky day! At last, something worthwhile to do. He kicked himself mentally for not having thought of it before. Of course he had blocked all that out of his mind. It was the last thing he had been looking for. Lost kids! And it was right under his nose all the time. He had a feeling he would be good at it. And the night-shift people sounded like a great bunch. He was looking forward to meeting them. He ran up the stairs.

There was a note shoved under the door. "Jack. Ring Jean," and her number. Jack almost fell down the stairs in his haste and excitement to get to the phone. He dialled Jean's office. It rang for ages. He checked his watch. Almost six. She must have gone home. *Damn!* Then Jean's voice on the other end, out of breath,' Hello...'

'Hello, Jean. Just got your message. Jack here.'

'Oh, Hi. Sorry, I just ran up the stairs. I was out for a take-away. Working late. Well I have good news for you. I was talking to a rep., from the midlands. He knows your woman, Shelagh Carr. Well it's the same name anyway. So I hope you're in luck. Have you a pen?' She gave him the number and the area code.

Jack thanked her. 'I owe you a pint.'

Jean laughed. 'If I ever get time. Hah! Things have really taken off here.'

'Well, keep it in mind. Thanks.'

'Good luck. And let me know when the next party is...' She laughed again and rang off.

Jack fished in his pocket for more change. His finger shook as he dialled the operator and waited to be put through.

A pleasant country voice answered.

'Hello, is that Shelagh Carr...?' He could hardly control his voice.

'Yes.'

'My name is Jack. I'm a friend of Rosemary's.'

'Oh yes. She mentioned you.'

'Would she be there...? Could I talk to her...?'

'No. I'm afraid not. She's out at the moment.'

'How is she?'

'Oh, she's grand. Did she give you my number?'

'Eh...No. I got it from a friend. She has a Natural Cosmetics Company. I hope you don't mind?'

'No. Not at all. I'm glad you called.'

'Could you give Rosemary my number here...'

'Yes.' Jack gave her the number.

'Thanks. Great...' He rang off and ran back upstairs. He was too excited to cook anything. He walked up and down the sitting room. He couldn't settle. He heard the phone ringing down in the hall. He bolted through the door again and took the stairs in a leap. Rosemary!

'Is that Jack.'

'Speaking...'

'Sheila Carr again. I just had an idea.' Her tone was very sweet. ' Rosemary is away to-day. I think she's in the city.'

'In the city...here ?'

'I'm not sure exactly where. She went up with a friend of mine. But I was thinking after you put the phone down, it's her birthday on Sunday, and I was going to give a little surprise party for her. I'm sure she's probably forgotten all about her birthday. But why don't you come down. I'm sure she'd love you to. But don't say anything. We'll keep it as a surprise...'

Jack was a little downhearted, but it was only three days to wait. Yes it would be a great surprise. 'OK. Yes! I'd love to. On Sunday....great...I'll just turn up then. Don't say I rang!'

'I won't.' She gave him the address and told him which

bus to take and rang off. He thought it was obviously a small village because she had said when he got off the bus to just ask anyone and they'll tell him where she lived.

Jack tore back up the stairs. What an interesting woman Rosemary's aunt was! To think of that! A surprise birthday! He couldn't believe his luck. The prospects of a job and Rosemary's address all in the one day. It was too much! Too much to absorb all at one time! He threw up his eyes to Heaven. *Mother Imelda you're a Saint*. And Jean, you're an *Angel*! And *Jack-In-The-Box* Weasel. You are a lucky man.

He couldn't wait for Sunday to come... And Rosemary.

27

When Jack arrived at Shelagh Carr's door on Sunday, shortly after lunchtime, he hesitated for a few seconds before knocking, waiting for his excitement to calm down. Would Rosemary answer the door? How would she look? How would he feel? How would she react?

He had borrowed a suit from Paul for the occasion. It was a navy blue single breasted suit with a grey pin stripe. He felt like a traveling salesman in it, but he wanted to make a good impression, and his experience with Maureen and the denim jeans and jacket still stuck in his mind. He wasn't going to get caught out again. This was a special occasion and he didn't want to create a wrong impression. But Rosemary had never seen him in a suit and she had never remarked on his usual jeans and jacket.

So who was he wearing the suit for, he asked himself? He didn't know. It certainly wasn't for himself because now he wasn't so sure if the suit was such a good idea after all. It was a little tight and he had been uncomfortable on the hour long bus journey. When he looked down on himself the suit looked alien to him. Not him at all. And the tan brogues were totally out of place with the dark material. But he wanted to appear different and neat. He certainly looked different all right, but he felt unreal. He hadn't worn a tie. He had tried one of Paul's but he felt as if he were choking so the tie was out.

The suit was new. Aisling's idea for the new Paul. She didn't know *he* was wearing it. *God!* If Aisling found out before he got back to-night Paul would have hell to pay. But Paul had said not to worry, he'd sort it out with Aisling. He knew it looked good, neat, clean cut, sensible. But it wasn't him. *Dammit!* Why didn't he just wear his own clothes. At least he'd feel comfortable. At least he'd feel like himself! But it was fifty miles too late now. He patted his pocket for the hundredth time to check that the little box of imitation, *but they looked real,* drop-pearl ear-rings - a present for her birthday, and the end of his savings - was still there.

He knocked.

When the door opened he got a shock. He was about to say, Hi Rosemary, but caught himself just in time. The woman who stood in front of him *could* have been Rosemary. He hadn't seen her for almost four weeks now, and he didn't know what to expect. His last image of Rosemary was a pale skinny girl in a hospital bed wanting to be somewhere else. The woman in front of him had the same heart shaped face, the same long black hair, the same pale blue eyes with their cat-like upward slope at the edges...it threw him for an instant, Rosemary could have changed in the country. Of course she would have changed. But the resemblance was uncanny. This woman must be her aunt, but her youthful appearance belied the fact that she was almost twice Rosemary's age. Of course this wasn't Rosemary. This woman looked far too healthy.

She smiled - Rosemary's smile, too - and held the door wide. 'Jack. You're very welcome. Come in. I'm Shelagh.' She held out her hand and Jack took it. 'Well,' He said bashfully, seeing a picture of himself standing in the doorway in *this* suit. 'I made it...' He went in.

The front door led straight into the sitting room. There was a large turf fire blazing in the hearth. The aroma added a friendly warmth to the small room. The walls were painted white - Rosemary's white - and the furniture was all wickerwork, two fireside chairs, a small round table, with four chairs tucked in under it and a delicate wicker sideboard. Although they almost filled the room, you had the impression that they took up less space in that you could see through and under everything.

Shelagh motioned to one of the chairs beside the fire. 'How was the journey?' She smiled knowingly, and sat in the chair opposite. She obviously had experience of the old bus; it had rattled the whole journey. 'We call it the *Bone Shaker*,' she said. Jack nodded and grimaced. 'Ye-es. I can see why.' It certainly had been the shakiest bus ride he had ever experienced. 'It reminded me of that old record by Duane Eddy,' He said. *'Forty Miles of Bad Road.'* Shelagh smiled, her head cocked to one side, surprised, 'You'd hardly remember that record,' she said. That was years ago, well before your time..?' Jack nodded. 'My last flat-mate, Paul, he used to collect Sixties records. That was one of his favourites.' Shelagh smiled and asked, 'Would you like a coffee or tea?'

'Coffee's fine.'

She left the room. Jack noticed all her movements were graceful and unhurried. And her voice was even pleasanter to listen to in reality than it had been on the phone. She hadn't mentioned anything about Rosemary. Was she here? Would she appear, suddenly, and be standing in the room? Was she going to jump out and surprise him. Jack braced himself. He didn't know what he would do or say when Rosemary did appear. And when she saw him in the suit...? Ach! The suit was a mistake, but he'd have to live with it now. He wondered what Rosemary had told Shelagh about him. This was all a mistake. He should have spoken to Rosemary on the phone first. What if she didn't want to see him? After all, she hadn't contacted him. Why had he agreed to this wild scheme of just turning up for her birthday party? It was madness.

Shelagh arrived back with the coffee. She was carrying a wickerwork tray with a coffee pot and two bulbous mugs, a milk jug and sugar bowl with chips of cane sugar. The crockery looked handmade and all had the same pattern of dark earth brown with a light blue brush stroke that resembled a bird. There was a plate with some cut slices of fruit cake.

The whole thing, the room, the turf fire, the wickerwork furniture and now the hand-made delft gave Jack the impression of being in a different world. From the outside the bungalow looked to him just like a million other country bungalows, but inside it had the ambiance of the interior of a Grimm's Fairytale. *And the Witch would arrive at any minute and ask him to test the heat of the oven...!* He stood and offered to take the tray from Shelagh, but she motioned him to sit and placed the tray on the floor in front of the fire and knelt down beside it and poured the coffee.

'It's decaff, ' She said as she handed him the mug. 'I hope you don't mind.' Jack shook his head. He indicated the cosy room. 'This is a lovely little house,' He said. ' Not like what we have to live in, up above.' He nodded in the direction of where he thought the city might be.

Shelagh smiled and accepted his compliment. 'Yes. I like to surround myself with natural things. Wood and wool and pottery. I can't bear the feel of synthetics.' She shuddered. 'Synthetics build up static around you. You can feel it. I'm sure it's unhealthy.' She looked around. 'But I suppose it's what you make of it. Landlords are usually sadly lacking in taste. It's the fast buck! I've lived in flats and bed-sits myself and I swore, never again.' She smiled reflectively. 'How is your coffee?'

'It's nice. You wouldn't know it wasn't...' He was about to say, wasn't real. '...was decaff. I've never had it before...'

Shelagh proffered him the plate with the fruit cake. 'Would you like some cake. Rosemary's baking. She's getting quite good.'

At last she had mentioned Rosemary. Yes, Rosemary. But where was she? Shelagh read his thoughts. 'Rosemary has gone out for a walk. She shouldn't be long.' She looked towards the door as if she expected Rosemary to walk in any second. Jack felt his anxiety rising again and was even more aware of the suit and the thought that Rosemary was about to walk in any minute and see him, sitting here, in it, she would probably have a good laugh at him or make some caustic remark.

'How is she?'

'Very well, I'm pleased to say. The country hasn't done her a bit of harm.' Shelagh sipped her coffee. 'We had an early lunch. She's taken to going for long walks. It's made all the difference. The fresh air has put the colour back in her cheeks. You probably won't recognise her...' She smiled as if she was amused at the idea.

'She probably won't recognise *me*.' Jack grinned. 'This is the first time I've ever worn a suit.' He shouldn't have said that. Now he felt more uncomfortable. Why did he have to draw attention to the fact? It was his nerves. Shelagh laughed. 'You look grand.' And she smiled to herself again.

Jack imagined himself and Rosemary scrutinising each other. She, looking country and healthy, like her aunt, and him in his suit, like a salesman, and both of them feeling like they were from different planets. Now he was certain this was all a mistake. His euphoria of two days ago, when he had spoken to Shelagh on the phone was now seeping out through his tan brogues. He wished he was back on the *Bone Shaker* bus, heading back to the security of the city and his denim jacket.

Just then the door opened and Rosemary walked in, letting a sudden draught of cold air brush in behind her. She stopped dead in her step. Jack was caught unawares with the coffee mug up to his mouth. He started. This was Rosemary? *Jesus!* She *had* changed. She looked...*God!* He couldn't think what! Radiant! Like a fashion model out of a magazine page. She was wearing a bolero style jacket and a long skirt of heavy royal blue velvet with a bright buttercup yellow blouse underneath and a long knitted scarf of angora wool in muted colours of brown and red and gold. Jack froze with his mug still to his mouth. Her long hair was swept back from her face from her walk and her cheeks glowed. She looked, fuller, not the slim pale Rosemary he remembered. She stood taller and straighter and stronger and more beautiful than he could ever have imagined.

'Jack...!!!'

He put down the mug and struggled to his feet in the suit. 'Hi. Rosemary...'

Rosemary glared at him, up and down, grimacing at the tight suit. 'Jack, what are you doing here..?'

He grinned sheepishly, 'I was just passing like...'

But before he could say another word Rosemary darted a look of venom at her aunt, then swept past and out of the room behind him. He swivelled on the spot and watched her disappear down the back hallway. He was speechless. Her sudden appearance, the startled look on her face, her stunning beauty, her eyes taking him in, her dart of hate to her aunt and her sweeping past leaving behind only the cold vacuum of air carrying the fragrance of her perfume, left Jack frozen on the spot with his jaw hanging like an idiot. He looked at Shelagh, appealing for help, but she sat with a faint bemused smile on her face and just shook her head gently from side to side as if to say, well, that's Rosemary!

Rosemary closed the door of her room behind her and leaned back against it. What was Jack doing here? How did he find out? Some birthday party this was going to be! This must be her aunt's plan. She had invited him to drive a wedge between her and Frank. Well, it was just as well Frank couldn't come. His mother wasn't well, she had had a restless night, and he didn't want to leave her. The day nurse couldn't come to-day and he would stay at home with her, himself. Rosemary had walked out to the house to see him. They had agreed to postpone the party and the engagement announcement until some other time. Somehow it didn't seem so important anymore.

They had driven up to the city for the ring and to get her some new clothes, the outfit she was wearing, and now that they had purchased the ring and the clothes it didn't matter whether they announced it or not. It was done. They had agreed to meet later. She thought she only had to tell Shelagh about canceling the party, oh, they could eat the cake anyway, but it wouldn't be a celebration or anything. But now she had to contend with Jack as well. What was she going to do? Well, she wasn't going to let Jack or Shelagh see that she was rattled. She took a deep breath but she was shaking. *Blast Jack and damn Shelagh!*

She took off her bolero jacket and the scarf and flung them on the bed. She sat down at the dressing table and brushed out her hair with vigorous strokes of the brush. That had been a mistake, sweeping out of the room like that. But the shock of seeing him sitting there, so unexpected! The suit had thrown her for a second. But now, both he, *and Shelagh,* would have to be faced. Well, she wasn't going to let it upset her. She was going to face them as cool as she could, get rid of Jack as fast as she could, and then leave. She didn't care where or what. But Shelagh had done this, and she couldn't be forgiven and that was that. She would go out to Frank and they would have to sort out something. *Oh, God!* This was a mess again just when she thought everything was under control...! Why did Shelagh have to do this to her...? Especially to-day! She threw down her hairbrush, took a deep breath and composed herself.

When she came into the sitting-room again Shelagh was smiling at Jack and explaining to him about herb growing. How every plant and bush in her garden was a cure for some malady. Jack sat, listening intently, perched now on the edge of his chair, the back of his suit jacket stretched tightly across his broad shoulders as if it would rip at the seams from the tension. Actually, she mused, he looked quite good in it. It's a pity he didn't wear suits more often. The dark material suited him. He looked quite handsome and mature, if it wasn't for the obvious discomfort he was now displaying. Shelagh and Jack hesitated for a moment before looking at her as she pulled a chair from the table and sat down.

'You're looking good.' She said to Jack, nodding at the suit. She could see the colour creep up into his face.

He grinned bashfully, fingering the lapel of the jacket, and had to turn awkwardly in his chair to reply, as Rosemary was seated almost behind him. Yes. 'Special occasion...' But the grin was forced. Once again he was beginning to feel like a spare piece of furniture.

Rosemary arched her eyebrows, nonplussed, as if she

had forgotten all about what day it was and what they were supposed to be celebrating..

'Happy birthday, ' Jack said standing up, fishing in his pocket and taking out the little wrapped gift. He took a step towards her and held it out, grinning self-consciously as she took it. 'Just a small...present.' He shrugged. Rosemary mode no move of acknowledgement and sat back down again.

'Thanks Jack.' She placed the little gift-wrapped package on the table in front of her but didn't open it. She was at a disadvantage. She didn't know what was in it, but guessed it was jewellery of some sort and she wasn't sure what to do or say if she did open it, because she never wore jewellery. And Jack should have known that.

Shelagh said. 'Aren't you going to open it...' She had a sweet smile on her face. Too sweet, Rosemary thought. She was obviously enjoying this.

Rosemary ignored her. She said. 'Frank can't come. His mother is not too well, so...' She let the sentence hang.

'Oh.' Shelagh exclaimed, looking from Rosemary's face to Jack's. But the implication of the statement hadn't sunk in on him yet.

'...So we've postponed the party...' Rosemary finished.

Shelagh was thinking, all the fuss for nothing. She had had to tell Rosemary that she had decided on a surprise party for her birthday, because she wasn't sure if Rosemary would remember her birthday or not. And Rosemary had admitted to her that she, too, was going to do the same thing. Only she didn't say anything about the engagement or why they had gone to the city for the day. She had only mentioned about buying clothes. It had been an awkward moment then, both pretending that it was only a birthday party. Because when Rosemary had mentioned that she had invited Frank, Shelagh wasn't that naive that she didn't suspect that if Rosemary wanted Frank there, it was for a special reason. She wouldn't have guessed about the engagement, would she? But if she did suspect something of the kind, she had covered it well. What Rosemary wondered now, was, did Shelagh invite Jack after she had told her about inviting Frank? And now Jack was sitting here, with a puzzled look on his face because he didn't know how his presence had complicated everything.

Jack looked from Shelagh to Rosemary. He was beginning to feel like a late substitute on the field when the game was already in full swing and the outcome decided and nothing he did would make any difference. It was already won or lost and he was simply the *piggy-in-the-middle*. He wasn't sure what was going on between the two of them, but it reeked of some conspiracy.

Shelagh said, explaining. 'Frank is an old friend of mine. He's one of the local doctors. His mother is over eighty. She's bed-ridden... He was supposed to come to the party...'

Rosemary glared at her aunt. Everything she said was true, yes, but it was the implications behind what she was saying that irked her. Frank was *her* guest, not Shelagh's. And this was supposed to be her birthday party. Her *engagement* party! Shelagh could sit there and smile sweetly and say, Frank is an old friend of mine... as if it had nothing to do with Rosemary. Well she would tell them. She would tell them and then they could sort it out for themselves. Shelagh and Jack. She was past caring now. She thought she and Shelagh had come to an unwritten compromise about their differences! But Shelagh was being a right bitch! Rosemary was making up her mind to say it out straight when the phone rang. Everybody looked at it for a second, then Shelagh got up and answered it.

Neither Rosemary or Jack spoke. Jack was at a disadvantage. The chair he was sitting in was at an angle to the fire and Rosemary had chosen to sit at the table which was to his left and behind him so that to talk to her he would either have to stand and face her or twist in the chair, which was difficult, because of the semi-circular arms of the wickerwork. Rosemary sat, fiddling absentmindedly with Jack's birthday gift, turning it over and over with her fingers, without looking at what she was doing. Jack could see her on the periphery of his vision. Shelagh replaced the receiver and said nothing until she was sitting again. 'That was Frank. It seems he can come after all. Mrs. Cosgrave will stay with his mother. She's much better. He's on his way.'

Rosemary stared stonily at her aunt. She took it as an affront that Frank had spoken to Shelagh and not asked for her. She knew Frank was nervous about this engagement party and the announcement. He had been quite sure last Monday morning after she had spent the night with him. But as the week wore on and the time drew near he had started back-pedaling. Something about a promise he had made to Shelagh. But he was very vague about it. He couldn't be drawn out on it. Rosemary had argued with him about it in the car when they had gone to buy the ring. She knew it was because of Shelagh, but, Rosemary had argued, Shelagh had to be told sometime, and the sooner the better so that they could get on with their plans. It Shelagh took umbrage, well then they knew where they stood. They couldn't put off telling her for ever, so, better to get it over with as planned. Frank had argued that it was a bit much having the announcement in Shelagh's own house. Perhaps at the hotel, neutral ground. Well, Rosemary countered, it was her house too, was hers after her aunt's time, and anyway after Sunday they would know where she stood. But one way or the other, Shelagh was not going to stand in their way. Frank sensed the challenge in her tone. He had to fight back his fears and his apprehension. It was a test!

But, Rosemary was right. It was now or never. Get it out in the open. Get it over with. But in Shelagh's own house! Even if it was to be Rosemary's eventually. That was beside the point! Did he want to marry her or not? There was no need to ask himself that! He did. Well that was that. Shelagh would be told. On Sunday. And his Mother being ill to-day wasn't an excuse. She had had a bad night, and Rosemary could see that he was genuinely worried. And the day nurse was away for the week-end. It was an unfortunate coincidence.

Frank arrived shortly after, all apologies. He hoped he hadn't ruined the day. It was unfortunate, his mother taking that turn, but she was resting comfortably now and Mrs Cosgrave was an old friend and had been a nurse in her time and his mother would be fine in her care. He was sure it was nothing serious. Would they mind if he only stayed until after dinner. He shook hands cordially with Jack. Rosemary rushed to the kitchen to make fresh coffee. She had to get out of the sitting-room. The atmosphere was thickening with every second. She didn't think she could stay in the house one more minute. The small sitting-room was now stiflingly cramped with four adults, their nerves stretching like piano wires. Shelagh, sitting poised like a Queen Bee. Jack squirming in his suit and now Frank, bubbling over with nerves and talking a mile a minute about the plans of the local

Conservation Committee....

When Rosemary arrived back with the fresh coffee, Frank was sitting in the chair she had vacated. Jack had moved his seat so that he was now facing more into the room. The three of them were chatting as if they were the best of buddies, but the atmosphere was one of artificial cordiality laced with presentiment. The three of them were smiling and pretending to be extremely interested in what the other had to say. Rosemary passed around the coffee mugs and when they had all completed the ceremony of milking and sugaring she had to pull out a chair on the opposite side of the table from Frank to sit. Now she was sitting behind Jack again. She felt left out of the company. The three of them in her absence had constructed a convivial triangle and she was now at a tangent.

Frank was chatting happily - *nervously* - to Jack about old buildings that the Restoration Committee were in the process of restoring. Jack was grinning and telling him about some little old church he was fond of in the city. Shelagh embraced them both with her smiles. Frank was wondering what Jack was doing here, neither Shelagh nor Rosemary had mentioned him before, and his youth, and the fact that his suit was a little too small for him so he seemed bigger than he was and bulged somewhat out of it threateningly, and the way he kept glancing at Rosemary...

Jack in his turn was wondering about this older man, who was closer to Shelagh's age, but not as well preserved, who Rosemary had mentioned couldn't come to the party, and now here he was... They both suspected, guessed, worried, that they were both here for the same reason - *Rosemary*. Nobody had to tell them. These too male dogs had already sniffed each other out. Shelagh,

Queen Bitch, had arranged this match. Rosemary fumed on the sideline. Well, enough of this, she decided, it was becoming unbearingly claustrophobic. She was finding it hard to breath in this fabricated joviality. She reached over and plucked at Frank's sleeve. He turned to her, still telling Jack about Ring Forts.

'Frank...?'

'...and of course the *Lios*, is not really a Ring Fort as some would have it, or a Fairy Ring, it's actually a...' He stopped as he noticed the blanched expression on Rosemary's face. 'Sorry, Rosemary...?'

Rosemary looked towards the door. 'I'd like to go out for a while... it's still bright and...'

'Of course...' He turned back to Jack. 'Would you like to see the old castle. It's quite magnificent. We just have enough time before it gets too dark...' He checked his watch. '...and I have to get back to take Mrs Cosgrove home at seven... Shelagh...?' He stood up. 'It should only take about an hour...'

When they got in the car Frank and Jack had managed to sit in the front. Rosemary was peeved. She sat in the back with Shelagh, her fists clenched tightly in her lap, staring daggers at the back of Frank's head. Frank continued to educate Jack on the difference between a *Lios*', Ring Forts, Cairns, Fairy Rings and related a story about his father, who claimed he had fallen asleep one night in a Fairy Ring and woken up in the morning with a little footprint on his back. Frank laughed, of course it was only a birthmark, but himself and his brother had believed the story when they were kids. In fact he had a similar birthmark himself. Only it hadn't been so prominent when he was a child when his father had related the event.

They arrived at the castle. It was still bright, although the pale, watery, winter sun was heading for the horizon and casting long shadows about them. The old castle stood majestic and solid against the wintery sky. There was a hint of rain on the wind otherwise it was a fine crisp evening.

They wandered around the perimeter walls. Solid slabs of limestone, ten feet thick at the base rising at a slope out of the ground and then straightening and shooting straight up to sixty feet above their heads. Craning his neck, Jack could feel the power of the stones overwhelming him. He could see where slabs from the castellations had dislodged and fallen like dead soldiers in the surrounding field. Frank led the way inside and brought them to the spiral staircase that led to the battlements, warning Jack about the need for caution when he got there, because the back of the ledge was missing and the rail support erected by the Board of Works was only a temporary measure. He cast a glance back at Rosemary and Jack noticed him hesitate and a frown creased his forehead when she followed them to the entrance. Shelagh shook her head, insisting that she would stay on the ground. The height up there was too much for her.

They were out of breath when they finally came out of the low arched doorway onto the battlements. Jack stood for a few seconds to get used to the height. It was dizzying. Rosemary strode on ahead along the slabbed path between the castellations and the fence, her hair billowing out behind her as she left the shelter of the tower, striding unconcerned as if she was walking in the safety of the Main Street. Frank started after her, calling, 'Hold on a minute...' But Rosemary ignored him. Jack began to follow them, holding on to the wall for support. The wind whipped at his open jacket and he buttoned it.

Far below him in the stone courtyard he could see Shelagh watching them. She looked like a miniature. He waved and she waved back. He continued his journey, holding on to the stone wall.

Rosemary was now at the other end of the walkway and leaning up against the castellations which reached up to her waist. She had her head up into the wind and her long black hair streamed back like a veil behind her. Frank stopped beside her and waited for Jack.

When Jack reached them he was beginning to feel a little more confident. The strength of the wind surprised him and he was afraid that if he let go of the wall he could be whipped off and sent flying. Frank began to tell him about a scheme the committee were considering to put a huge wind-mill in this wall when the restoration was completed to supply the town with electricity.

'...Of course the committee are divided on the issue. Some think it would be a sacrilege. It would take away from the castle itself and the interior,' He gestured behind them at the empty space that fell to the floor far below. '...all that would be filled with machinery. But it could solve the town's electricity problems. But of course the Electricity Supply Board are against the idea too...' He turned back to the view, stretching out for miles before them. The sky was beginning to darken and they could see the last rim of light in the western sky where the sun was sinking fast below the distant silhouette of trees.

'It's brilliant,' Jack remarked. He was invigorated by the air and the bracing wind and the sight of the vanishing ball of the sun which was turning the sky a rich shade of orange. 'It certainly beats the city... So much space...'

Frank laughed. 'It certainly does.' He glanced at his

watch. 'Well, we'd better be going back.'

He turned to Rosemary who hadn't uttered a word since leaving the house. She was still leaning against the parapet, seemingly oblivious to the men's chatter. This was to have been *her* day. Her *birthday*. Her *engagement* day! She was annoyed with Frank. He had closed ranks against her back at the house when she had gone to make the coffee. He had allowed Jack to share the front seat of the car and chatted to him all the way. And now he was acting the tourist guide for him and all but ignoring her. Well, she wasn't going to participate in their idle chat. She wanted Frank's attention. She especially wanted his attention in front of Shelagh and Jack. This was his opportunity to show them. That she was his. That he was hers. That they were together. But he was avoiding contact with her. She needed him to touch her, to show her, to show *them*. She needed that more than anything. If he wasn't prepared to act on his own initiative she would have to do something about it. There was a way.

She stepped back from the wall and strode off, tossing her head, as if in a huff. Frank and Jack eyed each other and shrugged. They turned to follow her.

Suddenly, Rosemary, half way along the flagstone path, stopped and began to spin around, holding her coat out, catching the wind.

Frank swore under his breath. '*Christ....!*' And began to hurry towards her. Jack edged along the wall. What the hell was Rosemary playing at. He was afraid to look. It was bad enough standing up here at this dizzying height clinging on to the parapet for support. Frank seemed able for it. He didn't have to hold onto the wall, but he was used to it. But Rosemary was spinning there in the middle of the path with her coat held open and the wind whipping at her hair. It was madness!

He heard Frank call out sharply. 'Rosemary. Stop it. Don't start this again.' But Rosemary continued to spin and wail. Jack could feel his legs turning to jelly just watching her. Frank grabbed her and wrapped his arms around her but she struggled free and began to run back in Jack's direction. Frank shouted after her. 'Oh, for Chris'sake, Rose... Let's go...' But she ignored the caution in his voice and let out a great whoop of laughter. Frank roared. 'Jack...!' And as Rosemary passed him he let go of the wall with one hand and grabbed her coat. She tried to pull free. He could see her eyes blazing into his.

'Let go, Jack,' she hissed fiercely in his face and tugged at her coat to try and free herself. Frank came up and put both arms around her again, clamping her arms to her sides.

'Rose. Please. Stop,' he commanded, but Rosemary continued to twist and turn. And then she began to giggle uncontrollably. They could hear Shelagh screaming at them from below to be careful, her voice echoing in the hollow between the massive walls.

'Now, that's enough, Rose.' Frank gripped her as tightly as he could and attempted to walk with her back to the exit. 'We should be getting back...' Jack was still holding on for dear life, one hand holding the edge of her coat, the other gripping the top of the wall. Rosemary was giggling and struggling with Frank as if this was just a great game. But, her struggling, and Frank's attempts to keep her still were too much for Jack and he felt himself suddenly pulled away from the safety of the wall. Rosemary was in a fury and wouldn't calm down. They had her between them now, but she continued to twist and turn in her attempts to free herself, laughing in their faces, her eyes wild, her teeth bared. Now they were both grappling with her and they forgot where they were, up so high, and the sheer sixty foot drop to the flagstones below. Rosemary seemed oblivious to the danger.

Jack felt a surge of rage rise up from the depths of his being. A rage he never knew he possessed. But what he did know was that he had to put a stop to this madness, which seemed to have taken a grip on her, and was putting them all in great danger. In his new found strength he took a step towards her and, reaching out, grabbed her coat in both hands and pulled her free of Frank towards him. His strength and determination took them both by surprise and they stood inches from each other breathing heavily and staring into each others eyes.

"Rosemary," he said, his voice low and deeply commanding. "This has got to stop." She jerked back as if to free herself from his grip. But he held her fast. "Now," he breathed.

The power with which he held her seemed to break her nerve and as suddenly as she had started she calmed. In this new condition between them Rosemary and Jack totally forgot about Frank and Shelagh. It was as if Rosemary's fit of craziness had brought to the fore a strength in Jack which neither had been aware of previously. And in Rosemary a clearing of past obstacles. It was as if they realised at that moment that there was no future for them if they carried on as they were. It was so sudden and so deep. This new insight into their feelings shocked them. But shocked them in a way that showed a new way forward; at the same time, shaking off the dolefulness that had, up to now, engulfed them. And in that instant, after all that had happened, it cleared a space for them which they both now realised could be filled with a real and understanding togetherness stretching into their future.

Jack gently pulled her to him and she responded as if melting into his embrace. They held each other for a long poignant moment. Frank reached out and touched her on the shoulder but she was not even aware of it. That they were standing in the wind sixty feet above the flagstones where Shelagh stood horrified at the scene unfolding above her seemed to elude them.

"Let's go." Jack breathed the words gently into her ear and she nodded in acceptance.

They turned and headed for the turret staircase and, hand in hand descended to the ground below, happy and content to put the turmoil of the past behind them. A togetherness that they both felt had been that something special that had eluded them all along, but they had known was buried deep inside them. It now rose to the surface and enveloped them like a comforting blanket. It brought lightness to their hearts and minds and they felt this moment as a new beginning.

About the author

Dick Donaghue is a writer and film maker. Many of his short stories have appeared in magazines and newspapers in Ireland and have been collected together in one volume, *CRASH and Other Stories*.
He was deeply involved in many of the arts organisations in Galway where he lived for many years, before retiring to the east coast where he writes and makes short films with a local drama group.
He is married to artist, Marja van Kampen and they live in Enniscorthy, Co. Wexford, Ireland.

Happy Reading

Komal